ACKNOWLI

There's a saying that originated from

name that "you can't go home again." These words have become an American dictum, embodying the idea that nostalgia harbors a flawed bias, and that we can't return to the places where we grew up because our recollection of them will always surpass what they've become. In this book, I've done the reverse with my hometown of Wakefield, going back in time even, past my '80s childhood and into the last half of the 1960s. I chose this idyllic time in the town's history as the backdrop for my story to offset the imperfections of the decade itself: a volatile moment in our history full of war, death, and social unrest.

In my first novel, *The Vitruvian Heir*, I took the angle of looking at these present issues from a future standpoint, begging the question, "What will happen if we stay this course? If we don't address these problems?" We could absolutely regress as a society if we allow ourselves to live fear-based lives and choose leaders who would repress us in the name of protecting us. But the problems we face today aren't new, either; and with *The Clothes That Make You*, I wanted to shine a light on that. For years, we've put a bandage on problems like racism, sexism, bigotry, and hypocritical political administrations instead of facing ourselves and our part in the way things are. Generations long for the "good times," but if you look at them, were they really that good? The answer is no. But the second and sadder part of that answer is that now, they're not very much better. *The Clothes That Make You* could just as easily be set in this current political and social climate, marking distinctly the inability of our human spiritual evolution to match pace with technology.

There are several people I have to thank. First and foremost, my mother, Mary Ann, who lost her father when she was seventeen like my protagonist, Sally. And like Sally's mother, Lorraine, my own grandmother, Angela, went to work at the laundry and dry cleaners in downtown Wakefield to keep the house and put my mother through college. When the idea for the larger story came to me, weaving it in with this moment in their lives made sense to me. For this is truly a snapshot of "a year in the life," a coming-of-age story of a young woman during, and in spite of, a time of great upheaval in our country and the world.

Next, to the two most important men in my life, my father, Vincent, and my husband, Steve. I was blessed to grow up seeing my dad revere the women in his life, almost to a fault. He's been my biggest fan and the best father a girl could have. And Steve, who is the kindest, most patient and loving man. I'm blessed to love you, and to call you my best friend and my favorite. Thank you for your invaluable feedback, and for always supporting my dreams and keeping me close.

To my supportive friends who read drafts for me: Chrissy, Damiana, Lori, and Mary; those of you from Wakefield who weighed in on the nostalgia, namely, Wendy and Jean; a special thank you to Cheryl, Kathleen, and the ladies of their book club for not only reading a draft, but also hosting a fantastic summer gathering to discuss it with me. To Linda Rubin and her late father, Allen Rubin, the founder of Adrian's Decorating, who were kind enough to speak to me about their family business that formerly had a location in Wakefield – I hope my description of the old store does it justice. To the late Sal Orifice, longtime owner of the Wakefield Bowladrome and his daughter, Sally O'Neill, thank you so much for reminiscing about the town and your business, which is still very much alive and as retro-fabulous as ever. And to the late Patty L., who inspired the character Sam in looks and spirit, thank you for your candid thoughts and for being you. You brightened this world and every time I see a rainbow in the sky, I'll think of you.

I'd also like to recognize my designer, Elizabeth Bonadies, who's done another stellar job with the book's cover, layout, and marketing materials. To my fabulous editor, Jennifer Rees, you've done amazing work making sure this second novel is its best self and are always a delight to work with! And Nick Santaniello, my web guru, you always give so generously of your time to help artist friends.

A lot goes into the making of a book – the actual writing is only a small part of it. This story is a special one for me because it's been decades in the making, made up of slowly accumulated truths I've learned, mistakes I've made, revelations I've had, and intimate anecdotes from my family twisted into fiction. Favorite places in my hometown like the Colonial Spa will always be embedded in my heart. And whenever I go into Cravings, the ice cream parlor that now occupies that space, I can't help but grow nostalgic at the preserved mosaic tile floor and the Spa's old sign still above the soda counter. The high school building, which, by the time I was in school, had become the junior high, was bulldozed a few years back to build a much-needed, gleaming new school. While echoes of chatter in the cafeteria, the velvety seats in the auditorium, and rows of gray, metal lockers have all faded into dust, they are not forgotten by the people who walked those halls. Main Street isn't at all what I remember, just like it wasn't the same for those who hung out there in the '60s during the '80s and '90s. Just like it still wasn't the same for me when I taught high school there back in the mid-2000s. My downtown Wakefield had a Royal Discount Books where my mother would buy me a paperback almost every week, a Cafe Maccora, a Mary's Beauty Shoppe where my grandmother had her weekly appointment on Thursdays. It had Jewel Craft, Santoro's, Smith's Drug, and Kline's with its two floors that after became Alano's. And some places are blessedly unchanged – the lovely Beebe Library, the WWII memorial, the old band stand, and of course, beloved Lake Quannapowitt. But the town itself is new, full of young families who'll make their own memories. We take for granted with nostalgia that nothing stays the same, that nothing is permanent. The world changes and adapts, and we're borne along with it, some more reluctantly than others. So, let's not reminisce. Let's do something else instead.

Perhaps it's true that we can't go home again in the sense of clinging to the way things used to be, or the way we've romanticized that they were. But maybe together, we can all return to that same place of goodness that resides deep within to create something even better – something that includes everyone.

Happy reading!

"She was a wild, wicked slip of a girl.
She burned too bright for this world."

— Emily Brontë, *Wuthering Heights*

"Everything may be labelled – but everybody is not."

— Edith Wharton, *The Age of Innocence*

Prologue

Domenic Fiore hadn't been feeling well the last week or so, with bouts of nausea, excessive sweating, and conversely cold hands and feet. He shrugged on his pale blue, short-sleeved shirt and pulled up his dark navy pants. Illness was a sensation he wasn't used to, but he wasn't going to let it ruin his day. Because it was a beautiful day, and he loved his job. He fastened his tie and combed back his thick hair that had just started graying at the temples. Then, sitting in the corner chair of the bedroom, he laced his worn shoes. His family kept pushing him to replace them, but these shoes were solid and had served him well over many neighborhood blocks. Parting with them because they were old seemed capricious and unfair, even though they were just inanimate objects. He'd grown used to this pair and, above all, he was a person who appreciated routines. The final touch was a spritz of Old Spice around his neck. He grabbed his blue jacket and mailman's cap and headed to the kitchen, tiptoeing past Sally and Paul's rooms, trying his best not to wake them.

Lorraine served him breakfast: two eggs over easy, three sausages, and toast with butter and jam. She'd been making him hearty food since last Thursday when he was sent home for dizziness. She moved around the kitchen like a fluid angel, tending to breakfast, packing school lunches, planning that night's dinner.

Domenic had decided to marry Lorraine when they were children. They'd grown up next door to each other and, as a boy, he watched her from the heights of the bedroom he shared with three brothers. From his perch, he could see down into the Spinosa's kitchen where Lorraine was the only one of four sisters devoted to helping her mother on a daily basis. Even as young as nine, she'd been capable of running a house. Capable, loyal, smart, and beautiful. He quickly learned about her active mind when their third grade teacher paired them up to do a project on the Pilgrims. Lorraine took charge from the start and executed every detail with an almost obsessive care. Because of her, they delivered the best presentation and received praise for having the most creative poster – Lorraine had insisted they make the figures three-dimensional, like a pop-up book she'd once seen. Their teacher asked them to pose with their poster while she took a photograph. He remembered looking over at her face, so serious for the picture, and feeling his heart swell with pride. By some, they were considered dumb, Italian immigrants, and a recognition like this, small as it was, had the power to disprove such ignorance.

She looked at him now with those dark, flashing eyes, and her milky skin still smooth even at forty-two. "What are you smiling about?"

"Oh, I was just thinkin' about when we were young."

"We're still young."

"I mean way back in grade school."

"What made you think of that?"

"I don't know. Watching you mill about our kitchen like you used to in your parents' house."

"When you would spy on me, you mean?" she teased.

"I was admiring. There's a difference. Either way," – he stood, put on his jacket, and zipped it up to a couple of inches below his tie knot – "I'm glad I finally won you over, Rainy." He bent and kissed her cheek. It still carried the scent of Pond's moisturizer.

"You feeling okay?"

"Sure," he lied. "Are you? How's that headache?"

"Oh, it's lingering, but manageable. You sure you're okay?"

"I am. It's a beautiful day. I'm sure the fresh air will do me good. Tell the kids I'll see them later. I love you."

"I love you. Here's your lunch."

With that, he set his cap on his head and proceeded out into the morning. The smell of bologna in his lunch pail brought on a fresh wave of nausea, but Domenic wasn't a worrier, so he banished any troubling thoughts of recent symptoms. When he arrived at work, he focused on arranging the mail for delivery as usual, which was a welcome distraction.

On his route, he walked a little slower than normal, but he still stopped to smell the roses that peeked over the top of Mrs. Anderson's fence. He still stopped and chatted with little Danny Stodges, even though his house was just one off his route. And he still thought about what to do with Sally, his teenage daughter. They'd had a terrible disagreement yesterday, which was unlike them. He wished he'd stopped in on her this morning to kiss her forehead and show her that he wasn't cross. What a stubborn creature. Arguing with her was like confronting Lorraine's temper inhabiting a younger, female version of himself. A funny phenomenon it was, having little parts of you wandering around in other people. That's what a miracle was, and he and Lorraine had made two beautiful ones.

Consumed by this happy thought, Domenic didn't even notice that he'd fallen to his knees, the letters in his sack spilling out like so many unseen days.

Chapter I

The custodian was wearing her father's old shoes. She knew this because she'd looked at those shoes every day for the past two years. She knew from the scuff on the left one. As she peered at him from behind her locker door, her thoughts wandered back to last week – the worst week of her life.

Last Monday, those shoes were on her father's feet while he suffered a massive heart attack. Two days later, the shoes sat on the floor of her parents' bedroom seemingly watching as she struggled to find another article of his clothing. The scent of cedar hung in the air as Sally sifted through the pile of handkerchiefs. Where was it? His favorite one, pale green with faint dots. Her fingers rifled through them, disrupting the elegance of her mother's pristine folding. The pile spilled over onto itself like a stack of cards.

"Sally? Have you found it? We need to leave," Lorraine's voice floated down the hall, still muted with grief and fading at the end of its sentences.

Sally hated that her father was dead. She hated looking for his favorite handkerchief so he could wear it into the grave. A familiar powdery sage flashed for a second from underneath a garish paisley. She snatched it up and brought it to her nose. It still smelled like Old Spice. And, for a moment, it felt like he was there.

"Found it!"

She held the small piece of fabric a moment longer, pressing it to her face. It was softer than when she'd given it to him one random Father's Day years ago. Because of all the wear. For every special occasion, it was his choice.

When she was younger, she always noted this and felt pride at his selection. But later, she took it for granted. She figured maybe it was just easy for him to choose that one. It left out the thinking. He'd always ordered maple walnut for ice cream and fettuccine alfredo for Italian. Always fried clams for seafood. Always bleu cheese for salad dressing. He'd worn the same pair of shoes for the last two years, even though they were getting run down. Because it was easier than buying something new. That's what she'd thought of him, even though she knew it wasn't true.

He wore the pocket square because it was a present from his little girl. She knew that. She closed her eyes, taking in the scent, imagining him standing in front of her.

"I'm sorry," she whispered. She waited for his answer, but it didn't come. It would never come.

Earlier today, before school started, before she saw the custodian wearing her father's shoes, everyone was staring at her. She could feel the weight of their looks, billowing out behind her like the train of a gown. Clusters of girls in her grade turned to gawk as she passed to get to her locker at the end of the junior corridor. Some of their looks were empathetic, some curious, and while a small percent were mocking, their impact fell heaviest. Once she made it by those snub-nosed cliques, laughter was sure to follow.

Sally wondered at their callousness. She was only just back at school following her father's sudden death and funeral. Why such cruel treatment when before everyone had just ignored her?

Father's funeral had been last Friday and today was the following Wednesday. Sally begged to be kept home for another full week, but Lorraine said no. She was starting her now necessary job at the laundry downtown thanks to the kindness of Mr. Crawford. And if she could be brave enough to do that then Sally could be brave enough to join her brother at school. Sally didn't think it was all that necessary. There was a pension, wasn't there?

But she couldn't argue with her mother. She couldn't protest when Lorraine wasted no time at all getting rid of his shirts, pants, suits – the shoes even – at the local thrift. Her mother was a machine not to be trifled with under such circumstances. And, if questioned, she would argue that despite his pension, she now had a mortgage to pay and two children to put through college. Maybe it was just that she didn't want to sit within those walls every day in the middle of all of his things. Even so, Sally had wanted to rip his clothes out of her hands and hide them in her room.

But whatever her repressed feelings, she saw her mother trying to be kind. Here was a new cardigan she could wear that Lorraine purchased with a few other pieces while she was unloading Domenic's clothes. Because that's where they'd have to shop in the future, especially since Sally kept sprouting up and outgrowing her older, well-worn outfits. She knew her mother, who was a naturally fashionable woman, had felt the pang of being a teenager with only two dresses during the Depression and liked being able to give her own child options. But no more Parke Snow. No more Sears. No more Elizabeth Hines. The cardigan was lovely, hardly worn and a deep cranberry with rhinestone buttons. In truth, it was finer than almost anything else Sally owned so she didn't mind putting it on over her plaid day dress of autumn hues. She liked how her dark hair, with its natural auburn sheen, fell against it. Early October in New England teased with a few warm days, echoes of summer, and that morning she left her camel suede jacket at home.

Her locker neighbor, Heather, regarded her with a look of wry pity. Heather was less than quiet, but more an outcast than herself. She was short with a thick mass of dark hair and even thicker eyebrows that sat like two caterpillars above her expressive eyes. She still wore braces and played the clarinet in marching band. The two of them were always partners in science class and in physical education, mostly because no one else wanted to pair up with them. Sally didn't mind.

Heather popped a butterscotch into her mouth and immediately slung it to the side so she could speak. It stuck out of her cheek like a tumor.

"I tried to come to the funeral, but my mom said things like that are only for family."

"You could've come. Paul's friends did."

Every Italian wake was a reunion of sorts on the same level as a neighborhood summer block party, and her father's was no exception. She stood in line next to her brother, who as usual, was a pillar of silent strength, while the loud gesticulating, tears, and melodrama unfolded before them like the spectacles under a circus tent. To keep from looking at her father's corpse, Sally made a game of watching her brother's changing expression. When someone greeted him and apologized, he nodded his head with solemn deference. When the same person moved on to Sally to express their sympathies, Paul set his hand on her shoulder in support. When there was a fresh outburst of over-the-top grief, his lips drew up tight and disappeared, a half-laugh sometimes escaped, and he'd shake his head in disgust. In response to Aunt Bianca sobbing so hard that she nearly fainted and had to be carried out by her rheumatic husband, Paul's reaction was to bend and whisper to Sally, "I'm starting to wish we were born into a repressed Protestant household." Under normal circumstances, Sally would have laughed to hear such dark sarcasm leave her brother's lips. But she knew this wasn't like a joke that her favorite cousin, Nick, would make. Her brother was perfectly serious.

And after the funeral, there was another party at the house of the deceased with the same cold cut platters and pastries each time. The same homemade wine. Sally wandered ghost-like, asking people if they needed anything, her cheeks sticky with lipstick smears in a rainbow of colors. She overheard stories about her father that she already knew.

"Remember senior year when Domenic hit that homerun and then ran straight off the field because he saw Lorraine talking to Salvatore Guilio? We lost the game, but he asked her to marry him."

"Remember when he came back from the war and surprised his mother by sleeping on the couch like his father? She went to whack him with the newspaper, and he threw back the blanket and grabbed her. She almost fainted in his arms."

"Remember when the Waterson's dog knocked him down and, instead of biting him, it just licked his face off?"

Sally felt like chiming in, "Remember when his only daughter fought with him and the next day he dropped dead before she could apologize?" But of course, she didn't.

Heather stood before her now, sucking her candy and arching her caterpillars. Sally grabbed her books for math class and slammed her locker. She could still feel a sea of eyes on her.

"What are people laughing at me for? Do they think it's just hilarious that my father's dead?"

Heather sighed. "No, they're laughing because when you got out of your brother's car this morning, Tammy Gallagher noticed you were wearing an old cardigan that her mother had just donated. She called you 'Secondhand Sally.' She thinks she's such a clever trick."

"Ain't that just great."

Heather shrugged, biting into her candy. "Who cares? Besides, making fun of you won't erase the fact that your brother has no interest in dating her. Homecoming King and Queen and all...Well, I have English class. *Othello*. Sitting through Rhonda reading for Desdemona is like listening to a goat trying to speak French. The Bard is rolling in his grave. See you in science."

Heather stormed off in her surly gait, passing the new custodian who was cleaning up a small river of coffee, still steaming where it spilled. Sally hadn't noticed him before, but she did now, along with the thin volume tucked in his back pocket. *The Great Gatsby*, she noted on further inspection. He resembled someone out of the twenties with his sandy hair, the lines of a lean silhouette filling his tidy uniform. He was sinewy like a farmhand and a deep intellect shone in his eyes. A thoughtfulness. Sally forgot about the judgmental stares burning a hole in her back. She could only think of wandering around one of those lavish, twilight parties and running into this mysterious man by a champagne fountain.

And then, there on his feet, were her father's shoes. She was sure of it – that scuff. He must have gotten them from the thrift right after Lorraine had taken them there. How curious to see them on someone else so soon. A pang of betrayal shot through her for an instant, as though the shoes had moved on far too quickly. But that was silly – she almost smirked at the thought – to be upset with a pair of inanimate objects like they had any choice in their fate.

He looked up and saw her watching him.

"Good morning."

Before she could answer, a gaggle of cackles erupted from the stairwell next to her, and who would emerge from the swinging doors but Tammy, and her Tammettes, as Heather coined them: Donna, Rhonda, and Marie. Tammy slowed her perky strut and took in the full length of her victim with cold, blue eyes that reminded Sally of the baby dolls she never wanted to play with as a child. She'd always felt like they were judging her in this same way for her dark, European looks, like she didn't belong in their plastic, Anglo-Saxon world, even though they belonged to her.

Tammy drew closer, inches from her face like when they were in elementary school. Even back then, she used her height to establish dominance. Because she was tallest and had a single hair budding under her arm by fourth grade, she won the other girls' reverence. And she'd never liked Sally. For what reason?

Sally had beaten her once in a race when running was Tammy's only talent. Sally was quiet and never fought back when picked on. She preferred to be off by herself coloring. For someone like Tammy, whose unfettered charisma commanded the attention of all – even those so far beneath her notice – it just infuriated her that Sally wasn't interested in being another sycophant in her growing collection.

As she stared at the tiny, blonde hairs protruding from the beauty mark above her adversary's lips, Sally comforted herself with the knowledge that

Tammy had always seemed so much more mature and sophisticated than everyone in grade school because she'd stayed back in first grade and then again in second.

"Nice sweater," she hissed in Sally's face and continued by.

The Tammettes burst into a peal of hysterical laughter that reverberated as the closest group of loiterers repeated it to those beside them and, like a roll of thunder, it found its way to the other end of the hall. Marie, whose family had faithfully sat next to Sally's in church every Sunday, turned back when the others were out of earshot.

"I'm sorry for your loss."

This small semblance of remorse smacked Sally in the gut with much more force than the teasing about her thrift store cardigan. She felt the proverbial lump in her throat, but her mouth was too dry to swallow it. Their eyes were still on her, like row upon row of vacant, baby doll stares. She spun on her heel to leave, but found the custodian still watching her, although now his rugged face and kind eyes were full of concern.

"Morning." Sally put her head down and walked past him, hugging her books to her chest.

There was a loud rumbling outside. Sally threw back the living room curtain.

"What's that noise?"

Her mother paused, holding her tray of perfume bottles. Sally never understood this ritual. The bottles teetered together while Lorraine moved like molasses to reach the kitchen sink and wipe each one free from its minuscule layer of weekly dust. Sally wanted to ask why she didn't just clean them with the dust rag where they sat, but there was no point. Her mother would continue on with her regular balancing act regardless of whether it was practical. And especially if someone had the nerve to point it out to her.

Sally peered back outside. "It looks like Joey got himself a new GTO."

Lorraine smiled and resumed her crawl. "Well, he's a boy. They like their cars now, don't they?"

Of course, because "he was a boy," that excused any bad behavior in her mother's eyes, besides the fact that his father was a prominent doctor and they lived in one of the nicest brick houses in neighboring Medford. He could be a communist, and Lorraine would still be wishing for a future marriage.

Sally tolerated Joey's presence and attention for one reason: out of respect. He was the son of her father's best friend, Teddy Mosca. Teddy had grown up in Winchester, down the street from Domenic and Lorraine, until his family moved one town over to Medford when he was eleven. Still, he and Domenic had remained best friends.

The two had kept in touch through school and even throughout her father's service in the Army. While Domenic married Lorraine and shipped her out to join him where he was stationed at a Prisoner of War camp in California, Teddy's flat feet precluded him from serving his country. He was well on his way to becoming a surgeon by the time the war ended. But he and Domenic had written letters full of childhood reminiscing, continuing their age-old feud about whose mother made the best sauce, and sending pictures. Teddy and his young fiancé, Carla, even honeymooned out that way so they could pay a special visit. And, after Domenic and Lorraine came back east and settled in Wakefield, the Moscas were always invited over for holiday parties, barbeques, and birthdays. They were like family.

Sally remembered Joey as a boy, small for his age and wiry, sitting across from her on the living room rug. A boy who chose to play quieter games with her and Cousin Nick, instead of causing mayhem like the other rambunctious male cousins in her mother's family. In fact, what Sally had liked about him was his shy nature, the gentle way he combed her Barbie doll's gold-spun hair and handled her tea set with such attentiveness. They played hide-and-seek and he counted so softly they could hardly hear him.

But then a change happened when they were around twelve. It was as though he realized his family was well off, and that did something to him. He became stuck-up at these gatherings, and while he still favored Sally's company, it was more so he could brag about himself and his possessions. This quality hung about him even now, especially when he had something new.

Sally didn't believe in the same excuses as her mother and turned icy as she watched him sprint up the front steps of their raised ranch with a smug smile resting on his face.

"What are you doing?" she demanded, opening the door.

"Is that how you greet your boyfriend?"

"You're not my boyfriend, and this is a residential neighborhood. Pull up to the house like that again and I won't even answer next time."

"Ugh." He scrunched up his face so that all his babyish features were just a little too close together, congregating in the middle like they were having a meeting. His high forehead, with its mass of slicked-back hair, presided over this activity. "It's 1967. Stop being such a square. It's just a new car."

"Just a new car? Just like that? How nice it must be to snap your fingers and have Daddy spring for the latest model. I bet my brother would really appreciate that since he had to slave three summers at my uncle's gas station to buy his used Nova. Look, Joey, I don't have time for this. Whatever this is."

She felt immediate remorse for her words. What if her cruelty one day drove him to never come back? Then what, she asked herself. It would just be another part of her father gone.

He dug his shoe into the slate of the stone steps. "I came to see if you could use some cheering up. Maybe go get an ice cream or something?"

"Did I hear someone say ice cream?" Nick appeared from behind her.

The warmth of his hands squeezing her shoulders provided instant relief. In a swarm of rowdy male cousins, Nick was nearest to her in age and her best friend since they could speak. He was closer to her than her own brother. Paul was always so serious like their mother; Nick was silly and jovial like she wanted to be.

They made up their own language when they were seven. They "ran away" together when they were eight to their Aunt Marion's garden shed. Their provisions were cans of baked beans, Chef Boyardee, and a bag of Kraft caramels. Aunt Marion found them the next morning, snuggled together in a sleeping bag with bellyaches after everyone had spent all night searching. Sally was going to get the belt for the first time over this, but Nick had insisted her father dole out the punishment on him. Now here he was, rescuing her yet again, this time from the peril of Joey's irritating company.

"Where'd you come from?" she asked.

"Came up the side walkway. Mom is here with me. She's out on the back porch now with your mom. So? What are we waiting for? I heard ice cream, and now I'm set on it. Paul around?"

"No, he's out with some football friends after practice."

"Brigham's then? That okay with you buddy?"

Joey's wellspring of machismo seemed to have dried up. "Sure, man. That's cool."

"We can take Nick's car," Sally said. "I don't want to make a spectacle downtown."

"Aw, really? But Joey's car is so boss," Nick whined.

"See?" Joey piped up. "At least someone appreciates it."

Wakefield center was the place to be on a Friday night. There was the movie theater, the Bowladrome, and Brigham's. Sally watched out the car window as the familiar storefronts of downtown scrolled past. They sat in a parade of teenage drivers, their cars like colorful floats, moving in a slow line to check out the Friday night action. The Mustang in front of them honked at a flock of girls congregating on the wall of the Beebe Library, and one redhead with a swinging ponytail ran over and hopped in the back. They looped around past the bandstand, the crown jewel of the town green. On balmy summer nights and weekends, bands played, and their melodies drifted out over the droves of picnicking families as little ones grew heavy-eyed with approaching slumber.

Her favorite spot in all this was the Colonial Spa. Mr. K., ever the gentleman, presided over the soda counter, turning out raspberry lime rickeys that were uniformly perfect in their tart sweetness and a fizziness that tickled your nose. One time, he revealed that the raspberry syrup came from berries grown in his own family's garden. She preferred to visit the Spa alone, though. It was a special haven where she could sit for an hour and lose her thoughts among the tiles in the mosaic floor, Mr. K's old stories soothing her like a melancholy lullaby. It was the kind of place where you could forget that a war was going on outside your door. A place that safeguarded the wholesome innocence that seeped out from underneath as fast as the sugary concoction ran up your straw and flooded your mouth with sweet distraction. There was nothing you could do to hold onto it.

"So, Joey, how's your junior year going?" asked Nick as they sat down with their treats.

They squeezed into a small area enclosed by wooden panels and frosted glass. A symphony of other conversations filled the air, and Sally half-listened to Joey while eavesdropping on the tables around them.

"Oh, you know. School's okay, kinda boring. My band has some upcoming gigs, though." He smirked at Sally. "We're playing the Topsfield Fair next weekend, and I'd really like you to come."

"I don't know." She swirled the ice cream around in her bowl until it became softer. "I'm not much for going out lately."

Joey's face fell, and he immersed himself in eating his banana boat. Nick gave Sally the same reprimanding expression that his mother, Jo, was famous for.

"Sally, I think it might be fun for you to get out to the fair," he started in his upbeat way. "See the animals, eat some kettle corn. You can't ditch every fall tradition. This time of year is your favorite."

"Was."

"I'll take you. Maybe our moms want to go."

"My mom definitely won't, but I'll consider it," she conceded.

"Well, look who it is," a snide voice interrupted.

Sally looked up to see Tammy. She only had one of the Tammettes in tow, but there she stood, regal in a dress the same electric blue as her spiteful eyes.

"What's that you're wearing? Another of my castoffs? Did your desperate mother follow mine into the thrift store?"

Sally looked down at the violet sweater set she had on with a pleated, plaid skirt of forest greens, reds, and the same purple, and instantly cursed herself for not suspecting the rest of the clothes her mother had brought home. How careless. Tammy laughed again.

"Poor little Secondhand Sally."

Some nearby tables full of peers overheard this time but didn't join in on the laughing. In fact, after her somewhat rocky start back to school last Wednesday, the rest of Sally's week had been met with sympathetic looks and pats on the back as she walked to her seat in classes. Nick and Joey both paused mid-spoonful, and Nick now set his down and began to stand. But before he could say anything, Tammy scooped a runny heap of mint chocolate chip on her spoon and flicked it onto Sally's chest.

"Oops! Sorry!"

"Hey, that's enough!" Paul's voice boomed from behind them. Her brother stood in the doorway of the ice cream parlor, tall and imposing, flanked by two of his bulkiest teammates.

Tammy's mean-spirited grin faded into embarrassed guilt as Paul strode over to their table with a look of paternal rage carved into his already brooding face. Brooding and serious, most of the time, but he could also be warm, especially once he got to know people. A natural leader and such a fine athlete, none of his teammates seemed to mind that he was also studious and less silly than the average teenage boy. Instead, they looked up to him and had his back on and off the field with a fierce loyalty. His eyes, which were velvety sable like their mother's, burned like coals in his head, the white showing all the way around them. If he wasn't her brother, Sally would've been terrified herself.

"What the hell is wrong with you?" he barked at Tammy, who seemed to be shrinking like Alice in Wonderland after taking the magic potion.

"Aw, Paul, I was just joking with your sister here. No harm done," she answered in her most syrupy voice.

"Like fun." His voice grew deeper and he pointed a thick finger close to her face. "I've heard about this nickname you have for my little sister, 'Secondhand Sally.' Because she's wearing your old clothes? Because our father dies, like that," –he snapped his fingers– "and you think it's fun and games to put a grieving person through more pain? What kind of monster does that?"

Tammy looked at the black and white tile floor.

"Answer me!" he bellowed. Any remaining chatter in the place halted at this. Everyone waited for her answer. Even the workers underneath their wedged caps stayed transfixed instead of admonishing. Darcy, the manager, who normally didn't stand for any antics, stood doughy in his white uniform, his belly poised above his belt buckle as though it, too, anticipated the moment.

Tammy shook her head.

"You got nothing to say now? Well, I'm not done yet. The taunting stops this second. Understand?"

She nodded, now looking up at him with imploring orbs.

"My sister may be stuck in your old clothes, but at least they have the chance to be worn by a decent human being," he finished and marched up to the counter to place his order as though he hadn't just told someone off.

Tammy and the Tammette scurried out of the shop, and the talking resumed in quieter tones. Nick gave an approving nod in Paul's direction.

"You gotta hand it to him. He may be a serious bastard, but he speaks like a goddamn president."

Sally laughed and looked out the shop's front window. The rest of the Tammettes had arrived, and she could see them commiserating. Tammy caught her eye and formed a scowl that promised retribution. They walked off, but she held Sally with her poisonous gaze until she was out of sight.

"I'm not wearing these clothes anymore!" Sally screeched at Lorraine on her way to her room that night.

Lorraine barely glanced up from her latest historical romance. This was one thing mother and daughter had in common at least. Books. It was something that drove her father mad. Instead of finding Lorraine in bed next to him most nights, he would find her hiding in the bathroom devouring prose. She would sit there on the hard porcelain of the closed toilet seat, because from the outside no one could see the light on in the back of the house, and God forbid a neighbor see that she was up until all hours of the morning – that would be embarrassing.

Sally was the same way. When she was little, she'd sneak out her flashlight and sit up under the covers reading and re-reading *The Secret Garden, The Little Princess, Anne of Green Gables, The Lord of the Rings, The Hobbit,* and *The Lion, the Witch, and the Wardrobe*. She would turn to these whenever she needed comfort. Soon the romance of classics drew her in, though, and *Wuthering Heights, Jane Eyre, Pride and Prejudice,* and anything else by Jane Austen replaced old favorites.

She flung herself on her bed in a rage. Of course, she hadn't betrayed her emotions to anyone that night, not even Nick. Maybe this was, in fact, another part of her mother's disposition she'd inherited. She could hold in feelings and appear unperturbed when her insides felt like a roiling mass of hot lava.

She'd never again sport another Tammy original at school, home, or anywhere else around town, she promised herself as she reached for the scissors in her sewing basket. From her bureau and closet, she snatched out the items she knew had once belonged to Tammy. The beautiful cranberry cardigan, another butter-colored sweater with a lovely quilted pattern, two black skirts that weren't even saved by their plainness – Tammy would know and would find a way to remark. The violet sweater set and plaid skirt needed to come off, too. She stood there, shaking with anger in her underwear, using her small scissors to cut up the despised garments and wishing instead that she was doing violence to their previous owner. The darker side of her wondered if this activity may have some type of voodoo doll effect. Maybe Tammy was at home right now going through her nightly beauty regimen and couldn't even lather up with cold cream because she was doubled over in pain at the sensation of little cuts all over her body.

She looked up to see Lorraine hovering in the doorway. Her mother had aged during her one week of work so far. She had dark circles under her eyes and her face was sunken and dull. If only five days at the laundromat had produced this level of deterioration, Lorraine would be an old woman by Christmas. Sally looked down at the pile of tattered rags she'd made out of her mother's gesture and started to cry.

Lorraine came close and hugged her. "I know," she said. "I miss him, too."

She cried into her mother's neck, dampening the shoulder of the modest, black dress she wore. It was a dress Sally remembered from at least a decade ago, and Lorraine still wore it. She'd refreshed it several times, adding on a new collar and a lace trim at the hem. Growing up during the Depression had made her frugal. She could stretch a dollar into ten, and she could salvage like no one else.

"Paul told me what's been happening at school," her mother said in her ear. "I never liked that Tammy. Her whole family are a bunch of snobs. And the father...Humph," she began and stopped mid-thought.

"What?"

"Oh, I shouldn't say."

"That's so unfair. You have to tell me now."

"Well, you have to promise you won't repeat this. But the father has a wandering eye, let's say."

"How do you mean?"

"I've learned a few things at work this week and more about people's dirty laundry than – well, than their actual dirty laundry. If you know what I mean."

"Yeah, he's given me a couple of looks at events."

"Me, too," admitted Lorraine. She brushed Sally's hair behind her ear. "Look, I won't get your clothes at the thrift store anymore, but we still have to be economical. So maybe…" She paused to think and Sally could see something visionary forming in her impressive brain. Sally thought of it as impressive since Lorraine dropped out of school after eighth grade to help her own mother, who'd been ill. And still, she was one of the smartest people Sally knew, always able to find a solution. Her sisters all came to her whenever they had a problem that needed fixing.

"Maybe I can take home some of the clothes that people forget to pick up – if they're old enough. After a few months of neglect, they become our property by default. I could ask about this, and if so, they're all yours. They may be a hodgepodge, though."

"Okay, I don't mind that. And I can even sew on some collars or something if I want."

"That's a wonderful idea," her mother said. "I'll give you a few dollars to visit Adrian's. You can buy some embellishments – fabrics, buttons. You know, odds and ends." She touched Sally's face once more then moved to her bookshelf and, with the tip of her finger, slid out *Wuthering Heights*. "Once you're out bashing along the moors with Cathy and Heathcliff, you won't even remember that any of this happened."

Chapter II

It was the end of the day, and she stalled as the building emptied, hopeful to have a moment with the custodian. For days now, she'd been watching him, especially once she'd noticed the shoes. That was a sign, she thought. He was a person to know. As though the fact that he was wearing her father's shoes somehow marked him as good, approved by the Universe. One of his supply closets was right across from her locker and adjacent to the first-floor girls' bathroom, so there were many opportunities to talk to him.

Sally planned what she would say to reference his reading of *The Great Gatsby*. It was casual but clever, she thought. It would make her seem mature beyond her years. Her line would be, "Did you get to the sad part yet?"

The last of the students spilled out and rays of afternoon sun flooded in from the tall windows behind the stairwell and through the wired glass of the swinging doors next to her locker, illuminating her path. Dust particles mingled in the light, and Sally indulged in the fantasy that they were flower petals, floating and adrift on the breeze at the hazy twilight of a Gatsby soirée. She approached as he exited the closet with his mop and bucket to clean the intersecting trails of dusty footprints that now marred the floor.

But as luck would have it, Sally never had the chance to unleash her wit on him. Voices trailed from behind the girls' bathroom door as it swung open, and the inane chatter emerged as if from a cavernous dungeon into the air in sharp, crisp notes. Tammy was once again in front of her with two of the Tammettes this time. Marie wasn't there. She looked as taken aback as Sally, but there was also a sharp resentment, as if behind her tight, pursed lips, she was biting down as hard as she could to keep from lashing out at her favorite target.

She managed to hold her wicked tongue, though she stood there for a long minute, sizing Sally up with those piercing eyes. At least, Sally thought, I'm no longer wearing her clothes. Today she put on another favorite burnt orange dress, a medium wool weight because it was chilly. On top of it was a creamy Irish knit cardigan, given to her last year by their neighbor, Mrs. McNamara. There was nothing unbecoming about this outfit, nothing offensive or outdated that Tammy could latch onto. In place of a snarky comment, she strode past and knocked so hard into Sally's left shoulder that her unfastened book bag fell to the floor and spilled its contents at the custodian's feet. The other two followed suit and by the time Sally could crouch to the floor to retrieve her belongings, he was already down there.

Their hands touched once as they grasped for rolling pencils. Neither spoke. He reached to scoop up her books: Algebra, Chemistry, U.S. History, and *Othello* for English class. She held her bag open as he placed them inside.

"I'm reading a bit of Shakespeare myself," he said, yanking from his back pocket a worn copy of *Twelfth Night*.

"Ohhh, I love that one," she said, thankful now that she hadn't made a fool of herself with a joke about Gatsby. "I used to read it aloud to myself."

"Really? You should audition for a play or something if you like that sort of thing."

"No." She blushed and shook her head. "I'm too shy."

He smiled, revealing deep dimples in the light scruff on his cheeks. They were both still crouched down, and now he stood, as if realizing some impropriety. She copied his abrupt action, and he formally held out his hand.

"I'm Arthur, by the way."

"Sally."

They shook. His hands were rough and calloused from all the chemicals, but his nails were clean and trimmed.

"It's nice to meet you," she said, now growing self-conscious. She couldn't use her planned joke, and she was never effective off the cuff.

"You too," he said, "and don't worry about those girls." He tapped his book and quoted, "'Such as we are made of, such we be.' And let's face it, some of us just aren't made as well as others."

Sally laughed at the irony. "Like clothes…if she were a dress, she'd be defective."

"Exactly," he said. "It's like you can't fake quality with frills. For instance, I bought some wonderful clothes recently. They're older but they're well-made and sturdy. They'll last. They're better than anything new I could have purchased, and I paid less."

She smiled knowing that he likely meant her father's clothes. Again, she felt a lump rise.

"Well, I should go. It was nice to talk to you."

His animated features flickered and dimmed but then surfaced again as he looked down the vast stretch of hallway.

"Right, and I must conquer this before my day can end." Arthur gave her a wry smile as he positioned his mop. "See you around, Sally."

That night, Lorraine came home with a twinkle in her eye, toting a plastic bag full of discarded, forgotten laundry. They were all workable items, but a few would need tailoring. Among some plain, white blouses, a goldenrod top with a turn-down collar, two A-line skirts with pretty prints, and a green, tweed pencil skirt, were two lovely dresses, one mulberry and the other yellow.

"I just took what looked to be in your size."

"These dresses are beautiful quality."

"Well, I tried to select the nicest pieces. What was left of it, Mr. Crawford was about to donate to the thrift. He does that when the clothes are left for six months. So, there were other nice clothes, but their time wasn't up yet, see. Do you think you'll want to alter these much?"

"Mmmm, definitely not the dresses, but these white blouses could use some embellishments, maybe ruffled collars or something. And I might put a contrasting trim on the pencil skirt, like black or purple."

"I can spare a few dollars so you can go to Adrian's tomorrow."

"Thanks, Mom."

Lorraine put some homemade sauce in a pan to simmer, set the water on for pasta, and began to assemble a simple salad while it boiled.

"How are things between you and Joey?"

"Mom…" Sally warned.

"I'm just asking. Can't a mother ask?"

"There's nothing to ask about. We're friends. He wishes we could be more. I tolerate his unwanted affection out of respect for his father's friendship with Dad." Sally folded the clothes and shoved them in the bag as fast as possible so she could make a swift retreat to her room, but Lorraine couldn't be put off.

"Someday you may feel differently, dear. You know, I wasn't always crazy about your father. We grew up next door to each other on Olive Street. And we were from immigrant families, so we all stuck together. Our families were particularly close. We each had a slew of children – six in mine and ten in his. Our fathers both grew their own vegetables right in the joined backyard. We had chickens and rabbits, we made wine. Even though it was the Depression, we were still able to enjoy a quiet, simple life. Well, maybe not quiet," – she smiled – "but always together, laughing and eating and playing. And your father loved me from when we were children. He always said he would marry me. Personally, I thought he was a bit annoying, a big show off. But in the end, he was tenacious, and I had to give him credit for that. I see the same perseverance in that Joey and, well, someday he just might win you over."

Sally stood aghast at this tale. "You've never told me this before. How am I sixteen and just hearing that you married Dad because he bugged you until you caved?"

Lorraine simpered, stirring her sauce. "Humph, well…I also did think he was quite fetching. He had that little cleft in his chin just like Cary Grant."

"I'm home!" Paul came through the back door wearing his football jacket but absent of his school bag.

"Where have you been? It's nearly six-thirty!"

"Practice."

"Practice ends at four."

Paul shrugged his way past his mother. There was a sturdiness about Lorraine's petite frame that still intimidated even a bulky quarterback of almost six feet.

"I was just with some friends, Ma."

"You know I hate 'Ma.' What about your homework?"

"Done, thanks to last period study hall." He lifted the lid off the sauce and took a deep whiff, grinning at them. "Are we done with the inquisition now? Because I'm starving."

Lorraine's dark eyes narrowed, and her lips clamped themselves into the most formidable line. A look of sheer terror passed over Paul's features, but before he could apologize, the wooden spoon she was holding had already made contact with his behind.

"Ow! Ma! I'm not a toddler. You can't spank me anymore!!" He clutched his stinging backside.

Their mother now stood with her hand on her hip, pointing at him with her weapon. "I'll tell you this. When you move out into your own house that you pay for, then I'll no longer spank you. But until then, your rear is free game. And don't ever talk to me in that tone again, or this spoon will hit you so hard in the mouth, you'll be brushing splinters out of your teeth for a week!"

The next day, Sally walked out of school with five dollars in her pocket and headed straight to the fabric store downtown. The top floor of Adrian's was her favorite part to visit. Bolts of the finest fabric in every color of the rainbow rose to the ceiling. She remembered coming with Lorraine when she was a little girl and hiding in the rows of silk, pretending to be a spoiled daughter selecting the materials for her latest seasonal wardrobe.

But she was older now, and maturity had dulled her sense of imagination. Maturity and reality, she guessed. The fact of the matter was that she would most likely never be in the position to buy luxurious silk or have custom designed clothing. And that was fine. *At least*, she thought, *I have a few dollars to spend here*. She stuck to the bottom floor where the cottons and linens made a less impressive, though still vibrant, display. Down here there were also buttons, fabric to use as trim, and sewing tools.

A woman with thick, honey-toned hair piled high on her head smiled from behind the counter as Sally perused. Another group of ladies gathered around a small table with their own sewing machines set in front of them while a matronly woman at the head of the table instructed in a patient tone.

Sally picked out some squiggly purple trim for the pencil skirt and then moved towards the woman at the counter.

"Could you help me pick out fabric? I want to spruce up some plain, white shells by adding collars and I was thinking of prints."

"Of course. Let's have a look. My name is Rose."

Close up, Rose was younger than Sally had speculated, maybe only in her mid-twenties. But the way she moved reflected an older grace, and her voice was girlish in contrast to her sensuous, hour-glass shape. The violet dress she wore hugged her curves, fabric swishing in time with her steps. *She must get asked out a lot*, Sally thought as she followed behind, nearly hypnotized herself by Rose's swaying hips.

"You like sewing?" Rose asked, looking back.

"I do, but I'm not very skilled."

"You should take a class here. I teach one on Wednesdays at about this time."

"That could work."

"Now, let's see. Here are some lovely plaid linens. There's also some floral cottons that might be nice for a collar."

In the end, Sally decided on a plaid of dark pink, purple, and teal, a pink cotton starburst, and a charming print of navy antique cars over a green and white swirl pattern. The last one wasn't quite as practical, but she thought it was too adorable to pass up. She bade good-bye to Rose and mused over a cherry Coke at the Colonial Spa before she started for home, swelling with pride that she even had some money to spare. Her joy was fleeting, though, when she spied Tammy and the Tammettes in her direct path as they headed uptown after cheerleading practice. There they were, a line of only three with Marie once again missing, all in matching white sweaters brandishing the emblematic "W," and pleated, red skirts.

Sally cut down Armory Street so they wouldn't see her. She was about a third of the way down when she noticed a familiar face through a window across the street. Slowing down and taking cover under a leafy tree, she pretended to inspect the items in her bag while casting her eyes at the grand house. There was Arthur, sitting in an upstairs window and wearing one of her father's favorite plaid, short-sleeved shirts while typing away furiously on a typewriter.

She felt a pang of anger at the sight of him that wasn't directed at him, but at her mother. Why did she have to get rid of everything so fast? Save for a few pieces Paul could inherit like his watch and his ties because her brother was, in fact, a much larger person than Domenic, it was like her father never had a physical existence in their home. Old pictures hinted of his presence, his tools were still in the garage, though covered with a tarp, some personal belongings like books and albums still haunted shelves in the living room, but none of his clothes. Sally didn't linger now in fear of being spied herself. She hurried home and decided on the way to keep the bit of extra money Lorraine had gifted her.

When she walked into Adrian's again the following afternoon, Rose beamed at her from behind the counter. The jade dress she wore seemed just as striking as the previous day's violet, but maybe it was just Rose who made the dresses look even better when usually it was the opposite.

Before school that morning, Sally had raided her savings. Along with the dollar fifty left from yesterday's spree, she had twelve additional from Christmas and her birthday that she hadn't yet spent. That made thirteen fifty. She felt rich all day at school with that amount in her pocket.

"I see we're back."

Sally nodded. "I was wondering how much that sewing class is."

"Well, it's discounted a little since it's a group class. Eighteen dollars for three sessions and the sessions are each two hours long. So, you'll receive six hours of instruction at three dollars per hour."

"Oh." Sally felt her face grow red. How foolish to think the small bit of money she had saved would be enough. "I – I don't have enough for that."

"What's your name, dear?"

"Sally Fiore."

Rose's smile didn't falter. Instead, she leaned over and spoke with sage composure, notes of her floral perfume scenting the air between them. "Well, Sally, I think I might have a solution for you. Did you happen to see the sign in the window as you came in?"

She looked at the front windows of the shop and noted, albeit backwards, that the sign read "Help Wanted." Rose's suggestion registered with her.

"I could work here?"

"Sure. Mr. R. put me in charge of hiring a part-time girl, and I can't think of anyone better for the position. He loves giving young people a chance. And, at your hourly wage," – she paused here doing the calculations in her head – "you could work from two to six Monday, Tuesday, Thursday, and Friday, and make enough to pay for your class on Wednesday with even a little to spare."

"That would be great."

"Can you start Monday?"

"Sure. I mean, I'll just have to check with my mother, but I don't think it will be a problem. She works right over at the laundry. We could even go home together on those days."

"Is your mother Lorraine Fiore?"

"Yes."

"Of course, I see the resemblance now. I chat with her sometimes when we're getting our morning coffee." Rose's face blanched. "Oh, Sally." She reached across the counter, grabbed Sally's hand with her soft white one, and looked at her with sorrowful blue eyes. "I'm so sorry…about your father."

Sally withdrew her hand from under Rose's and gave a solemn nod. "I'll see you Monday, Rose. Thank you for the opportunity."

She sighed as her feet hit the pavement and felt a necessary detour was in order before her almost daily sojourn to Colonial Spa. The laundry and dry cleaners was bustling as she stepped inside. Women hauled clothes out of the washing machines and loaded them into dryers. Others sat at stations folding. Sally didn't see Lorraine anywhere and stood near the entrance, unsure of what to do, until a brassy woman wearing a yellow kerchief addressed her.

"You lost?"

"I'm looking for my mother, Lorraine. She works here."

"Ohhh, it's Lorraine's little girl!" the woman shouted to some others close-by, who sat wearing similar kerchiefs like a row of pastel birds. They smiled and nodded over the din of their work. "She's out back on the steamer. Follow me."

The woman led Sally to a back room where her mother stood waving the steam machine around a royal blue scalloped dress until the wrinkles disappeared. Lorraine paused to wipe her brow before noticing her daughter.

"Oh! What are you doing here? Is everything okay?" Worry erupted on her face, and in the tense rigidity of her posture.

"Yes, I'm sorry. I didn't mean to pop in like this. I was just at Adrian's again, and I wanted to tell you that Rose – she says she knows you from morning coffee – offered me a job after school in exchange for sewing lessons."

"Oh?"

"I'd like to do it, but I wanted to run it by you."

"I think the responsibility of a job is a valuable experience, and learning to sew well is a skill you'll use for the rest of your life."

"I figured you'd agree."

"Rose is something, isn't she?" Lorraine smiled.

"She sure is."

"Her kind of beauty is a blessing and a curse. I can tell from speaking to her that she's a fine, moral woman, but with that face and that figure, she'll always be an object to men. One can only hope she finds a good one. So, where are you off to now? Home?"

"Might stop at Colonial Spa for a cherry Coke."

"Don't spoil your appetite."

Mr. K. assembled some cucumber sandwiches for two elderly ladies while she nursed her drink. He set their order in front of them like it was lobster on a silver platter. As she watched, a tune glided through the air from the radio, the same station her father listened to. The song was "Fascination," an instrumental version, but she knew the lyrics because they were some of the last words she'd heard her father say.

It was the Friday before he died, and they both had a dentist appointment. He already hadn't been feeling well and was sent home from work the day before. Sally sat next to him in the car, sulking because she hated going to the dentist and taking every moment for granted as people do. But she now remembered this scene in detail, wishing she could go back and relive it. He turned to his favorite station, and this same song came on.

He started singing, "It was fascination, I know. And it might have ended right then at the start."

"Dad…"

He eyed her sideways as he drove. "You like this song?"

"It's a nice song, I guess."

"It's a waltz. It may be a good song for us to dance to when you get married someday."

She snorted.

"Would you like me to sing some more of it?"

"No, that's okay." She giggled and shook her head at him.

The melody now crept into all the sad cracks of Sally's heart, filling them and expanding out into an even greater pain, a pain so intense she wondered if this was what a heart attack felt like, if this is what her father felt as he lay dying. So many realities were dawning on her lately, so many corners of her life clipped shut without her knowing – without her consent. She would have no father to walk her down the aisle, no father to dance with at her wedding. There would be no more mundane drives to the dentist's office together. She would never hear his voice again, let alone the treat of him falling into song. Mr. K. must have noticed her distress because he came down to where she sat at the other end of the counter, gave her a gentle look, and touched her wrist with his hand.

"How are you doing, Sally? Are you doing okay?"

As she walked home, she wondered if the pain would ever dull as people continued to be sympathetic. She assumed it eventually would. Perhaps some future day down the line, she'd be able to hear his name spoken or the word "father" itself even, without feeling such an ache inside. But not anytime soon.

While she thought, her body retraced its steps from the other day and trudged down Armory Street instead of favoring Main. She slowed again at the same house and looked up at the top right window. There he was again, in another of Domenic's casual shirts, typing away on the keys and sipping a mug of something. This time, Sally's grief was fresh and didn't give way to anger. Instead, she felt content that some part of her father was still here where she could see it. She watched for a few moments until she felt well enough to press on.

October continued to unfold in flashes of bold crimsons, daring golds, and vivacious oranges. Sally's favorite tree was the sweeping sugar maple in front of their home, its leaves burning so orange that from down the road it looked like it was on fire. Second to that was the scarlet red Japanese maple on the other side of the house, a delicate but equally striking counterpart. But this year, she let her favorite season pass her without much notice. Savoring the riches of autumn when her father could no longer do so left her insides twisted with guilt, so she ignored the beauty around her and tucked herself inside.

It was the weekend, and Nick dragged her to the Topsfield Fair to listen to Joey's band perform. Paul planned on coming, but, at the last minute, changed his mind. Her brother was quiet lately and more serious than usual. He and mother plodded along like two work horses, her mother at the laundry and Paul at school and football. They ate their meals as a family, but no one spoke of the empty place. Every so often, one of them would look at the unoccupied chair, usually in the midst of a laugh or a shared anecdote from the day, and the recollection that the full audience would never again be present robbed the moment of its potential. Heads dropped down towards plates and reticent eating replaced conversation.

"So, tell me again why you hate the fair?" Nick asked with the intent to annoy.

"You know why. You're just trying to irritate me by making me repeat myself."

"Why would I ever do such a thing? In fact, that's a horrible trick to accuse someone of. I'm so mad at you right now."

She laughed outright.

"What?! And now you're laughing at me? I'm offended. I'm going to leave you in the cavy barn by yourself."

This was the beauty of her cousin's wit. He was able to end his banter with the exact known reason for her aversion to the fair and act like he had no idea the two were related. Sally didn't hate the fair exactly, but a traumatic experience when she was about six years old in said cavy barn certainly warranted its avoidance for a few good years. She had watched as a little boy stuck his finger into the cage of one fancy rabbit with wild, long hair that made it look like a crazy bag lady, and sure enough, it bit him in one speedy motion, startling her so much that she wet herself.

"You're a jerk," she said to Nick for forcing her to remember this humiliation.

"Never mind that. It was over a decade ago. Let's live in the present, shall we?" He was starting again, she could tell. He was about to launch into yet another exhaustive diatribe.

She decided to cut him off. "What's this outfit you're wearing? Is this the London look? Because personally, I think it should only be worn in London."

He looked down at his clothes, flustered. It was getting chilly, and he wore a dark navy pea coat over an olive-green ribbed turtleneck sweater with plaid dress slacks.

"Look, I can't help it if I'm stylish."

"Did your mom pick out those clothes?" She knew that would strike a nerve since his mother very much tried to control his wardrobe in quintessential Italian mother fashion.

"I will give you the worst noogie of your life in front of all these people," he said, but laughed. "So, are you excited to see Joey and the Love Bites perform tonight?"

"Ugh. How does he expect anyone to take him seriously when his band sounds like a group of hormone-crazed boys? Why didn't they just call themselves The Boners and get it over with?"

"Santa Vittoria Fiore!"

"Hey, don't call me that!"

"It's your given name." He smirked.

"Well, don't use it. I'm Sally. And stop acting all fake shocked at my language. I'll talk how I want in front of you."

"That makes me feel shameful and special at the same time. I think only you could rouse such an odd marriage of feelings like that. It's a gift you have, young Sally. Don't ever let it go." He touched her arm for added melodrama.

"Likewise. You're the only person I both love and hate in equal amounts."

"Cotton candy?"

"When in Rome."

Sally mused later as they drove home in the sleepy lull of a busy day. Joey and the Love Bites were actually somewhat of an enjoyable listen. Joey wore a black turtleneck and rust-colored leather bomber jacket with his jeans, his hair slicked back as always. They tried to mimic the sound of The Beatles, but their attempts were pedestrian at best and aside from Joey's adequate vocals, his other bandmates weren't so musically inclined. Watching him, Sally could see his frustration with the lot of them in between songs as they goofed around. He took himself so seriously even in this.

She could see him pointing her out to his friends, and she grew self-conscious about her appearance, which she had taken little care about that morning. For a brief interlude, she found this sort of attention flattering. Then she remembered his supreme smugness, and this barred any attraction she might have felt. There was an underlying immaturity, like that of a pouty child, about Joey (even the fact that he still preferred to be called Joey instead of Joe) that turned her off.

Her mind wandered to Arthur, clearly the opposite. Arthur was a fully grown man, though, and it was probably wrong to imagine him in a romantic way. Sally would have confessed this at church, but since her father was buried, Lorraine had silently boycotted the institution. Sally assumed it was because she was furious with God, and that was just fine. Her mother would never speak it, but the last few Sundays she'd conveniently suffered from migraines. Her absence exempted Sally and Paul from having to attend. Sally had never liked church that much, anyway. What was the point of being devout when you were so bored that you blanked out five minutes into a sermon? But part of her was considering going alone despite her mother's blatant defiance.

"A penny for your thoughts," asked Nick, now perking up since they were a few streets off.

"You would need a dollar."

Sally found herself happily immersed in a new world of fabrics, needles, thread, and all the trimmings with her job at Adrian's. She'd watch the clock during last period as it ticked with too sluggish and obstinate a pace towards one-fifty, counting the seconds until she could spend time with Rose. The high point of her workday was when someone had a request for quality buttons. Rose made a ceremony of taking out the silver box that held these treasures. Its lid was adorned with a sample of each, making it a medley of color to behold. The buttons were sorted by color first then by shape and separated by small compartments within the box. And the drawers pulled up and out to reveal more levels of buttons – ones made out of glass and metals. Sally liked the white cabochon dome-shaped ones best.

She responded well to Rose's thorough training, and when she wasn't helping someone to find an item or shadowing the former as she advised customers on fabric choice with an effervescence Sally feared she would never possess, the two of them spent a peaceful time chatting behind the counter. She learned that Rose was twenty-six and had given up on marriage after a string of failed relationships.

"I guess I'm just unlucky in love," Rose sighed during one slow day.

"I'm the last person to give advice. For whatever reason, I've never really been that interested in having a boyfriend. But maybe you're looking in the wrong places and that's why you keep finding these men who are no good."

Rose listened with her customary poised and attentive expression. Sally wondered if she was only being polite by letting a teenager, who clearly had no experience on which to draw, attempt such advice.

"You could be right," she admitted. "But I'm running out of places to look. And you know," – she grew wistful, gently brushing a curl out of her dreamy eyes – "I think my great love came and went in high school and maybe there just isn't anyone else."

"Your great love? In high school?"

Sally couldn't hide the disbelief in her voice. She was nearly through with high school, and she couldn't fathom finding a great love in any of the boys there, nor even in poor Joey whom she'd known her whole life. Maybe I just don't have it in me, she thought, to love like that. Maybe I should just become a nun.

"Yes. But don't worry. Love happens to all of us at different moments. Just because you may not have felt anything big inside you yet, that doesn't mean it won't happen someday," Rose answered as if reading her mind – or her skeptical expression.

"But mine came early, and it would have lasted a lifetime, too, I'm sure of it." The loftiness of her face darkened a bit here but brightened as she continued. "His name was Roy DePrizzio, and he was kind of a bad boy. Oh, not in a delinquent sort of way, just in his looks. He came to our school junior year and already had a motorbike. He wore a white t-shirt and a leather jacket, his hair was slicked up, and his jeans were cuffed. He was just as you'd imagine. And even though he was new, no one hazed him. He was too cool for all of that, and everyone knew it. We were in English class together, my favorite class."

"Mine, too," Sally interrupted, excited to have another thing in common with Rose. Rose smiled patiently and continued.

"It was his, too, actually. And we sat next to each other. Before class, we would chat about best loved books. He was into Fitzgerald and Hemingway, of course, but he also loved D.H. Lawrence. Our friendship consisted of these daily pleasantries, and I was nursing a large crush, of course, but I didn't yet look like this." She gestured to herself. "I was a bit gawky then, I hadn't bloomed, as they say. Things didn't get romantic until we were cast as the leads in the senior show. Do they still put that on?"

Sally nodded. Yes, the senior show. In fact, auditions for that would be in January, and people were already abuzz at the likelihood of her brother being this year's lead. The senior show was different than the productions of the drama club. There was still a fall straight play and a spring musical, but in March, the seniors would get together and perform a variety show and excerpts from a musical. It was an annual tradition that unified the senior class even more before they were to inevitably part ways.

"Well, that year we did *Oklahoma*! We were cast as Laurey and Curly. And, you know what happens on sets. People fall for each other, and we were no exception. He looked so cute in that cowboy hat. After rehearsals, he'd give me a ride home on his bike. My parents didn't like it, but they could see in my face that I was smitten, so they didn't harp. They're sweet like that. Then one night, after our last performance, in fact, there was a cast party. We went and had ourselves a time. He dropped me off at midnight, walked me to my front steps, sweetly kissed me and said, 'Someday Rosie, I'm gonna ask you to marry me, and I hope you'll say yes.' And he walked back over to his bike and gave me a long look before he took off." She stopped and looked at Sally like she was coming out of a trance. "I never saw him again."

"What happened?!"

“He was struck by a truck driver who’d fallen asleep behind the wheel. He was three hundred yards from his own house. They had to pull his body out of a neighbor’s tree.”

“I’m so sorry.”

“I shouldn’t be talking about it.” Rose smoothed the bow on the neckline of her blouse in an attempt to compose herself. “But see, after a romance like that, all these other men pale in comparison. So, it doesn’t matter whom I choose, really. I’ll only ever be settling. Some men take me to dinner and then expect something just because they’ve paid for a meal. Some even get rough and pushy when I say no. Others seem all right, and then after a month or two of dating they’re mean just to be mean. Maybe it’s because they want out, and they’re not sure how to end things. Others are nice but so uninteresting that I might as well be talking to a sewing machine. Oh, speaking of which, how is the Singer I’ve lent you working? You seem to be acclimating well in class.”

“It’s wonderful. I appreciate you letting me borrow it and store it here. It’s much nicer than the one my mother has at home.”

“Don’t mention it. My friend gave that to me because she tried sewing and had no talent for it. I’m not surprised – she has too much going on up here to focus.” She pointed to her head. “So that was just collecting dust. As a matter of fact, why don’t you just keep it? I have no use for two.”

“Really?”

“Sure. It’s yours. For being such a good little listener.” She winked and stood to attend a new customer.

It was a crisp Sunday late in the month, and Sally sat on the enclosed back porch sipping hot cider and delving into *Wuthering Heights* for about the fourth year in a row. They hadn’t gone to church again, and Lorraine busied herself baking apples pies for the family get-together that evening. The intoxicating aroma of hot apples and cinnamon sugar wafted through the house and brought the kind of contentment that only her father's presence could make whole. But, Sally thought, this will have to do. Apple pie was his favorite so maybe that feeling is here because he's here. And that was somehow enough.

She once again became absorbed in the tale, wishing she was more tempestuous like the lively Catherine, but her longings were cut short when her brother stepped out on the porch in his school jacket.

"Come on, I want you to come with me."

"Huh?"

"There's a rally about the war downtown on the Common."

"Oh...to protest, you mean?"

"No, haven't you heard about this? It's a rally in support of the war and our troops. Everyone is sick of these hippies protesting, so we're doing something different. Let's go, then. Okay?"

Sally set down her book, grabbed her coat from the rack by the door, and was about to follow her brother outside when Lorraine emerged from the kitchen.

"Where do you think you're going?"

"Ma, there's a rally downtown in support of the war. Can we go? We'll be back in time to go to Aunt Jo's for dinner."

"You'd better be."

They weren't prepared for the mob on the Common. The policeman who directed them to a parking spot said they estimated that about twenty-five thousand people were there. Sally believed it. In the sea of faces, there were young and old, men and women, straight-laced folk and bikers alike, all mingling as one mass in support of American troops in Vietnam. Sally and Paul squeezed into a spot next to the bandstand and watched as a group of men lifted a biker with long hair, a leather jacket, and a bandana tied around his head. He held up an American flag in solidarity.

Sally looked around her and strained to hear through the din of so many voices. Her eyes tried to focus on more points beyond the hundreds of waving flags, and she zeroed in on one sign that read, "Join the holy war against godless communism. Fight red anarchy in the USA." Another sign instructed, "Love & Support U.S. Soldiers in Vietnam." Other than listening to her uncles and cousins rail on about the war – a few of her cousins had enlisted including Nick's older brother – she hadn't thought much about it, but it seemed silly to her for this country to be inserting itself into another nation's civil war.

Now she wondered if there was more to it than that. She glanced up at Paul, who looked even more intense than usual. He was always grave, but this was outside of his temperament. There was a feeling igniting behind his eyes, stirring with the energy that ran through this crowd like an electric current. His jawline twitched and his eyes grew watery. As the crowd transitioned from chanting "Support our troops! Support our troops," to singing "America the Beautiful," he fervently joined in.

After a few bars, he caught her watching him and stopped. He looked guilty, like she had discovered a great secret. In the moment that passed between them, no words were exchanged, but Sally was able to see Paul clearly for the first time, to see the determination behind his firm mouth and his forthright gaze – to understand him. While the crowd's voices echoed above, the reality gripped her core in the same way as her father's passing, for it was the same type of news in the end. A death sentence.

Her brother was planning to enlist.

Chapter III

Since that day, Sally carried the burden of Paul's secret, but she took some comfort in the fact that it brought them closer together. Where before he had been standoffish, perhaps keeping his little sister away from his more forward friends, he started welcoming her into their company. As though if she were nearby, she couldn't be at home spilling her guts to their intuitive mother. Sally didn't mind. She did mind, however, the several occasions where he managed to include Joey in these plans.

In fact, she sat next to Joey now at the traditional Thanksgiving Day football game. It was a sunny but raw morning, and he threw a blanket over them to keep warm. As she watched Paul artfully throw the pigskin to his most trusted receiver, she felt Joey's hand worm its way over to hers under the cover of the red and black Buffalo plaid and close to the hem of her skirt. He entwined his clammy fingers with hers before she pulled away and feigned scanning the crowd so she wouldn't have to meet his wounded eyes. She landed instead on a most welcome face several yards away. Arthur. He wore a thick, fisherman knit sweater over another of her father's shirts. Her favorite actually. It was a long-sleeved plaid of black, cream, and a lovely forest green. He looked over and caught her watching him. He smiled and waved.

"Who's that?" Joey's voice fell with warm breath on her ear.

"He's our school custodian."

"Oh." The way he said this irritated her. As though any jealousy he might have had was dispelled because Arthur was only a lowly janitor.

"He reads a lot," she said with purpose.

"Good for him," was Joey's uninterested reply.

"And I think he's quite handsome."

At this, he was at attention. "He's your school's janitor," he began. "If you have a thing for him that's kind of strange."

Sally blushed because she knew he was right. How Lorraine would disapprove of her even mentioning something like that, and to a member of the opposite sex even. She sighed.

"I'm just kidding, anyway. I'm trying to ween you off me," she joked and told the truth at the same time.

Joey laughed. "You're wasting your time. I made up my mind about you a long time ago, Sally."

"Yes, but I haven't. And everyone knows it's the woman who decides. My mother told me."

"I have faith that you'll choose me. Someday. Maybe years from now, but that's okay. I'm going to stick around and wait it out. You can't blame me for that, can you?"

"I guess not."

"Besides, it's not like I'm some creep. You and I are old friends. Are you forgetting?"

"No..."

Sally watched again as her brother threw a long pass. The receiver, Foggarty, caught it and made a touchdown. The crowd screamed. It was a home game and there were more "warriors" in the stands. On the sidelines, the cheerleaders chanted, "Who do we love? Warriors! Who's gonna win? Warriors!" Then Tammy, in all her bouncing, bosomy glory, shouted, "Give me a W!" The girls replied "W!" This continued until the word was fully spelled and followed by squeals and giggles and free kicks.

Joey drove her back home where their families were gathering for the meal. Before they got out of the car, he glanced around for bystanders, then leaned over and quickly kissed her mouth. This surprised her because she'd been somewhere lost in reverie, thinking instead of Arthur. How clean he looked and with fragments of boyishness about him, though complemented by the hard edges and angles of his face. His hair was thickly parted, the color of the hardy sand found on beaches up north. These musings were still in her mind when Joey's lips met hers, and she couldn't help but pretend they were Arthur's.

"Your parents are here for God's sake. What if they were looking out the window?" She gathered herself enough to chastise him.

He shrugged. "I'm sorry. You look so pretty today that I couldn't help it."

Any concern she had of their kiss being witnessed faded as they walked into the kitchen and, instead of Lorraine bustling about cooking a Thanksgiving dinner for all to enjoy, she and Dr. Mosca were immersed in a sea of paperwork at the table. Joey's mother sat off to the side sipping tea and looking sympathetic.

"Oh," Lorraine looked up startled. Her eyes were red. "I didn't think you two would be home so soon." She stood and sighed. "Teddy was just helping me go through our finances while I have him here."

"Mom, what can I help with?" Sally asked, spying the empty pie crusts on the counter, the yams that hadn't been peeled, and the ingredients for green bean casserole still unassembled.

"If you can get the apples ready and into the pie crusts, I can do the rest."

Lorraine put on her apron and reached for another to tie onto Sally. Watching her mother, Sally went through the automatic motions of peeling and slicing the apples, tossing enough for two pies worth into a glass bowl with generous helpings of cinnamon, nutmeg, ground cloves, sugar, and brown sugar. At the end, she stirred in some plump golden raisins and a spoonful each of bourbon and maple syrup. She noted that Lorraine's normally fluid movements around the kitchen seemed stilted as she boiled and mashed the yams, mixed them with a bit of cream, brown sugar, salt, and an egg, then poured them into a pan to be covered with marshmallows and crumbled pecans before being baked. Every once in a while, she made a noise. Not the pleasant sigh that so often came with cooking, but more like the plaintive moan that escapes during a nightmare. The kind of guttural sound you have no control over, but your body expels it without first consulting your mind.

Mrs. Mosca offered help, but it was only obligatory. She knew Lorraine would say no and invite her to go relax in the front parlor with her husband and son. No woman was ever allowed to hold domain over her kitchen. Even Sally was resigned to sous chef. And Lorraine accepted this rule when she visited her sisters' homes as well.

After the final pie went into the oven, Sally and Lorraine joined their guests for light conversation and resting. An hour later, Paul was home, showered and dressed, and Nick and his parents arrived with his middle brother, Louis, who was on break from college. Her mother's other sisters were with their in-laws and Nick's older brother, Ralph, was stateside out in California. Dr. Mosca's younger brother, Father Carl, a soft-spoken priest whom Sally had always felt kindred to, also joined their table. He was a pastor at their local parish and said the Saturday mass. Back when her mother went to church, she'd been adamant about going on Sunday because it was God's day, and so times were few and far between when Sally got to hear Father Carl give his enlightened sermons. Only when he was standing in for the presiding pastor, was she granted that pleasure. Though she did often have him for confession.

The first thing she'd noticed about Father Carl was his gentle eyes. They were the same light brown as his hair and always kindled with sincere beneficence. He bowed his head, covered with soft waves made lighter now with flecks of gray, and said a lilting grace that warmed the corners of Sally's heart. She always felt shy about confessing, even though her sins were minor, and wondered if he recognized her voice. Sometimes she would try her best to disguise it.

"We thank you, Lord, for allowing us this special time together, for this bountiful harvest to nourish our bodies. We thank you for our health, for keeping our loved ones safe. For all of this, we are grateful and today, we'll be thinking of those less fortunate than us and praying for their luck to change. In the name of your son, Jesus Christ. Amen." He lifted his head and smirked, "Can we eat now?"

He ended with this same joke each year, and it never failed to provoke a chorus of laughter. Although, this year Paul's laugh wasn't quite as robust, and Lorraine only smiled. Sally did nothing but felt stricken by the sight of Paul sitting in her father's chair for the first time. She caught Father Carl's sympathetic eye as he watched her with the innocence of a field mouse. Come to think of it, that's exactly what he reminded her of. She stopped filling her plate with yams mid-spoonful to make this curious observation. His wide eyes, his upturned nose, his slightly longer two front teeth that rested themselves on his bottom lip when he wasn't speaking, and his little ears that stuck out just enough to reflect light from behind them.

"There she is," he said.

"Excuse me, Father?"

"You. You were smiling that dazzling smile I remember."

Realizing her face had been mirroring her cheeky thoughts, she blushed and finished plating her food. The dining room reverberated with the sounds of utensils clinking on plates. For good reasons, this was one of the more taciturn Thanksgivings in the Fiore home. Nick's father, Ralph, Sr., talked football with the boys, but he was also a muted form of his gregarious self. Aunt Jo and Lorraine quietly talked, and Mrs. Mosca joined in somewhat, but mostly listened to them gripe about their jobs. Aunt Jo cleaned houses. Mrs. Mosca related more with the kind of women on the receiving end of their professions, so she couldn't contribute much except to look guilty and ashamed of her status in life.

Bored of that talk, Sally's mind transgressed to baser things as she moved the turkey around on her plate. She watched Joey engage with her uncle in what was becoming a lively debate about the Patriots. She thought of what it felt like only a few hours ago when his lips were on hers, and she felt herself wanting it to happen again.

"So, Sally, your mother tells me you have a job?" Father Carl's tenor sliced her fantasy in half.

She jumped a little in her seat. The priest regarded her again with his naïve features, though underneath it there was something that made her feel ashamed. It was as though he knew what she'd been thinking and he was saving her from it by inquiring about quotidian matters. She collected herself.

"Yes, at the fabric store."

"How are you liking it?"

"Very well. I'm learning to sew."

"She made that collar on the blouse she's wearing," bragged Lorraine.

Father Carl pretended to look longingly at the bright plaid around Sally's neckline and touched his own immaculate, white collar. "Oh, if only."

Her mother and aunt broke into peals of laughter. Finally, Sally allowed herself the same indulgence, and her body remembered the sensation of a full belly laugh. Her parts shook and she almost didn't know what to do with herself. It was like learning how to walk again. She glanced over at Joey, who watched her with a look that spoke of anguish and elation, like falling and flying at once. And soon, she felt her own heart plummeting to the bottom of her feet.

As the days grew shorter, Sally's mind revolved around learning to sew, and it proved a blessed distraction. She grew patient and exact, so her stitches would be as meticulous as Rose's. She completed her first blouse using a woven plum fabric expertly selected for her hair color and complexion by Rose's discriminating eye. The sleeves billowed out and then tapered again at her petite wrists, her ivory collarbone was set off to perfection by the swooping neckline, decorated with the daintiest of Peter Pan collars and tied in the center with a bow.

The day she wore it to school, several classmates stopped at the lunch table she occupied with Heather and some of the other less popular girls to mention how much they liked her shirt.

"Yeah, well, you won't find that at Parke Snow," barked Heather. "She made it herself."

Even Tammy, who usually walked by and at least giggled at Sally and her misfit crew, couldn't quite bring herself to affect laughter. And Sally suspected she was too preoccupied with winning the lead in the senior show to be bothered with torturing the few lucky victims she'd carefully selected over the years. Since Paul had been including Sally more in some of his plans, people began treating her less as Paul Fiore's strange little sister and more just as Sally Fiore, quiet and stylish, which didn't matter to her either way. She wasn't about to switch lunch tables over it.

It hadn't started to snow yet, but the evenings were cold. One Thursday, Sally lingered in the shop after closing to finish a plaid skirt she was making for herself. It was a cozy material, part cashmere and so soft to the touch, but the colors were practical – cream, beige, and black. It could be worn with almost any other shade. Lorraine had stopped in to tell Sally she was headed home. They usually commuted back together, but Sally begged to finish. Rose or someone would give her a ride. But now, as Rose emerged from the ladies' room trailing a new cloud of perfume and blotting her refreshed berry lips, it was evident that she had an engagement.

"I forgot to ask if I could have a ride home," Sally practically whispered, gazing out the window at the piercing dark.

"Oh no! I can't believe I didn't mention I had a date. How stupid of me when you've been staying late."

"It's okay. I shouldn't have assumed anything. I can walk. It's only a couple of miles."

"But it's so cold!"

"I'm bundled up," she said, pulling up her boots.

As the air bit her face, she regretted her decision not to go home with her mother. Sally hustled. If she got home too late, Lorraine would never allow it again. She still cut down Armory, though, for a quick glimpse at Arthur. She hadn't seen him as much in the halls and wondered what book he was reading now. The light was on, but he wasn't in his window. She squinted as a bit of blustery wind stung her cheeks.

Instead, he was standing in front of her. He wore a heavy wool coat and held a garbage bag.

"Hi, there. What are you doing out in this cold?"

Sally felt like she'd been caught doing something bad, but her guilt concealed itself as surprise.

"Oh, hi. I'm just walking home from work. I stayed late and my ride had to leave."

"How far do you live?"

"Couple miles."

"You can't walk in this. You'll get frostbite." He swung the garbage bag into a nearby can and turned back to her. "I'll drive you."

"No, really, it's okay." Sally started to panic.

If her mother saw her pulling up in Arthur's red Ford truck, she would never hear the end of it. Alone like that with an older man. And how exactly did she run into him? Sally supposed she could make that part up well enough, but lying to her mother was not ideal, mostly because Lorraine could always wheedle out any kind of deception. She discovered this when she was in first grade and had been throwing her lunches away at school. Well, she ate the cookies and discarded the sandwiches. When her mother asked if she'd eaten her lunch, she said yes because she figured the cookies counted as something. Lorraine stared the truth out of her, though. Guilt must have been written on her then chubby face. Once she confessed the entire truth, Lorraine had said, "Remember, Sally, a half-truth always becomes a whole lie." After that, there were no more cookies packed in her lunch-box for a full three months.

He smiled. "I insist. Come in while I get my keys, so you don't freeze out here."

She followed him up the side steps to his separate entrance. Warmth flooded her, and she felt immediate respite at being indoors. The apartment was lit with the amber glow of a small desk lamp. A typewriter sat by the window, stalwart and waiting to be used with a paper inserted and black letters inked halfway down it.

"Can I get you some tea or something?"

It felt odd to be in a space with him that was not a sterile corridor lined with lockers. Here there were no social barriers, nothing that outwardly screamed, "This is not a man for you. This is wrong." The sensation of strange possibility coupled with the foreboding image of Lorraine's disapproval made her hands, just ice-cold moments ago, start to turn clammy.

"No, thank you. We should really go, or my family will wonder where I am."

"Okay, then." He grabbed his keys and gave his typewriter a parting glance before ushering her out the door.

"Are you writing something?" she asked as he started the truck.

"Sure am."

"Well, what is it?"

He paused. "It's hard to explain. I guess it's a memoir of sorts. About some of my experiences. Where am I taking you?"

"Just follow Main Street straight into Greenwood. Have you always written?"

"What are you, seventeen?"

"Almost."

"I've been dabbling since I was about your age. Maybe a little younger. It started with some very bad poetry and then progressed to bad prose."

Sally laughed. "I'm sure it's not as bad as you say. Aren't all writers supposed to be self-deprecating?"

"You know. I've had no formal training, so I'm sure my form is somewhat unorthodox, but it's an activity that brings me joy. Whatever comes of it is fine with me. I'm not trying to write the next Great American Novel. I'm doing it to stay sane in a mad world."

"I feel that way about sewing."

"Really? What kind of sewing? Like darning socks or making actual clothes?"

"Clothes. But I'm just learning. I've finished a blouse, and I'm almost done with a skirt."

"What do you like best about it?"

"I like the slowness of it. Starting with a fabric and taking methodical steps to transform it into something else, something beautiful that you can put on to transform yourself. And it relaxes me, I guess. I can do it and pay attention to detail, but I can also have time to sit and think to the rhythm of the sewing machine."

"And what do you think about, Sally Fiore?" he asked with a teasing in his voice.

Sally sighed, lamenting that her honest answer would prevent her from flirting back. "My father."

"Oh?"

"He passed away in September."

"I'm sorry to hear that. Very sorry."

"Thank you. So, how far along are you with your book?"

"About halfway. I plug away on it every night. It's hard with working full-time, but something needs to pay the bills."

"Oh shoot, we passed the turn. You can turn right down here, and I'll hop out just over the bridge."

"How come? You don't want me dropping you at your door?" He pulled over on Myrtle Ave after crossing the short Cooper Street bridge.

"My mother is very proper. She would think it inappropriate for me to accept a ride from you. So, I'd just rather her not know."

"I see. Because I'm an older, single man?"

Sally snorted at the formality of his statement. "You're not that old. But the other part, I guess."

He smiled. "You don't live very far from here, do you? It's still freezing, and I don't quite feel right leaving you by yourself on a night like this."

"I live around the corner and down the street a bit. It's not half a mile."

"Okay, goodnight then. Get home safely."

"Thanks, and thanks again for the ride."

Sally started the trek home. It wasn't a long walk, no, but it was certainly cold, and her feet were already feeling like blocks of ice in her boots. Better move fast. How had her father done it? Every day, rain or shine, and through abominably harsh winters, faithfully delivering the mail? While ruminating on this point, she briskly rounded a bend in the road and took two lovers in mid-kiss by surprise, almost running smack into them.

"Oh! Sorry! Oh…" She stopped short in her tracks.

Her brother and Marie looked as shocked as she was, then their faces simultaneously morphed into dual guilt.

"Sally!"

"Paul? Marie?" Sally screwed up her face and thought to play with them a little. "So…this explains everything. Why you're always late from practices. Why Marie is never with her girlfriends anymore. I get it. You two have been sneaking around."

"Sally, shhhhh!" Paul looked wildly around the desolate street.

"Canoodling. That's what the kids are calling it these days, right?"

"Now, Sally, you listen here." He wagged his finger in her face. Marie had to stifle a laugh.

"Uh-uh, you listen here. You're acting as though you caught me doing something bad when clearly, the opposite is true. And if certain people at school ever found out about this secret love affair," – she rolled her eyes for emphasis – "that would just be a mess."

"Sally..." Paul's voice was stern, but his eyes betrayed him and for a second he was himself before September.

"Well?" She crossed her arms. "What's it worth to you?"

"Sally, you're only joking, right? You'd never tell on us?" Marie asked, now serious, pausing on the front steps of her family's handsome mansard.

"Of course, I'm joking."

"Yeah, didn't you know, Marie? Sally here is a regular comedienne. A real Lucille Ball."

"Har, har."

"And anyway, what are you doing walking this way? Why wouldn't you have cut up Greenwood? Hmm?"

"Um..."

"'Um' isn't an answer," he said meanly. "I hope you'll be able to do better than that when I inform our mother where I found you."

"Hey!"

He smirked up at Marie. "See? She'll keep quiet."

"I would have kept quiet, anyway, but only for Marie's sake!"

Paul smiled up at Marie's dark beauty once more and then grabbed Sally playfully by the hood of her coat. "Come on, weirdo. Let's go home. You keep my secret, and I'll keep yours, whatever it is." He opened the door of his Chevy Nova and unceremoniously pushed her in.

Sally bristled at this dominance. It reminded her of when they were children and he would boss her and Nick around at play, overseeing their every move. After he settled in behind the wheel and belted himself, she chose to strike.

"Actually, I'm keeping two of your secrets, so it's a bit uneven, see."

"What are you talking about now, brat?"

“This Marie development is the second.”

“Oh really, is it? And what could possibly be the first, do tell?” He sparred with a dark sarcasm that wasn’t reminiscent of either of her parents, but could be traced back to their great-grandmother, Santa Angelina.

“That you’re planning to enlist after you graduate.” She hoped that in saying this, he would dispute it as untrue. She hoped.

Instead, he stopped the car right in the middle of the road and looked at her. “What did you say?”

“Paul, there could be a car behind you!” She looked back, but there were no headlights in the distance.

“Answer me.” He sounded upset.

“You’re planning to enlist, aren’t you?”

“How the hell would you know?” His changeable face now wore a look of worry as easily as it wore its confidence.

“The rally. The rally in support of the troops. I watched you during it, and I could just tell by the look in your eyes. You wanted to be there. You knew that I knew.”

He was silent but put his foot back on the gas. The car crawled the rest of the way up the street and into the driveway. The lights were on and the smell of cooking onions led them up the side steps. Before they entered the back porch, Paul turned to her again, this time with a look she could only read as a mix of staunch resolve and deep compassion.

“Don’t mention it again, okay? Not yet. She can’t know yet. Promise me.” To bind her, he held out his pinky.

She looped hers into it with a gnawing dread. “I promise.”

The tiny line between her brows when they were knit together in concentration was there now, prominent as ever, while she finished the

stitching on the final scarf. Her tongue poked out between her lips, too. Lorraine had spoken to her about this trademark look of concentration on several occasions through the years, warning of what it could do to upset the alignment of her naturally straight teeth, and how a wrinkle could form between her eyes that resembled the crack of someone's behind. Sally never cared to heed this advice as a child, but now as vanity began to have its way with her, she tried to coerce her offending tongue back into her mouth and smooth out her face. She'd made scarves for Lorraine and Paul as Christmas gifts and was finishing a third that she intended to keep for herself. She'd selected rich plaid wools for all of them: rose, beige, and cream for her mother; red, navy, and white for Paul; and maroon, forest green, and cream for the last.

"Well, this is fine work, Sally." Rose beamed.

"They're nothing fancy. I wasn't sure about adding fringe to the ends, so I just went for simple."

"And why not? Fringe just gets all tangled, anyhow. These are quality scarves, made with love, and full of the warmth of your heart."

"Gosh, Rose, you sound like a greeting card."

"Ha, I missed my calling. You should jot down that line in your cards to them."

"Speaking of cards, let me shoot to Woolworth's and buy some cards and boxes for these. I'll have to hide them when I get home. Do you want to come?"

"No, I have yet another bad date lined up."

"How can you ever expect to like anyone with that attitude?"

"Well, how interesting can he be? He's the son of my mother's bridge partner. He's thirty-one and still lives at home, and he's an accountant."

"Sounds ghastly. Why bother going at all then, if you've written him off?"

"Oh, my mother's been hounding me about it. I guess he saw me through the window once when he came to pick up his mother, and he's been after her to get a date. Plus, I have a sneaking suspicion that my mother is getting sick of her friend, and she's hoping if I don't like him, maybe her friend will come around less."

"Now that's an ulterior motive if I ever heard one. How wicked of her!"

"She's something all right. So, I'll try not to disappoint her."

"Okay, well, have fun. Or don't."

Sally rolled up the scarves and tucked them into her book bag. At Woolworth's, she considered her options. She settled on red boxes and shiny red paper printed with tiny Christmas trees topped with snow. Careful not to overdo it, she chose green ribbon over bows. Her mother refused to decorate this year. Sally tried to understand, despite her inner disappointment. She knew Lorraine probably felt it was disrespectful to Domenic's memory, or she was simply too sad to bring any cheer to the house.

But Christmas was his favorite holiday, and no one was as jovial as he was throughout the month of December. At home, out of his uniform, he wore starched shirts and sweater vests with festive bowties – his best one had a print of tiny Rudolphs. He knew all the songs and would freely belt them out. He'd sing Nat King Cole's "The Christmas Song" and badly mimic Bing Crosby's "White Christmas," but Frank Sinatra's album was the one he loved best.

As she was holding her scarf out to see if it would fit the dimensions of the box, someone tapped her on the shoulder.

"Hi, Sally." It was Arthur, wearing his bulky fisherman knit sweater again with jeans and Converse sneakers.

"Hello."

"Getting your Christmas shopping squared away?"

"I guess you could say that. Just really for my mom and Paul. A small list this year."

"Really? Not that boy you were with at the football game?"

He asked this in such a natural way that Sally couldn't decipher any jealousy in his voice. But why should there be, after all?

"No, no. He's just a family friend."

Arthur continued to smile at her until his eyes fell on the scarf she held, the maroon and green present to herself.

"Did you make this?" He reached out and let his fingers glide across the fabric.

"I did. They're simple."

"I bet you have your big, Italian family over for Christmas dinner."

"Usually, but this year may be a little quieter."

"I used to love Christmas. I mean, I still love this time of year, but it's nicer when you have a family to spend it with."

"Oh, are you going to be alone?"

"Not quite. My landlady, she has two elderly, spinster sisters who live in the Berkshires, and this is their year to come have the holidays with her. So, she's insisting that I spend it with them."

"That doesn't sound so bad."

"No, I'm sure they'll be a jolly group. I just – I miss my mom. She loved this time of year, too. It was our special thing."

Sally wasn't sure how to react without crying or pouring her heart out since she felt so utterly simpatico. Instead, she fumbled with the boxes and almost dropped all her items. Arthur looked embarrassed for having revealed so much, and quickly departed with one last compliment.

"Anyway, lovely scarves. Your family is lucky to have them."

The aisles of decorations at Woolworth's had reminded her keenly of so many happy Christmas seasons, and, as she walked into the bare house, she grew more upset about this lost holiday. She loved trimming the tree with decades of homemade ornaments, stringing up lights, placing the tinsel, painstakingly threading popcorn and cranberries for garlands, and smoothing out the felt tree skirt to line with presents. Late at night, after the carols were turned off, she'd nestle into the plush armchair next to the tree and stare into the lonely peace of gleaming lights, their facets promising the many different adventures a new year would bring.

This deliberate absence of cheer plagued her while she started dinner. Lorraine had been working late, helping Mr. Crawford close and keeping the books for a bit of extra money around the holidays. She'd come home, her body dragging, her feet swelling out over the tops of her shoes. On these evenings, Sally would make dinner. She kept it simple with dishes like beef stew with potatoes and canned carrots and peas, franks and beans, and tomato soup with grilled cheese. Tonight, she found herself leaving the Lipton noodle soup simmering on the burner and marching to the small side closet in the living room where some of the more delicate decorations were kept.

She reached up to the top shelf for a white box that looked like it might hold pastries. She set it on the bench of her mother's organ, one of the focal points of the front parlor, and gingerly opened it. Inside a layer of tissue paper was a ceramic Christmas tree that stood about ten inches high when mounted on its base. It was a rich, spruce green, and tiered branches held a coating of powdery snow. All about it were holes that Sally filled with the colored bulbs as fast as her fingers would allow in hopes of finishing her project before her mother ambled in.

Before plugging it in, she snuck into her brother's room for a special item. She dug through the top drawer of his bureau, scooting aside some bundles of socks until she found it. It was a much faster process than months ago when she scoured for a pocket square. Now she held the Rudolph tie in her hands and returned to execute her brilliant idea. The tie was pre-tied and had an adjustable neck strap. She wound it around the top of the tree until it was fastened, the ideal topper – better than a star or an angel in her view.

When she plugged it in and clicked the small switch attached to the plug, her eyes filled. This Christmas without her father at the head of the table slicing the ham would not be a Christmas. She thought of her favorite heroine Jo March's rant in *Little Women* about how Christmas wouldn't be

Christmas without any presents. Sally would rather have no more presents for the rest of her life if it meant having her father back even just one more time. No, for her, Christmas wouldn't be Christmas without her dad – ever again. Somehow, this little tree made it better. As tradition dictated, she broke out into a timid rendition of the song they sang whenever they lit up this decoration.

"Oh Christmas tree, oh Christmas tree, thy leaves are so unchanging."

"What are you doing?"

Sally turned to see that her mother and Paul had both just walked in the door. It was her brother who asked the question, but he didn't wait for an answer before he took in the bowtie and processed her reasoning. He came over to her and put his hands on her shoulders, prompting her to sing again with his own deep baritone.

"Oh Christmas tree, oh Christmas tree, thy leaves are so unchanging. Not only when the summer's here, but also when it's cold and drear. Oh Christmas tree, oh Christmas tree, thy leaves are so unchanging."

Lorraine didn't join in but stood with reverence at the sight of her children. When they finished, Sally turned to her. "I'm sorry. I know you didn't want to put anything up, but he loved Christmas. I felt like he would want at least one small thing."

Her mother smiled as if the effort pained her after such a long day. "I think you're probably right, dear." She moved wearily out of her beige wool coat and hung it in the coat closet, glancing at the tree once more before heading to her room. "It looks very nice."

"It's perfect. Just perfect."

Rose stood next to her while they both stared into the full-length mirror. They'd closed the store and, while Sally waited for Lorraine to walk over from the dry cleaners, Rose had begged to see her completed skirt. She was still inspecting it, wearing a look of satisfaction as though she had made the garment herself.

"I'm so proud of you, Sally. You're really becoming quite the seamstress."

"Thanks to you."

"Oh, stop." Rose laughed and lightly slapped her shoulder.

"How was your date the other night?"

At this inquiry, her proud countenance grew haughty, and her movements became more abrupt in tandem as she balanced the cash register.

"Humph, just like all the others. What about you? Any more consideration of Joey?"

"Mmmm, I don't know. I like him well enough, but I'm not entirely sure he's boyfriend material. I wish I could date an older boy. These teenage boys are so thick."

"Really? How much older?"

"Not very, just someone more mature. Someone who has interests other than trying to look cool and score chicks."

The jingling of the bell on the front door signaled Lorraine's arrival. Her cheeks were flushed, and she seemed anxious, but made sure to compliment her daughter's handiwork before setting into her news.

"Mr. Crawford just did me a big favor, and I'll need your help."

"What kind of favor?"

Lorraine pulled off her hair kerchief for a moment while Rose handed her some tea that she'd made in the break room. Outside, a mix of rain and snow coated the streets, settling over everything like a quilt of heavy slush.

"Well, a new family has moved into town, a wealthy family. The father is a distinguished judge, and they've moved here from Cambridge to that beautiful white manse by the lake. Anyway, Mr. C. was at his country club hanging about, and the judge was there having himself a scotch in the lounge, and he was asking the bartender about caterers in the area. See, they're having a Christmas party in a few weeks and plan to invite a lot of prominent townspeople to properly introduce their family. Well, you know Mr. C. He butts right in and says, 'I know the best cook this side of the Mississippi, and her name is Lorraine Fiore.'"

"Wow! And the judge just said he would hire you like that?"

She nodded. "And he's paying five hundred dollars plus the cost of the food!" Lorraine's eyes crinkled up and began leaking.

"Oh, Mom," Sally said, hugging her. She knew this had to be a huge burden off her mother's shoulders.

Lorraine sobbed with relief into Sally's shoulder, and then as abruptly as she'd started, she stopped and looked up into her daughter's face. "I have to go home and plan the menu."

As with every aspect of her life, Lorraine carried out this event with the same attention to detail and quality of product – even more so, if that were possible. In the week of the event, the two women sat together at the kitchen table, covered in a cotton cloth for ravioli making. Sally balanced a textbook on her lap to squeeze in homework, turning the pages with her left hand, and with her right, sealing the sides of each ravioli with careful fork pricks.Mr. Crawford allowed Lorraine to leave work early to prepare more of the food. Fortunately, it could be stored in the large icebox Domenic had kept in the garage for his hunting kills – mostly it had been fowl, but the occasional deer made it back once or twice. When Sally arrived home from work on these evenings, her mother was already covered in flour and seemed like she was about to snap. Sally asked for Thursday and Friday off to help her with the desserts: eight pies – two apple, two pumpkin, two custard, two ricotta; two large trays of tiramisu; two large trays of cannoli; and three big plates of assorted holiday cookies.

Lorraine had recruited Nick and his mother to help out at the event, along with Sally. Early that Saturday afternoon, they took three separate cars brimming with the delectable items.

"What are you giggling at over there?" Nick asked.

"Oh nothing. I was just thinking, it's funny, isn't it? This is literally a moveable feast."

"You are such a bookworm."

"What's wrong with that? Anyway, who's a bookworm? You got the reference, Einstein."

"Well, who doesn't like Hemingway?"

"Me."

"What? You just made a pun using the title of his book. How can you use someone's book title in a pun if you don't like them?"

"Why should I have to like him because of that? It was a clever pun. Anyone with half a sense of humor would have thought it up. That doesn't warrant my allegiance to an overrated, drunk misogynist. Now, Dostoevsky – there was a true genius."

"You know what I think, Sally? I think it's a crime what you're saying about Hemingway – a crime that needs some punishment."

"So much for puns."

"Here we are. This is the place? Geez, these people must be loaded."

They'd arrived before her mother and aunt and stayed in Nick's Dodge Dart, gazing up toward the imposing, white house. The stately structure boasted an elegant open porch on one side of the main house and an enclosed sunroom on the other. At the very top, a widow's walk with a delicate cupola.

"How beautiful. I never really noticed that little room up on the roof. If I lived there – "

"Oh wait, I know this one," he interrupted. "If you lived there, you'd sit up in that tiny room and…and…" He closed his eyes and pinched the bridge of his Roman nose as though he were fraught with concentration. "Read!" he shouted after a few seconds.

"Oh, shut up."

"Am I right?"

"If by right you mean ridiculous, then, always."

Their banter was cut short by her mother and aunt pulling up behind them. As Sally hopped out of the car, her eyes landed on a window in the upper left corner of the house. A curtain fluttered and a pale face looked out on them, but quickly disappeared.

Sally rested for a minute against the counter, one eye on the oven and one on the wide, kitchen window where outside snow fell softly and silently, casting a sparkling incandescence across the lawn. It couldn't have been a more perfect welcome for the guests who would soon be carefully making their way up the front walk.

Aunt Jo poked her curled, raven head around the corner. "Sally doll, your mother needs extra toothpicks for the passed hors d'oeuvres and Nick is asking for more maraschinos and grenadine. Grab those from the pantry while you wait on that last tray of garlic bread, will you?"

Sally nodded and forced herself to move, pushing with her palms against the edge of the counter to launch her body forward. She had to hand it to her godmother for being such a master delegator. Next to the refrigerator was a small alcove that served as a pantry. It had shuttered doors the same golden, knotty wood as the rest of the space.

While she knelt there sifting through the paper bags of their supplies, harsh voices trickled down the stairs across the room that led to the kitchen from the second floor. Sally peered out of the pantry to have a look. Angry footsteps descended and attached themselves to a startlingly dapper teenage boy. He wore a cream-colored dress shirt with the sleeves rolled up, a forest green sweater vest, dark wool pants, and a cranberry bowtie with cream dots. His hair was cut short around the sides, except for a lively pompadour on top, and he defiantly smoked a cigarette while he paused to lean on the bannister and address the other person.

"What have you done to yourself? You can't do this to us. You can't be at the party like this," the upstairs voice pleaded.

A gauzy lamplight sifted down and illuminated the boy's face. It was a delicate face with wide eyes, a slender nose, and a pert mouth that now set itself in a smirk in contrast to the otherwise fraught look Sally could place in his furrowed brow. A deep pain rooted itself behind the dark eyes, just subtle enough to go unnoticed with the right bravado in front of it.

"What's wrong with the way I look? I'm comfortable," he stated flatly.

"I laid your clothes out for you...and your hair. It's all in the sink!" the tremulous voice argued, growing more desperate with each word. "You didn't even bother cleaning it out after you mutilated yourself!"

"Well, sorry. I'll clean it now."

"Never mind that, I already did. But people will be here soon, and you need to change. I don't know what can be done about your hair."

"I'm not changing."

At this time, the boy looked over and met Sally's gaze. She froze. He pretended not to notice her and resumed his battle.

"There's nothing wrong with my outfit."

"If your father sees you like that..."

"Like what?" The boy now grew cross and stood a little more defensively, his hand gripping the bannister and his other dangling with the cigarette by his side.

The voice didn't answer at first. Then said almost inaudibly, "Why are you doing this to us? We moved here for your sake."

"I'm not doing anything to you. I'm just being myself. But that's the problem. It's always about what you and other people think. It's never about me, is it? It's fine, Mother. I'll put on your stupid outfit, so you don't have to be humiliated at your first party."

He winked at Sally, took a drag from his cigarette, and climbed back upstairs. The owner of the voice hurried down from the opposite direction and peered into the kitchen, mortified at a witness to the argument. She sighed and came the rest of the way. Dorris Pettyfer was an attractive woman in her late forties, tall and graceful with a blonde coiffure and wearing a beige, satin dress. The double strand of pearls knotted down her front was undoubtedly genuine.

"I'm sorry. I should have figured someone would be in here. Sally, is it?"

Sally set down the toothpicks and cherries and stood quickly, jutting out her hand. Dorris took it.

"Yes, I'm Mrs. Fiore's daughter."

"Well, thank you for the work you're doing. I have to say, the house smells wonderful. We've heard plenty about your mother's cooking, and we hope our guests will enjoy it."

"She's done her best, so I think they will."

Dorris frowned. "And you'll have to excuse us for the outburst you just overheard." She smiled and tried to make light of it. "You teenagers, always rebelling…Is something burning?"

"Oh! The garlic bread!" Sally hastened to the oven. She threw on her mother's quilted floral mitt and pulled out the aromatic bread, now slightly charred around the edges. "Ugh! She's going to kill me."

"It looks fine to me."

"Technically it is fine, but you don't know my mother. She's a perfectionist."

"Doll, where are those things?" Her aunt stuck her head in again, and, seeing the mistress of the house there, decided to come in the full way. She shook her pretty head over the garlic bread. "Ohhhh, wait until your mother sees that."

"You can tell her it was my fault," Dorris interjected. "I was having an argument with my child on the stairs, and it must have been a huge distraction for her."

Aunt Jo gave this woman the same once over, only Sally assumed she was forming a slightly snarkier opinion of Mrs. Dorris Pettyfer. She could tell by the shrewdness dancing in her aunt's black eyes.

"That so?" she said.

Another set of heels reverberated on the stairs, and a heavenly being emerged wearing the most beautiful emerald party dress with a creamy tulle petticoat peeking out from beneath it. Her delicate face was accentuated with a rosy lip, and her hair was combed down into an elegant pixie style evocative of Audrey Hepburn. Sally almost dropped the tray of garlic bread when she realized it was the same young person as before.

This young woman reluctantly flounced over to them as her mother cooed, "There now, that's so much better. And I even like your hair like this. It suits you."

The girl glared at her from under a thick fringe of lashes, but no longer protested. Dorris turned to Sally and her aunt. "This is my daughter, Samantha."

"It's Sam," her daughter corrected.

Dorris laughed nervously and squeezed Sam's shoulders. "I'm going to go see how everything is looking," she said in overly cheerful intonations, sweeping out of the room.

"I'll take these." Aunt Jo picked up the needed items from the pantry floor and followed, leaving Sam and Sally alone.

She half-smiled as she spied the tray in Sally's hands. "Looks like you burned the bread."

In spite of the garlic bread, which garnered a look of slight consternation from Lorraine, the party was a success. The house, still warmly lit and glittering with its holiday festoons, left a pleasant imprint in the memories of the guests as they departed in a languor of satiated merriment. Lorraine glowed under the praise of Judge and Mrs. Pettyfer while they presented her with a tight wad of cash for her efforts and a one hundred-dollar tip, of which she generously gave Sally, Nick, and Jo thirty dollars each, keeping only ten extra for herself.

Aunt Jo held her finger to her lips for Sally to keep quiet as she snuck her share back into Lorraine's purse. She then glared at her son until he mimicked her gesture. Sally followed suit with her own tip and, before her mother caught on, Aunt Jo distracted her with good-byes and congratulations. Sally let Nick continue nursing a leftover cookie and started taking the garbage out back. As she was hoisting two large bags into some empty cans, she heard a footstep crunch in the snow behind her.

It was Sam. She had a fancy wool coat draped over her shoulders. It was a deep berry with black piping and a black fur collar and cuffs. Against her ivory skin, the berry and emerald tones were like jewels in the snow. It was arresting. She smiled and lit a cigarette.

"So, you go to the high school, I hear."

"You hear correctly." Sally shoved the lids on the cans and then stood facing this enviably dressed girl, unsure yet what to make of her. She didn't quite understand how anyone gifted with such a stunning wardrobe should prefer boy's clothes, but it seemed more complicated than just a matter of style.

"I'll be starting in the New Year," Sam said, looking out into the yard. "Maybe we can hang out, if you wouldn't mind."

"I wouldn't. But I'm not popular or anything. Kind of the opposite, if you don't mind that."

Sam looked at her with a raised brow. "Popular? Really? Is that a thing in this town?"

"I mean, isn't it kind of a thing everywhere?"

"Only if people allow it. That's what everything comes down to. What people allow. What they tolerate. You do know there's a war going on out there?" She nodded out into the immediate landscape for lack of a better gesture.

"I know," Sally snapped. "I watch the news and read the paper just like anyone else."

"My point is, there are more important things to worry about than trifles like who has the most friends and the best clothes."

"I think you'd win in the clothes department."

Sam snorted. "I won't be dressing like this, that's for sure."

"What's wrong with these clothes?" Sally asked, trying to sound innocent so she wouldn't sound ignorant.

"Humph. These clothes. This dress is a Sarmi of New York. Most of my other pieces are custom. My mother's commissioned the best designer in Boston to make me an entire new wardrobe for school, but I'm not wearing any of it. I'll change in the bathroom if I have to. These clothes," she said, fingering the shiny silk of her dress, "these clothes just make me feel foreign in my own body. That's all. Like a tourist in my skin. And I don't like that. I prefer to be comfortable at all times. To just be myself."

Sally looked her over once more. Maybe she was one of those girls like her mother had told her about. The kind of girls who like other girls. She supposed it didn't matter much.

"I think that's fine. If there's any place in the world you should be able to be yourself, then I guess it's here."

"I guess. But here isn't perfect. Here is far from it."

Sally could see Nick waving her inside through the French glass doors of the dining room.

"It looks like I'm being summoned to leave."

"Okay, well. I guess I'll see you next year." Sam smiled.

"Happy New Year."

She nodded, and Sally left her outside on the back patio, blowing smoke circles into the frigid night air.

During the week of Christmas, the mail was fat with holiday cards as usual, though in most were scrawled words of sympathy. When rifling through the red and green envelopes that weekend, Sally started recognizing addresses from streets on her father's former mail route. A new ten-dollar bill fell out of the first card she opened and the note inside read, "We wanted to make sure we sent Dom his holiday thank you."

"Mom?! Mom, come and see this."

"What is it?"

She handed it to Lorraine, who looked it over with the crisp, green note and grew teary-eyed. "People loved him. Everyone loved him."

"There are at least twenty more here."

Lorraine's face flushed. "Well, let's open them, then."

As she said this, the doorbell rang.

"Who could that be on a Saturday morning? Will you get it, Sally? I'm still in my house dress."

A thin, older man stood, shifting from foot to foot in a wool coat that was too big for his frame. He held his hat in his hands, and, even though it was freezing outside, tiny beads of perspiration dotted his forehead.

"Can I help you?"

"Is this the Fiore residence?"

"Yes."

"Is your mother home?"

"She is. Hold on just a moment." Sally walked down the hall to see if her mother was dressed. "Mom, it's someone for you. A gentleman."

"Did he say what it was about?" Lorraine emerged in a black day dress with a white lace collar.

"No, I didn't ask. Sorry. He seems nervous."

"Hello, I'm Mrs. Fiore. What can I do for you?"

"My name is Stodges, Bill Stodges. Your husband…" Bill started and became overcome with emotion. He looked down at his hat as if the details of the plaid might tell him what to say. "Well, our house wasn't on your husband's route. It was just off it by one. But see, down in the car there. That's my boy, Danny. He had a real bad accident when he was a little boy and hasn't been able to walk since, so he's wheelchair bound."

Down in the Oldsmobile wagon, a boy of about eleven looked up at them and waved.

"Your husband knew about my son, and he'd take time off his route every day to come over and talk to him about baseball and sports. It meant a lot to my wife and me. Danny's gonna miss those visits." He broke into tears.

"Sally, why don't you go down and say hello to Danny," Lorraine said.

Sally threw on her heavy coat while her mother invited Mr. Stodges in to sit for a moment. She walked down the front steps in her flats, careful to avoid icy patches. Danny saw her coming and rolled down his window. His wheelchair was folded up in the spacious backseat, and he sat in the passenger side with his much smaller legs pulled close together like matchsticks. If it weren't for those little legs, he'd look like a healthy, growing boy with ruddy cheeks and a toothy grin.

"Hi," he said, his breath drifting out of the car like he'd been smoking a forbidden cigarette. "Are you Sally?"

"Yes."

He smiled. "Your dad told me how pretty you are. He wasn't kidding."

"Well, thank you. What else did he tell you?"

"We'd talk a lot about baseball. That's my favorite sport. I wanted to be a pro when I grew up. Before…" he trailed off looking at his useless legs.

"I'm sorry. What happened to you?"

"Mom always told me not to climb trees. I never listened. And then one day, I fell." He half-laughed. "Doctors said I was lucky to be alive at all. I think they're right, so I try not to mind. Most days I don't."

"That's good."

"I'm sorry about your dad. He was nice to waste time from his day on me."

"I'm sure he didn't consider it wasting time."

Danny smiled. "Maybe you can come 'round some time? We live on the West Side, right on the corner of Prospect and Sheffield."

"Okay, I'll try. But we may have to find something other than baseball to talk about."

"I like music."

"All right, then. When the weather gets better, it's a deal."

"Promise?"

"I promise."

Just then, his father returned. "We better go now," Bill said, shaking Sally's hand before getting in the car. "Sally, it was nice meeting you."

"You, too. And thanks for stopping by."

"See you in the spring?" Danny said, laboring to roll up his window.

"Don't worry, you'll see me."

Sally entered the front living room to see her mother dabbing away wet marks on her cheek.

"These people have so many expenses with their son, but they still wanted to give us something. That poor darling."

Poor darling. That was Lorraine's universal nomenclature for anyone deserving of her sympathy. She even used it on those whom Sally herself would have judged harshly. Like that time when her mother took her into Boston to visit a great aunt in a nursing home, and they'd stopped in a store on the way to the train. Sally was about four or five and had wandered a few feet from Lorraine. A large, Black lady was pushing her cart slowly down the aisle, and Sally remembered being hypnotized by the darkness of her skin because she'd never seen anything like it. So, she stared without realizing it was rude. She stared at the rolls of skin that fell from underneath the sleeves of the woman's dress. She stared until the woman noticed, drew her brows together in anger, and shouted, "What are you looking at?!"

Sally had run back to the safety of her mother's cart and hid behind the folds of her skirt. "What's wrong, angel?" Lorraine asked, pulling her out of her fabric sanctuary.

"That woman over there yelled at me."

"Over where?"

Sally pointed. Lorraine, instead of starting an argument or even giving the woman a dirty look, simply looked down at Sally and said, "She probably didn't mean to upset you. Sometimes people are just having a bad day. Maybe this is hers. Poor darling."

Lorraine sat now with all the envelopes in her lap, looking unsure of how to repay the debt of so many kindnesses.

"I promised I'd go visit Danny in the spring," Sally offered in case this small contribution might relieve the new burden.

Her mother smiled up at her. "You've never been more his daughter than you are right now. Try to remember that."

Sally warmed at such praise, but in the moment, felt undeserving. There'd been something pricking at her in the past few days, and she only just realized it as Lorraine said this.

"Mom, would you mind if I run downtown to do an errand?"

"Go ahead, just be home for dinner."

With a hustle in her step, driven almost by a fever to accomplish this deed without being seen, she walked the two miles to Wakefield Center as quickly as she could. At Woolworth's, she grabbed another red gift box and rued not taking a swath of wrapping paper and some tape along. Maybe a card and a bow would make it okay. She picked out a greeting card with a wreath and bells on it, and a simple Christmas message. Inside her book bag, she pulled out the maroon and green scarf that she'd been looking forward to wearing when her mother and Paul had theirs, but this was a better purpose for it. She smoothed and folded the wool, set the lid on it, and stuck a green bow on top. On the inside of the card, she wrote: *Merry Christmas – I hope it's full of present joy and joyful memories of special Christmases with your mom. Truly yours, Sally*

Pleased with herself, she hurried over to Arthur's apartment and celebrated that he wasn't home. She climbed the stairs and gently placed the gift on the welcome mat outside his door.

Chapter IV

On the first day of school back from the holiday break, heads turned, all following the assured steps of the new person in school. Rumors were swirling around the enigmatic presence already, and the largest point of discussion was whether she was a he or he was a she. Sam didn't seem to care a lick. She strolled to her locker, smiling at everyone like she knew them, nodding and saying pleasantries like, "Hey, man," and "How's it going?" Her book bag was fat with the clothes she was dropped off in, most likely, thought Sally, remembering what she'd said last month.

"Did you see the new girl?" Marie whispered as Sally put her bulky chemistry and history books in her locker for later that day.

Since Sally had discovered Paul and Marie's secret, Marie had been forgoing her time with the Tammettes, and was spending more time around Sally and some other girls of less notoriety. Marie herself hadn't always been so popular until the one day she'd struck Tammy's fancy. She'd been quiet, bookish, and focused on her flute playing through lower school. She wore old-fashioned, long skirts and blouses with high ruffled collars. She sat at lunch with Sally and the other outcasts until eighth grade when Tammy decided her group needed a brunette member, and Marie was conveniently seated near her in homeroom.

"Girl, you say? That's one for the debate team," said Heather, snapping her gum as though in applause of her own snarky joke.

"I know her. She's nice."

"You *know* her?"

"Stop being like all the others, will you? It's unbecoming."

Heather shrugged good-naturedly and continued murdering her gum.

"But, Sally, she does dress like she's a boy," Marie pointed out in her kind way.

"What of it? She's not hurting anyone."

They both watched her, Heather like a small, brown, cud-chewing cow and Marie like a doe-eyed fawn. Sally felt the corners of her mouth curling into a smile as they started to appear like sidekicks in a Disney movie, turning to animation before her eyes and about to spring forth in a happy-go-lucky song and dance.

"How do you know her?" asked Heather.

"My mother catered a Christmas party at her parents' house – they moved into the big white one on the lake – and I was helping. We talked a bit."

As she said this, her two friends became abruptly silent and focused on a spot directly behind her. Sally turned around and Sam was there. She wore a navy wool turtleneck, brown corduroy pants, and dark blue Converse sneakers. Her smile was so easy and confident that it drew more confused looks than her clothes.

"There you are," she said, still grinning. "Knew I'd find you. Are you first or second lunch?"

"First."

"Excellent. We can catch up then. Do we have any other classes together?" She whipped out her schedule and handed it to Sally.

"Yes, English right after lunch. But I have to warn you, if you're a lover of books like me, the syllabus is – well – very rudimentary. And it takes us forever to finish anything because O'Hoolihan loves to beat a dead horse when it comes to analysis. I heard we're going to read A Farewell to Arms – that's another thing. He's also a Hemingway junkie. So, he'll sit at his desk and talk at us for entire periods at a time. At least you're coming in for this half of the year. Last half, we nitpicked through Othello and The Scarlet Letter. I wanted to poke my eyes out."

Sam took in this rant with the same cordiality that she'd emitted all day. Once Sally was done venting, she just said, "Yeah, I'm not really a reader. I sort of like science and math more. At least with them you're dealing with facts, not lies made up by some crazy author. Well, catch ya later." With that, she left.

"I like her," Heather immediately said.

At lunch, Sally scanned the busy cafeteria to see where Sam might be. Sally sat, as usual, with Heather and a few other girls, all clustered like shy hens at the end of the long table. The din of chatter, of metal chairs clinking and scraping, of plastic trays being set down, of giggles and bickering, hung overhead like a swarm of bees. Her eyes first landed, not on Sam, but on Arthur. Someone had spilled a bowl of chili and he sauntered in with a mop and bucket, catching Sally's eyes. He stopped before reaching the spill, smiled, and held her gaze for a few stray seconds of recognition before he nodded and continued with his task.

Finally, she saw Sam wandering around, craning her neck to find them. She was a few tables over and held her tray of Salisbury steak, soggy carrots, and hopelessly unseasoned mashed potatoes. But she had the staple of high school lunch, at least – the one decent item sold from that kitchen. The chocolate chip cookie. Wrapped in cellophane and still warm, the chocolate chips melted into the plastic as it was opened. Whatever mixture of flour, eggs, sugar, and oats came together to make these cookies for the masses was pure magic.

It was when Sam saw Sally motioning to her that it happened. As she made her way over, skirting around the big jocks at Paul's table, she accidentally bumped into Lenny O'Malley, a burly junior known for brawn and not brains. He was above six feet tall and a hulking presence on the football team. Sally knew her brother tolerated him for the sake of team spirit, but inwardly thought he was a brainless bully, something which Lenny was about to prove.

"Watch it, dyke," he yelled out in his booming voice, so ignorant and lazy that he always sounded like he was swallowing his tongue when he spoke.

And with that, the hovering cloud of bees fell from the air and landed like pebbles on the filmy tiles. All eyes turned on this scene. Some were full of mean-spirited mirth because they were thinking what he was heinous enough to say, but others looked on with concern and embarrassment. Sam faltered, if only for a second, and then recovered her unshakable aplomb. Lenny stood squinting at her and breathing through his mouth, like it was taking all of his brain power to try and anticipate another full sentence in case she had a comeback. She did.

"You know what? You can call me that when you can spell it, you goddamn Neanderthal," she said, laughed directly in his confused face, and moved fluidly over to the open seat next to Sally.

The cloud of bees ascended once more like nothing had transpired. Not a moment later, the football table erupted in a bout of good-natured hazing. After a few minutes, the linebacker couldn't handle it and was forced to leave in a huff. He stormed past them, glaring at Sam, his too-short shirt coming untucked and exposing a bloated, white gut that jiggled over his belt like custard cake just out of the oven. Sally watched for her brother's reaction. He smiled a little at the ruckus that came at Lenny's expense, but she knew he didn't like that Sam had cursed. He probably also didn't like that Sam was now seated next to his little sister. Catching his eye as he looked over at their table, she was reminded of the stern, black glare of their mother, and knew this to be true.

A few weeks passed. Sam had borne the stares, the whispers, the snide comments made under breath yet just loud enough to meet her ears, the giggles as she passed, and the suspicious looks of teachers without even acknowledging them. Now, though they still happened, it was with much less frequency. People became used to Sam's appearance and her almost unshakable positive attitude, and she melded in like any member of the junior class. Sally didn't quite understand how she did this so successfully but made a note to ask when they were together that Saturday. Sam had asked her for a personalized tour of downtown. She said she hadn't explored much, except a couple of trips to the Bowladrome since the month had been so snowy.

Sam waited for her outside Parke Snow department store, sporting a navy- and maroon-striped mod sweater, gray trousers with a slight flare at the bottom, and a navy pea coat.

"Hey. So, tell me about this tiny town," she demanded, and the cold air danced with her request.

"It's not that tiny," Sally defended. She wasn't even sure why she thought it an insult, but it felt it.

"It's tiny compared to Cambridge. I didn't mean it in a bad way. Good things come in small packages, right?"

"My mom says, 'the littlest peppers are the hottest.'"

"Ha, is your mom small?"

"Yeah, she's only about five foot two."

"Figures, she's tootin' her own horn."

"I guess. So, what do you want to see?"

"I dunno. You tell me. What's good to do around here?"

"Well, everyone hangs out on the library wall. It's kind of the meet-up place, not so much in this weather, though."

"Is that where you go?"

"No. I don't really hang out with any of those people. There's a couple of places to get food. There's Santoro's if you like subs, Hazelwood Cottage is more of a formal restaurant, Piece O' Pizza, Brighams. For stores there's J.J. Newbury's and Parke Snow here. There's the movie theater, if you want to catch a flick. Saturday matinees are twenty-five cents, and you can get candy at Woolworth's next door."

"Where do you hang out?"

Sally debated about telling her. Of course, Colonial Spa was her place of choice, but it was also her sanctuary. But that's silly, she thought, to keep it from Sam, who would most likely notice it, anyway.

"I prefer Colonial Spa to any other place."

"Then let's go there."

A few minutes later, they were at the counter waiting for Mr. K. to make their ham and cheese sandwiches and cherry Cokes after he greeted them with his customary warmth.

"Can I ask you something?"

"Sure, shoot."

They were given their food, and Sam took an aggressive bite of the dainty sandwich.

"Your clothes...Well, how do you afford the second set? I mean, you obviously have to hide this from your parents during the school week at least. How do you do it?"

Sam finished chewing before she answered. "Well, my old man makes a lot of money, and I get an allowance. I use that to buy clothes. It gets tricky, hiding them. My parents think I just wear them at home and on weekends, so they don't give me too hard a time about it. If they knew I was bringing a change of clothes to school, they'd do something."

"So, I'm trying to understand. You feel more like a boy than a girl?"

"You could say that."

"How does that happen?"

"It doesn't happen," Sam snapped a little. "I was born like this."

"Like what?"

"This." Sam pointed to herself. "I feel more like a boy than a girl. It's been this way since I can remember, so I know I was always like this. Because, really, who would ever choose this? Do you know how difficult it is to always be the butt of jokes? To get second looks from everyone? To be threatened, even? No. I came this way, which is why I refuse to apologize for it or try to change it."

"When did you really know?"

Sam grew contemplative for a moment and sipped her cherry Coke. "I guess it was during movies."

"Movies?"

"Yeah. Whenever I would watch a film and the heroine was having some sort of romantic problem. I would always think, 'I could treat her better than that guy. I could be the guy.' I guess that's how I finally knew there was something different about me, and it was unquestionable. It was me. If you can think back to the time when you first felt something for a boy, it's the same thing. Only I felt something for girls. I felt like the boy."

"I think I understand."

"That's why I like you. You don't judge. I could tell that about you when I saw you in our pantry, staring up at me as I was fighting with my mother. And I thought, 'I'll be friends with her. She's a good sort.'"

Sally laughed. "Maybe you overestimate me."

"No," Sam said matter-of-factly. "You're a nice person, Sally. And I think these last few weeks could have been worse. I met with some adversity, but it was nothing to the level that I imagined. I think the people in this town seem pretty decent. Anyway, enough about me. Tell me about yourself."

"There's not much to tell."

"Modest people always say that. Stop being modest."

Sam looked at her with such a genuine interest that Sally couldn't help herself from spewing out almost every detail of the past few months. Her father's death, Joey's advances and her conflicting feelings for him, Tammy's bullying, her job at Adrian's and Rose, her brother and his secrets, her mother's financial struggles, and finally, Arthur and her inappropriate longings. She was shocked at herself for revealing so much. So shocked that she felt like she had to admit even that.

"Gosh, I'm sorry. I shouldn't have said all this."

"See, that's your problem, right there. You're the type who walks around in this life acting like you've done something wrong by existing. Stop doing that. You're a cool chick. Act like it."

"Okay." Sally blushed into her second cherry Coke.

"And as far as your friend Arthur, I don't see any shame in that. You're practically an adult and he's not old. Besides, you're mature for your age. It's only natural for you to be bored with teenage boys. I've seen him, by the way. He hangs out at the Bowladrome. Let's go over and see if he's there."

"No, I should get home."

Sam snorted. "Don't be silly. It's only five, and I've seen him there at this time before. Come on. We'll scope it out, and, if he's not there, we'll play one game and leave."

Sally considered this, and the blood leapt in her veins. She'd informed Lorraine of what she was doing today, and there was no rush for her to be home. Her mother wouldn't look with a harsh eye on an innocent round of bowling. This was enough for her to accept.

"First, let's go in here." Sam stopped in front of the pool hall.

"No way. No respectable girl sets foot in that place."

Sam looked around her shoulders in mockery. "I don't see any respectable girls for miles."

"No, I heard bad men go in there."

"What are you so afraid of? Are you protecting your virtue? Come on, there's two of us, and I've been itching to play. I wouldn't go in alone either, but you're here now. It'll be quick and painless, I promise."

Against her better judgment, Sally caved. A stagnant wall of smoke hung in the air as they entered the dimly-lit main room. In the darkness, heads turned to stare. The room was canvased with drunken eyes and seedy leers.

"We should go. This seems bad."

"Nah, I want to have a competitive game with someone," Sam said loudly, strutting like a rooster around a neglected table. "Anyone in here care to play me?"

"I'll play ya," a gravelly voice said from the corner shadows of the room.

From a darkened recess, the man belonging to the voice stepped forward. His hair was the color of a burnt persimmon, his freckled face aged beyond his years, and his teeth yellowed from nicotine. He was Pat O'Malley, the older brother of the same Lenny O'Malley who'd verbally assaulted her new friend. Sally wondered if she should warn Sam about this. Their family was known not just for their imbecilic nature, but also for their fiery and unpredictable tempers. Pat was recently back from being wounded in the war by an RPG rocket that killed his captain and took his left leg off. His whole clan was touting him as a big war hero, and he now used it as a crutch to slough off all accountability.

"Whaddya wanna play?" he asked, moving towards them with a purposefully threatening gait, made more menacing by the heaviness of his artificial leg. Like his younger sibling, he was an inherent bully. Sam was unfazed, and this bothered Sally.

"How 'bout a game of one pocket, eight points? Five bucks a point."

A chorus of "oohs" echoed from Pat's crew, which was comprised of other burly deadbeats. Everyone in town knew that the pool hall attracted all kinds of riff-raff like this, and no one liked it. Trouble-makers, gamblers, addicts, all hung out here. Mr. O., who owned the Bowladrome, regularly lamented the pool hall's existence.

Sally started to panic as Sam set up the table. She could feel men staring at her from behind their curtains of smoke, while she was out in the open, unprotected and vulnerable.

"I'll take those odds," he said, taking up his pool cue like a weapon.

"Say, what's your name? You look familiar," Sam asked.

"Name's Pat O'Malley."

Sam paused. "O'Malley. Why do I know that name? You got a younger brother at the high school?"

"That's right. Best linebacker on the football team," he answered, puffing out his broad chest.

A wide grin spread across Sam's face as she positioned herself. "That's right. Great guy." She made her first shot.

In three more shots, she'd won the game. Pat paid her reluctantly. "What's your name, boy?"

"Sam."

"Sam, you're a decent player. But you better come here again soon and give me a fair shot to win back this money."

"Oh, I will. For sure."

"And next time, don't bring your girl." He nodded at Sally. "This ain't no place for ladies."

"Righto."

When they were outside, Sam fanned the cash out in Sally's face, but she whacked it away.

"What? Oh, come on. That was brilliant!"

"I don't care what it was. You never should have made me go in there."

Sam raised an eyebrow. "Please. Are you descended from the Queen or something? You need to get over yourself."

"I'm not high on myself. I just didn't feel safe in there."

"Did anything happen?"

"No, but – "

"Exactly. So, calm yourself. Let's bowl and find your custodian crush."

"I should be getting home. We wasted too much time in there."

"We wasted all of ten minutes. This stick-in-the-mud act isn't working for me."

"I don't really care what's working for you. If I want to go home, I'm going home."

Sam took her in for a minute without a word. Then conceded in her relaxed way and said, "That's fine with me, but do you really want to go home, or do you just think you should? It is, after all, not even six on a weekend. And if you stay, it'll be my treat," she finished, fanning her earnings back out again.

"Okay. But if he's not there, just one game. And if he is there, oh – I don't know. I feel weird about it."

"Stop worrying, sister. That's another one of your major issues. Why worry about things you have no control over? If he's not there, one game like we said. If he is, don't sweat it. Just leave it to me."

In complete contrast to the billiards, the immaculate Bowladrome was bathed in light and full of the hum of wholesome recreation. A ladies' league practiced in the right lanes closest to the door, milling about in their polyester jackets. There were some families with young children in the middle lanes, making it lighthearted fun instead of keeping score. Next to them was a spray of younger teens, some freshmen and sophomores Sally recognized. But there was no Arthur. Sally felt both disappointment and relief at his absence.

"Well, that's too bad," said Sam. "Oh, well. You wanna play or head home?"

"I think I'll just head home. It's dark now, and it'll be a cold walk."

"Suit yourself. I'll probably roll a few."

"Okay, well goodnight."

"Night. Thanks for hanging out. Maybe we can do this again next weekend if you're up for it?"

"Sure, that'd be nice."

As Sally turned to leave, she noticed a new family had taken up a lane. It was the Gallaghers – Tammy, her parents, and her younger brother, Trent. They looked like the idyllic American family. Tammy and her mother with hair like glossy corn, while her father and brother were dark-haired, all of them above average in height, and all with the same twinkling blue eyes. Yet there was something in their interactions with each other that felt artificial and forced. Her parents wouldn't make eye contact with each other. There was civility among them as they played, but their motions were automatic at best with no playful interaction or banter or even bickering. Just a stunted, false affection.

Tammy noticed her watching them and stared her down with a mean smile, taking note of whom she was with. This didn't bother Sally, especially as she noted Mr. Gallagher ogling the young freshmen girls in the neighboring lane before he turned back to his own daughter, and something in the pit of her sickened a little at the sight of his hand falling heavily on Tammy's shoulder. Then and there, she decided Tammy Gallagher was just like Lenny O'Malley, a pitiable bully who would peak in high school and never amount to much else. She held eyes with her nemesis until she reached the exit. The latter didn't quite know what to make of this brazen new version of the girl she'd tried to torment for the last decade. And Sally was able to meet her glare because she'd outgrown her like an old piece of clothing one finds tucked away at the dusty edge of a closet and long since out of style. She no longer cared what Tammy thought of her. She no longer thought of Tammy at all.

But Tammy still thought of her and apparently that was enough to cause a disruption in her life. Sally walked into school on Monday feeling like Audrey Hepburn in a pair of black cigarette pants and a turtleneck that were hand-me-downs from Rose. She'd brought a small bag into work last week full of lovely black clothes – two pairs of cigarette pants and three black turtlenecks. She said she was over her gamin phase and felt that dresses and nylons were part of being a grownup despite the whole pants revolution. The clothes were a little stretched from Rose's ample curves, but they still served their purpose and Sally had the dark hair and doe eyes to complete the look. Her hair was swept back in a ponytail, and she'd even put some of Lorraine's black eyeliner on her top lids.

Her confidence was quickly shaken by only loosely stifled giggles as she walked the length of the corridor to her locker, much like a few months ago when laughter had followed her to this same place. Heather was there again the same as before as well. She leaned against her closed locker, shaking her head and snapping her gum in time.

"What now?"

"You don't wanna know."

"Oh, but I do. So, so badly," Sally said with the most sardonic tone she could muster.

Heather snorted with delight at her shy friend's unusual mocking tone. "That bimbo Barbie doll fancies herself a poet now. She's made up a cute little rhyme about you and your new pal to the tune of 'Sam n' Sally sittin' in a tree.'"

Sally chose not to react. She grabbed her books for first period and walked through the double doors into the lobby by the auditorium where the majority of the student body socialized before classes started. Today, the sign-up sheet for senior show costume and crew was posted, and she intended to put her name down for costume mistress. It was hanging on the bulletin board by the auditorium doors right next to the sign-ups for auditions. The show was *Carousel.* Some of the seniors were congregating, jockeying for a position to pen in their names.

"Hey," a voice startled her. It was Sam.

"Oh hey, morning."

"What's going on?"

"People are signing up to try out for the senior show, and I'm about to put my name down for costume mistress. Underclassmen are allowed to be on crew."

"That's something people do voluntarily?"

"Hey, look!" Lenny O'Malley had spotted them and the crowded lobby turned to stare.

Sally could see Tammy's delight as she stood poised to write her name down for the lead role of Julie Jordan. Then a few of her cronies began chanting, "Sam n' Sally sittin' in a tree, k-i-s-s-i-n-g." Paul and Marie had quietly entered, and Sally could see the tick in her brother's jaw and the stormy look on his face that would not only guarantee him the coveted part of Billy Bigelow, but also warned of his propensity to lose his temper. Sam, however, beat him to come to Sally's defense.

"Wow," she shouted so the entire lobby could hear. She also gave an exaggerated clap and gesticulated to Tammy. "The poetic stylings of Tammy Gallagher everyone. Brava."

A weighty hush fell over the crowd like people knew what was coming. Somehow everyone did. It was inevitable, like they were watching David take up that small stone and place it in his sling. Even Tammy was a spectator in her own dethroning, her pupils dilating in fright.

"Gosh, Tammy. If you were any more original, you'd be Allen bloody Ginsberg."

Tammy said nothing but chewed her bottom lip and continued to look her aggressor in the eye.

"It's fun, isn't it? Having people to beat down so you can make yourself feel better for being so pathetic."

Whispers surged through their audience.

"That's right. Pathetic. Know why Tammy here is such a tragic figure?" Sam addressed the crowd.

"Why?" someone in the back corner called out.

"Hmm, let's see, shall we? There are actually a few reasons. The first is why Tammy has always been so much more mature than everyone else. One might think it's because she was just born sophisticated. No, it's because she was born two years before everyone else in her grade. How many times did you stay back in elementary school, Tammy? Once? No, twice. Two times. Aw…first and second grade are hard, aren't they? All that adding and subtracting."

Sally began to panic at what would come out of Sam's mouth next. The crowd watched, more out of a morbid fascination than enjoyment, it seemed. Tammy tried to be strong and hold her ground, but her impervious eyes were transforming into pieces of burning cobalt.

"What else? Oh, there's her family. Right. The perfect family, aren't they? I guess they are – when her father's not having affairs with every last desperate housewife in town."

"SHUT UP!" Tammy screamed, a red fury flushing her face as tears came spilling out.

"What about all the times you should have shut up? People are supposed to feel sorry for you, now? Well, I don't. You pick on my friend here, for what? Because you want to date her brother, but he'd rather date your best friend?"

At this, heads turned to Paul and Marie. Sally's heart sank at their betrayed faces. For Tammy, this news was worse than being taken to task for failed grades and a philandering father. It was such a shock to her system that she stopped breathing for a second while she observed them, and her brain put together the telltale signs of the last couple of months.

"No, that's not it. We know the truth, you and I, don't we, Tammy? You pick on her because you know deep down, right in the black, rotten center of that pretty outer package, that she's better than you in every way. She's better and purer than you'll ever be. And it just eats away at you, doesn't it? But oh look – you made up a clever rhyme today."

"That's enough." It was her brother's voice this time. Sam looked over at him, her face unreadable and passive. But she stopped.

The bell for first period rang and the dallying crowd ambled away, now lethargic from the day's premature drama. The Tammettes who hadn't defected ushered Tammy away to the girls' bathroom. Her brother frowned from across the room and stormed off with Marie, pulling her along behind him. Soon, Sam and Sally were the only ones left save for some flower children types who always straggled to class late.

"How could you do that?"

Sam raised an eyebrow and crossed her arms. "By 'that,' do you mean stand up to that heifer for you?"

"You could've stood up to her without spewing every damn thing I told you. I told you those things in confidence. Especially about my brother. Now he and Marie are upset with me."

"He'll get over it."

"Get over it? What do you know? Are you a member of our family? Do you know the inner workings of our relationships? And those horrible things you said to Tammy…"

"Those horrible things were true, and nothing less than she deserves after how she treats people. I can't believe you're actually empathizing with your enemy."

"I appreciate that you were trying to stick up for me, but I think how you went about it was wrong and cruel."

Sam looked her over once more, accepting this proclamation in her calm manner. "Maybe so, but look at it this way. She'll never make fun of you again."

Chapter V

Sally had been correct about her brother and Marie not speaking to her. At lunch, the collective gaze of their table felt like a punch to her insides, especially the hurt that still marred Marie's wide, innocent face. She dreaded going home later and being cornered whenever Lorraine was out of earshot. More than that, she prayed he wouldn't tell their mother. Although, he wouldn't risk her spilling his other secret, so maybe she was safe there. That only meant whatever he said to her privately would be even more severe.

But it was worse than that. He ignored her completely. At home, at the dinner table, on the car ride to school, at any point of interaction, she became a specter to him. Their mother was now too tired to notice things that she would've instantly picked up on just a few months prior. With no one paying her any mind, Sally made plans to hang out with Sam again that Saturday. This time, Sam had asked her to first come to her parents' house for lunch. To avoid any potential obstacles, Sally told Lorraine she was working a shift at Adrian's to cover for Rose and then planned to head to the library to do homework.

It had snowed, and there was a light coating, but the sidewalks were bare. Still, it was a blustery walk, and Sally wondered what awaited her at the commanding, white house. Would Judge and Mrs. Pettyfer be there? She pictured all of them sitting at the sprawling oak table in the dining room having genial, though inhibited, conversation over endive stuffed with crab or something equally pretentious. But only their housekeeper, Molly, an older Irish lady, answered the door, her face as round and blank as a pumpkin waiting to be carved.

"Hello, miss."

"Hello, I'm here to see Sam – Samantha."

"Oh," Molly faltered for a moment, turned and looked inside the house before turning back to Sally. "I don't think she can come out to see you, dear. They've had a terrible row, she and her parents and now she's locked herself in her room, though I probably shouldn't be tellin' you that."

"Who is it, Molly?"

Dorris Pettyfer appeared in the doorway with eyes glassy from crying. At the sight of Sally, she breathed a soft sigh of relief.

"Oh, it's you, Sally. Well, I suppose you and my daughter had plans today, then?"

"We did, but I can leave if it's a bad time."

"No, no. Why don't you come in," she said as more of a command than an option, shouldering past the now mum housekeeper and pulling Sally in by the sleeve of her coat. "Samantha is forbidden to leave this house at present, but I think perhaps a visit from someone who possesses common sense will do her some good. She's upstairs in her room."

Sally followed her through the front hall – its mirrors reflecting back the beauty of portraits in gilded frames that hung the wall opposite and its console tables standing like sentinels outside the rooms beyond them – the front parlor, another larger sitting room opposite, a small half bath, Judge Pettyfer's office, the door of which was very firmly closed, and the dining room. At the end of the hallway was the entrance to the kitchen.

"Are you hungry? Would you like Molly to fix you something – a grilled cheese?"

"Oh, no that's okay. I'll just go up and see her," Sally said as her stomach growled in protest. She half-laughed and made a hasty exit up the kitchen stairs to the second floor.

"It'll be the first door on your right," said Dorris, not looking at Sally anymore, but staring down at her own hand poised on a pack of Newport cigarettes.

Sally climbed the stairs and stopped in front of the one that led into Sam's room. She knocked.

"Go away!"

"It's me, Sally. Your mom let me in."

After a quick shuffling, Sam opened the door and yanked Sally inside in a similar fashion as her mother had just done, only slightly rougher and more desperate.

"What did she say to you?"

"Not much. Just that you're not allowed to leave the house."

Sam grunted and sat on her bed, the blanket still rumpled in her shape like a cast mold. Her room displayed a war of clashing worlds. In sharp contrast to the pale peach wallpaper covered in pink and blue flowers and the four-poster bed with a quilt and pillows of the same schemes, her closet door was covered with posters of the Beatles and James Brown, and quotes drawn on pieces of paper from Martin Luther King, Jr.'s "I Have a Dream" speech. On her vanity table, bottles of perfumes and glossy new makeups sat untouched.

"You like Dr. King?" Sally asked.

"Of course, don't you?"

"I like that he stands for peace."

Sam looked at her with amused condescension. "Have you ever even met a Black person or any person of a different race, for that matter?"

"Yes. What kind of question is that?"

"It's just mighty white around here. And back in Cambridge, I had a good amount of Black friends. They didn't live in my neighborhood, but a few went to my school, and I became close with them and their families. In fact, they felt more like family than my own."

"I see. What happened, anyway, with your parents today?"

"Oh, they found out how I've been dressing at school. I guess Tammy's slimy father goes to Father's country club and mentioned it, along with what happened this week." She got up now, walked over to her record player, and turned it on. "Sgt. Pepper's Lonely Hearts Club" blared out into the room. "So you know, they're threatening to take all my clothes away and send me to the nuthouse."

"The nuthouse? For what?"

"For the way I am, of course. They think it can be treated. They think they can 'shock' it out of me," she said, pinching Sally's arms.

"You mean that place in Belmont?"

"The very one."

"I've heard about it. One of my grandpa's cousins had to go there because she was manic depressive."

Sam swung open her closet doors to a display that looked like it belonged in a window at Jordan Marsh. "Speaking of depression, I'll be stuck wearing these clothes, at least in school, since Mother is now going to check my bag for extras when she drops me off."

Approaching the row of hanging dresses, Sally couldn't help but reach out and touch them. It was a sensory overload for her eyes and hands – custom pieces of the richest of fabrics, designer names, details she could never imagine being able to create herself. She counted thirty perfect dresses, followed by nearly as many A-line skirts of various prints and textures, and several blouses adorned with tie fronts and smart collars. On the shelves above was a rainbow of cashmere sweater sets, and below, several rows of exquisite heels. Sam watched her with amusement.

"Wow, you really dig this stuff, huh?"

"You're so lucky," Sally breathed, then quickly added, "I know it's torture for you to wear these, but really. They're breathtaking."

"I'll leave them to you in my will."

"Don't say things like that. Where's your bathroom?"

"Just down at the end of the hall."

"I'll be right back."

The room Sally ended up entering wasn't the bathroom, but a child's room. The walls were covered with pink chintz wallpaper that matched the bedspread and even the fabric that bordered the edge of the tiny vanity table. White curtains of delicate, sheer ruffles hung from the windows. Shelves built into the far-left wall held an assortment of books and dolls. Sally read the titles, noting her favorites. *The Secret Garden. A Little Princess. Anne of Green Gables. The Little Prince. Madeline. The Lion, the Witch, and the Wardrobe.*

The dolls were different from the hard, plastic variety with corn yellow hair and eyes like cloudless skies. This collection was far superior as their painted, bisque faces, though still vacant, exuded. There was one grander than the rest, with a cascade of golden ringlets, a rosy, bow-shaped mouth, and emerald glass eyes. She wore a violet Marie Antoinette-style gown with layer upon layer trimmed in white lace and billowing sleeves topped with dainty bows. This doll must be called something like Claudette or Veronique.

Over to one side was a small circular table, the same white wood as the other furnishings. On it rested an actual porcelain tea set hand painted with sweet rosebuds. The walls also held several framed flower prints featuring only pink varieties – roses, carnations, peonies. But the crowning glory of this little girl's room was the Victorian dollhouse that stood in one corner, next to a neatly packed toy box with the name "Charlotte" carved in fancy script.

Sally walked over and sat in front of the structure, mesmerized by the intricate details. Her own dollhouse, constructed and presented to her by Domenic on her sixth birthday, still existed but had been relegated with some embarrassment to the back of her closet last year after Nick tried to play with it by making the doll family speak to each other only in Pig Latin.

As she opened the front of the pale pink behemoth, its turrets and gables fringed with scalloped edges that resembled a gingerbread construction good enough to eat, hers seemed a badly conceived shack. Her eyes scanned the miniature world, lingering fondly on the carved, Queen Anne furnishings that populated the three levels. There were five bedrooms, a bathroom, and a sitting room on the top two floors, and, below, were the kitchen, living room, a dining room, and a second parlor. She noted that the mother, father, and daughter were all seated in the downstairs living room, and upstairs, a younger daughter was lying in bed.

Even the piano in the second parlor had individual keys. She ran a finger over them and thought of the instrument in her own dollhouse that Domenic had painstakingly carved with such attempted accuracy. There were no keys to be deciphered as he just painted that part white, but he'd taken time to form a piano book with the tiniest piece of paper and had written in some musical notes.

No one will ever love me that much again.

The thought flew across her brain in one sharp and fleeting revelatory moment. It was such a despairing thought, and so much worse for its indisputable truth that she was grateful for the interruption of Sam's voice.

"You get lost?"

"Oh!" Sally jumped up, suddenly conscious of her intrusion. For there was a much larger question looming in the air. Where was the child that belonged to such a room? "I'm sorry. I did. I – clearly this isn't the bathroom."

"No, it's not." Sam remained composed as always, but Sally knew she had somehow crossed a line, a line she hadn't seen drawing itself in the space before her, a breech that she didn't quite understand. She only knew she had messed up and she felt horrible about it.

"I'm really sorry. I shouldn't have been looking around. I don't know what I was thinking, really."

"Oh, it gets even better," Sam said, moving over to the closet doors. "You think my closet was a spectacle, get a load of this." She pulled them open, revealing a row of precocious dresses. Dresses with rounded collars, petticoats, sewn rosettes, and puffed sleeves. On the floor beneath this sea of cheerful pinks, creamy mints, and butter yellows were equally precious little shoes – a matching pair for each dress.

Sam looked back at her, tears foiling her impenetrable look of unruffled detachment. Sally didn't say anything as her friend sat defeated on the small bed and touched the stuffed bear propped up on the center pillow. Sally understood this, because it was a phenomenon she'd been growing accustomed to more each day.

"How old was she when it happened?"

"Five," came Sam's voice from someplace far away. "She had leukemia. I was ten."

"I'm sorry."

Sam continued, "They keep her room exactly the same as she left it. I was glad when we were moving. I thought, they'll have to get over it. They'll have to let go. But no." She shook her head, and a stray tear fell, dripped off the edge of her pointed chin. "Even the same wallpaper…They can't let go. And they won't let me. Because they wish it'd been me instead."

"That's not true."

Sam looked at her. "It is true. If it were me, do you think they'd have kept my things? No. They would erase me. They wish they could erase me now." She paused, looking back at the closet and around the rest of the room. "Sometimes I want to take everything out of here and burn it. Give my Lottie peace."

"I'm sorry. I don't know what else to say."

Sam stood with her back to Sally and took a deep breath. When she turned around, she was her old self. "Hey, how would you feel about living a little dangerously today?"

"How so?" Her nerves started going like they always did when she was afraid of getting caught in a lie by Lorraine. She was already pushing it with this outing, and now Sam was about to take it even further.

"Well, you go back downstairs and tell my mother you're leaving. Say that I'm still upset and want to be left alone. Wait for me out on the street. I'll sneak out down the trellis by my window, and we'll go into town as planned. They'll never even know I'm gone. When stuff like this happens, they don't check on me until morning."

"That sounds risky. What if someone sees?"

"No one will see. Trust me. I've snuck out before. Just do it. Where do you have to be?"

"Nowhere."

"Exactly. We can see if your Arthur is bowling today. But first, I want to go back to that Spa place and have a sandwich and cola."

Sally managed to keep herself composed on the way out. Pangs of guilt coursed through her as Dorris apologized for their ruined plans and humbly thanked her for speaking to Sam. She walked a few steps and loitered in front of the adjacent house until Sam appeared, breathing hard with rosy cheeks.

"Well, that was fun. The trellis gets shakier every time I go down it, but I think it'll keep."

"You're crazy."

When they strolled into the Bowladrome after their late lunch and some browsing in a few stores, it was already four o'clock. This time, in the far-left corner by the juke box and the machine that sold ice cream sandwiches, was Arthur, enjoying his own solitary game.

"Let's go," said Sam, making her way through the throng of bowlers.

"What? No!"

"Sals – can I call you Sals? Look, there are no other free lanes. Be cool. Please. Be the cool chick you are and just follow my lead."

Sally sighed, wishing she'd gone home an hour ago when she had the chance. Sam was so bold. Too bold. Waltzing right over to an older man and asking to share his lane, just like that, when she didn't even know him.

"Hey man, can we roll with you?"

Arthur had paused his game to retie his left shoe. He looked up, startled at this boyish youth in front of him, but broke into a grin when he noticed Sally.

"Oh hey, sure. Knock yourselves out."

"Thanks, pal."

"I've seen you here a couple times," Arthur said, swigging coffee from a Styrofoam cup. "You're a decent bowler."

"You're okay, too," Sam said while making a strike look like nothing but an effortless stretch.

"How 'bout you, Sally? You like to bowl?"

"Not really. The balls always feel too heavy in my hands, even these small ones."

Sam choked on a laugh. Arthur, all politeness, looked down at the carpeted floor to avoid any awkward eye contact. Sally felt herself blushing to the roots of her hair. She was furious with Sam, who was now handing her what looked like the marbled seeing-stone of an evil sorcerer.

"Here, see how this ball feels," she said, still smirking.

Sally snatched it and with a scathing look at her, marched to the line and took a moment to exhale before hurling her ball straight into the gutter, where it toddled the remainder of the way without even moving a pin.

"Shake it off," Sam said, with a dismissive wave of her hand, but then smirked again. "It's just nerves."

The rest of the game was uneventful. Arthur and Sam were much more seasoned and coordinated bowlers, but Sally was able to knock down a few pins in the end. When the points were tallied, Arthur emerged as the winner by only a narrow margin.

"Winner has to have the losers over to his place for drinks," Sam said.

"Really? And who made that rule?"

"I did. Just now."

"Sam…" Sally admonished from behind her. Sam waved her off.

"Whaddya say? One drink? Maybe a smoke? Then we'll be off home for dinner."

Arthur considered as he changed back into sneakers and wrapped the scarf Sally had given him around his neck. A look passed across his hazel eyes, a hesitance that nearly won over whatever he was wrestling with before a more powerful force subdued it.

"Just one drink, then?"

Sam nodded. A few minutes later they were seated on the couch in his apartment. He took off his gray wool coat that looked like another thrift store find. He wore his fisherman knit sweater again with a navy turtleneck and brown corduroy pants. Sally liked how he looked in street clothes and couldn't help admiring from her seat.

"So?" He stood in front of them smiling. "What can I get you?"

"I'll have a scotch, neat," Sam ordered.

"Just a cola for me."

"Oh, come on," Sam said.

"I don't want to go home smelling like alcohol," Sally defended.

"Throw some vodka in that cola," Sam instructed Arthur. "Vodka has no smell. She won't suspect a thing."

"You sure?" Arthur looked at her, poised with the Coca-Cola he'd just pulled from his fridge.

She looked at Sam's assured face – so assured even now that she would go along with this newest scheme.

"I guess so…"

"Atta girl. I swear, you need to loosen up. You're all wound up tight over this mother of yours. I'd like to meet her."

"Maybe you should be concerned with your own parents. I'm not quite sure how you get away with all that you do when they seem ten times stricter than my mother."

"Years of rebellion have started wearing the old goats down," Sam said, pulling three joints and a lighter out of her pocket.

"What's that?"

"Grass. Here." She put all three in her mouth and lit them at once.

"You mean, marijuana? I can't."

"If anyone needs this, you do. Arthur?"

"Yeah, sure. Where'd you score these?" He came around and handed them their drinks.

"Friends in high places."

"Ha, clever."

Sally held the strange-looking cigarette she'd just been handed, unsure of whether she should try it. The aroma was pungent, and already she was panicking about how to mask it when she returned home. She sipped her drink. It tasted like regular cola only with a sharp punch at the end. She watched Sam and Arthur slowly inhaling, closing their eyes, their actions shrouded by the skunky mist. Sally took another sip from her drink and felt her mind grow hazy. Her movements fell in line with theirs, and even though her logic told her not to, she couldn't help but watch Arthur's well-formed lips close around the thin paper and want to do the same. She did.

The scorching smoke immediately made her cough, but she didn't dislike it. She watched Arthur again. His lids looked heavy, and he smiled lazily at her. She inhaled a second time, fighting back the urge to hack. This time, it swilled around in her lungs, burning on exhale, but leaving behind a tingling, a delightful lethargy, a fuzzy reverie. She laid her head back against the fabric of the couch and closed her eyes, joint poised between her fingers.

"Hey...hey," Sam's voice floated in her right ear.

She opened her eyes and turned her head without lifting it from the cradle of the cushion. Sam took one look at her half-lowered lids and broke into uncontrollable giggles. Sally followed suit. Suddenly, everything was funny. She took another sip of her drink.

"I don't know how I'm gonna go home like this."

Sam waved her off. "You worry too much. Who cares? Your mother probably doesn't even know what grass smells like."

"She'll know I've been drinking."

"There's time to sober up. We're having one drink and one smoke. It's not like we're in Atlantic City on a bender. Arthur – tell us a story and sober us up. Tell us about what you're working on over there," Sam demanded, pointing at his typewriter.

Arthur laughed and took another drag. "Do you mean to say you think what I'm working on must be so boring that it's able to reverse the effects of drugs and alcohol?"

Sam burped unceremoniously. "I mean, I wasn't going to say it outright like you just did, but okay... Yes?"

"Fair enough." He regarded Sally. "And what do you think?"

"About what? Your boring book?" Again, they laughed.

"Well, that settles it, then. I'm just not telling you anything."

"No, come on. Tell us." Sam slapped her hand on the arm of the couch.

"Yeah, we're just kidding."

"Start telling Sally while I use your bathroom," Sam said, getting up. "Here, come and keep my seat warm." She grabbed his hand and led him over to where Sally sat.

He plopped down with a hint of reluctance, but there was no resisting Sam's overtures. Sally looked at him and tried to pay attention. Even in her state, it wasn't hard to watch the curve of his mouth as he spoke.

"What I'm working on is very personal," he started. "It's a memoir like I mentioned to you before."

"Right." Sally took another sip of her drink. "About your experiences."

"Yeah, basically from childhood to now. I – um – I've had kind of a shitty life until coming here."

"Where'd you come from?"

"A farm in California."

"Wow. What part?"

"Salinas."

"Oh...Like Steinbeck!"

"Yes. That's likely the only real thing I have in common with Steinbeck."

"Why did you decide to leave?"

"I had a stepfather. He'd get drunk and he'd beat on me. At least he wouldn't beat my mother because she was sickly. At least he had the decency to take it out on me. And maybe that's why I never left home. I was afraid if I wasn't there, he might turn on her, sickly or not." He sighed. "I don't know why I'm telling you this. Probably because I'm high. I don't like to talk about it. That's why I'm writing it – to get it out of me, to expel it. I think that's the only way I'll ever heal."

"That makes sense to me. What landed you here of all places?"

"When she passed a couple years ago, I said to myself, 'You don't need to stay here with this sonofabitch. You're free.' I'd lay awake at night, staring at my bedroom ceiling and wondering what it would be like to just find a lovely small town and start over. To have a clean slate like that, to become a brand-new person, the person I wanted to be – I think you only get those opportunities a few times in life, if at all, and they're a gift not to be squandered. So, I gathered up all my worldly possessions, which didn't amount to very much more than a small suitcase, and I made my way across country by all different means – trains, buses, kind drivers, my own two feet. First though, before small town living, I wanted to emulate Steinbeck and get myself to New York just to see what I could do there. And you know, it's funny, but I learned more in the getting there than the arrival – I felt like Kerouac and Ginsberg out there meeting all different kinds of people, seeing all manner of sights. I felt like I could do anything. I started jotting down my memories and new experiences all at once in a worn pocket notebook my mom had given me. Then when I got to Manhattan, well that was a different story. For one, I got scared out of my mind. It was wonderful, but overwhelming. I had enough money to get from there to Boston, and once in Boston I met a fellow who was hiring people to work on the grounds of a historic property, so I did that for a while. It wasn't bad, but it wasn't for me. It was seasonal and I needed something steadier if I was going to make it on my own. A friend recommended me to rent this apartment from the widow who owns this house – a friend of his mother's. My landlady, Helen – I mentioned her before – she's quirky, but for the most part she's nice and charges me little because she knows I'm writing. I think she fancies herself my benefactress. And when I moved here, I thought, boy wouldn't it be an easy commute to work at that school. I inquired and they just so happened to be hiring. This town has grown on me since. This town is the lovely little town I'd dreamed of starting over in. That's the whole story." He paused and shrugged.

"Well, I'm glad you're here."

His look changed as she said this. "Me, too," he whispered. "I'm glad you're here. That scarf you left me, Sally…That scarf meant -"

"Where's Sam?" She sat bolt upright, feeling a prominent absence in the space.

Arthur joined her in the alertness of the moment. "Man, you're right. Hey, her jacket is gone."

Sally let another giggle escape even though she was furious.

"What's funny?" He leaned against the couch, relaxed again.

"That girl, she's such a troublemaker. But I can't help liking her."

"Why is she a troublemaker?"

Sally sipped her drink, resting her chin on the rim of the glass and grinning down into it until the bubbles tickled her nose. "Leaving me here alone with you."

"Are you saying I'm trouble?" He feigned offense. "That I'm some kind of bad example for giving drinks and grass to a minor?" He laughed at his own sarcasm.

"No, silly." Sally shook her head, resting it again on the back of the couch. "It's because she knows I have a crush on you." Realizing what she had just admitted to, she drew in a sharp breath and immediately expelled a loud hiccup. "Oh gosh, why did I just say that?"

She forced herself to look and see if his reaction was horror, but he looked the same as he had the moment before she realized Sam had gone. And she knew what that meant. He bit his lip as though fighting an internal battle with himself, but in the end, he bent forward and kissed her. His kiss was different than Joey's. Where one was warm and safe, familiar almost, this new sensation burned deeper, like electricity. He cradled her cheek with his hand, his fingers threaded themselves through her hair. Time stopped her breath when she felt his tongue parting her lips and the kiss grew more fervent. And then he pulled away.

"I'm so sorry." His head was in his hands, fingers now running through his own hair, the strands rippling through them like fields of toasted wheat.

Her insides knotted with an ache different than grief, but not by much – a longing, the wanting of an emptiness to be filled and knowing at the same time that it would always just be empty in the end. It was the feeling of being with someone, but still being alone. He sat that way for what seemed an eternity before he spoke again.

"I knew that was wrong when I was doing it, but I couldn't help it. You're just – you're different. I don't see you as a teenager. To me, you're a contemporary. I always felt like that's why you noticed me."

"Well, kind of..." Sally began, the pot working now like a truth serum. "But mostly I noticed you because you were wearing my father's shoes."

"Come again?" His head snapped to attention.

"My father. Domenic was his name. Right after he passed away last September, my mother took all of his clothes to the local thrift. She said she couldn't bear having them as reminders in the house. So, she took them, all of them. He was a mailman, and he had this pair of black shoes he'd been wearing forever, but they were still in decent shape, so he refused to buy new ones. And the left one had a scuff because one time a dog chased him, and he fell. I would recognize those shoes anywhere. So, I felt like because of that, I wanted to talk to you."

"Oh, I see. That's – well, that's pretty odd, isn't it?"

"I guess. And then one day, I was cutting down Armory to avoid Tammy and her friends, and I looked up and saw you in your window typing on your typewriter and wearing one of my dad's plaid shirts. Somehow, it made me feel less alone."

Arthur slung an arm around her and kissed her forehead. "You've been through a lot."

"Not as much as you."

"Well, no one said it was a competition."

"What time is it?"

"A quarter 'til seven."

"What?!! Oh no! My mother's gonna kill me for being so late." She scrambled up and hurried to the door, carelessly throwing on her coat.

"Let me drive you."

"No, she'd go ballistic. You don't understand."

"Sure, I do. Your mother is strict. I get it. Let me make it easier on you and at least drop you close enough."

Because of the lateness of the hour, Sally consented. Arthur dropped her about ten houses away from her front door.

"I hope you don't feel weird about anything that happened," he said.

"No. I wanted you to kiss me."

"Do you want me to kiss you again?"

She opened the door of the truck to let the arctic air temper the hotness in her cheeks before she answered. "Only if you can kiss me with your soul instead of your lips. If you can kiss me not as lover, but as kindred spirit whose path has connected with my own, even if briefly."

He smiled and shook his head. "See what I mean? No regular high school girl could ever think something like that up."

"I never said I was regular."

"You're anything but. You're the saddest, most beautiful woman I've ever met."

"Worth turning into a character someday?"

"Definitely. You have all the melancholy charm of Daisy Buchanan without the unredeemable flaws."

"I like to think of myself as more of a Jo March or an Elizabeth Bennet."

"I'll just have to read those novels then. *Little Women* and *Pride and Prejudice*, right?"

"Yes, you won't be disappointed."

"He sat silent for a moment. Do you think we can still be friends?"

"I don't see why not."

He waved as she hopped down, then turned his truck around and went back the way they'd come just for safe measure. Her own house was lit up like a torch. To make matters worse, Joey's car was parked out front, and only then did she recall him mentioning coming over earlier that week. She climbed the back steps dreading this moment with the same pit in her stomach as the time in first grade when she got in trouble for sending Sandy Perkins down the slide and into a giant puddle at the base of it. Sandy had waded out crying, her white tights dotted with a few slugs. Lorraine was called by the principal. And that afternoon, Sally got off the bus and trudged up the side walkway to the back door, bracing herself for her punishment: the thickest wooden kitchen spoon against her naked backside.

In the kitchen, Lorraine was serving Paul and Joey dinner. Sally just had time to notice her mother wasn't wearing black and had put on her father's favorite plum dress when Lorraine and Paul unleashed on her like two angry hornets.

"You'd better have a good explanation, girl," Lorraine said. "A damn miraculous one. You'd better have been out saving someone from being hit by a bus or rescuing a basket of kittens from a fire. Well? What have you got to say for yourself? You think it's good manners to be tardy to dinner and stand up your date? Is that how I taught you?? Answer me! What were you doing today?"

Sally was still too high to effectively argue, but she tried. "I told you – I covered a shift for Rose and then went to the library."

"Oh, really? Is that why when I called the store, Rose answered and hadn't the slightest idea you were supposed to be working for her today?"

Sally's insides sank. She'd been caught in a lie by the only person she knew who hadn't lied in more than a decade. And now, Rose would know she'd used her as an excuse to go gallivanting. Well, at least I'm consistent, she thought. At least I've managed to get everyone in my life to hate me.

"Where were you? Tell me right now."

"Look, I just wanted to be by myself, okay?"

"I don't believe you," said her mother. "I don't believe you because your tone is false, but also because Dorris Pettyfer called here looking for her daughter about an hour ago. She said you'd visited and left, but that Sam has a tendency to get people twisted up in her antics. She said if you'd run off with Sam to hang around town that she wouldn't be a bit mad at you. So, just tell us and we can figure out how to deal with this."

"Can you just let it go? I don't feel well."

"That Sam is a troublemaker, Ma. She shouldn't be hanging out with her at all," piped up Paul, his voice ringing with vindictiveness.

"No, she's not. You're just mad because she blabbed your secret," Sally sputtered, feeling attacked from all sides, except from Joey, who stood there looking like a teen idol in his sport coat and skinny tie while she came unraveled.

"Oh my god, you reek of cheap alcohol. I can smell it from here," Lorraine said, inching closer to her.

At this choice moment, Joey chose to speak, and his words stung like a dagger to the back. "That's not alcohol, Mrs. Fiore. It's marijuana."

All the blood shot to Sally's face at this betrayal and cruelty rose from the bile in her stomach that she couldn't keep from escaping her lips. "Thanks a lot. Maybe you should take the hint, then. When a girl isn't home when you come to pick her up, that probably means she's not interested in dating you."

"Santa Vittoria, go to your room." The force behind her mother's voice was worse than any wallop she might have dispensed instead.

Sally tore her eyes away from Joey's lovelorn face and, without looking at her mother or Paul, turned and stormed off to her room. She stood in front of her mirror and fought the urge to cry. She was sick of everyone telling her what to do, of always being kept inside a safe bubble. More than anything, she wished she'd stayed with Arthur, or even better, that she was still out somewhere with Sam. A rapping at her window interrupted these mutinous thoughts. She lifted her shade to see Sam. The cold air stung her face and neck when she opened the window.

"What are you doing here?" she whispered. "You've already gotten me in so much trouble, and it sounds like you're in heaps of it, too."

Sam smirked up at her from a few inches below. "That's exactly why you're coming with me. I figured you'd chicken out with Arthur, so I took a little detour to see if you'd gotten home. Come on, then."

"Are you crazy?"

"Look, it's a Saturday night. It's still pretty early. And you and I are already in trouble. So, we might as well go out and have some more fun, right? What have you possibly got to lose?"

"Where would we go?"

"My friend is going to a party in Harvard Square and she invited me. We can meet her at her dorm."

"All the way in Cambridge? How would we get home after?"

"Just climb out here before someone comes to check on you. We'll figure it out as we go."

Running on spite, Sally opened the window as wide as she could and let Sam spot her as she jumped down the few feet, landing squarely in the inches of matted down snow. They skirted the back of the house and scuttled as fast as they could down the street until they could walk without arousing suspicion. The early dark made that easy. Sally looked back at her house, lit up and Joey's car still out front. How long would it take before they realized she was gone and started to panic? She thought about turning around, not causing her mother hours of needless worry, but it was too late for that now. She'd chosen to follow Sam whether it was smart or not, and now she wondered where the night would take her.

"Well, well, look what the cat dragged in."

The girl greeting them wore a turquoise mini-dress that set off her flawless skin to perfection and her hair was styled in a short, chic Afro. She grabbed Sam in an all-consuming hug.

"You're a sight for sore eyes, chicky. And you're freezing! Are you nuts, being out like this with no gloves or anything?"

"I was kind of pressed for time as I was leaving." Sam rubbed her hands together and blew on them.

The girl gave her a knowing once-over. "And by that, you must mean you snuck out, right?"

Sam laughed and skirted the question. "This is my friend, Sally Fiore. Sally, this is my best friend in the whole world, Dawn Elder."

"Nice to meet you." Sally stuck out her hand to shake. Dawn took it and returned the greeting.

"You're the first live Black person Sally's ever met or touched," said Sam.

Feeling her face drain of color, she let go of Dawn's hand. Dawn, in turn, snorted.

"Sam, really, why do you have to be such a bitch?"

"I'm just fooling."

"But you're not, really, are you? There's always a bit of truth in a joke."

Sam looked at Sally and kept instigating. "Well, Sally, was there truth in it? Is she the first actual person of color you've exchanged words with?"

"She's not, for your information."

"Is she the first you've ever shaken hands with?"

"What does it matter to you?"

"Your defensive tone answers for you."

"Leave her alone, now. You've had enough fun at her expense. Besides, it's not her fault she grew up in a predominantly white town. No one chooses their life circumstances, do they?"

"You're right on that one. Or I never would've chosen mine," Sam said, plopping down on the small bed.

The room itself was cramped, almost busting at the seams with clunky furniture. There were two small twin beds against either wall, and at the foot of each bed was an equally diminutive desk and chair. At the far wall, two identical dressers stood adjacent to each other. The walls were covered with posters of musicians – James Brown, Otis Redding, Aretha, Jimi Hendrix, the Beatles, Bob Dylan. Dawn's side of the room was strikingly more vibrant. A crocheted quilt of multicolored fabrics covered the bed, and above that hung some tapestries.

"Where's old Shirley?" Sam asked.

"Oh, that one has a date tonight. Shirley is my roommate," Dawn said, filling Sally in.

"Where's this party we're going to, in a dorm?"

"God, no. It's off-campus. Between here and Central."

"Is it that guy you're into?"

"Reggie? Yeah. Except last week we had this huge fight about the war."

"How so?"

"He supports it."

"What?!"

"His brother's there, that's why. He said he didn't feel right protesting anymore when his brother was over there risking his life."

"Well, his brother's an idiot for going."

"Don't say that," Sally interrupted.

Sam turned on her. "Oh, why? Just because your brother is also cracked in the head enough to want to go?"

"He's not cracked. He's just patriotic."

"This isn't about patriotism. This is about our government playing war games with other people's lives. Young kids. Black kids. All this junk about Communism being a threat to our freedom is nothing but fear-mongering. You think North Vietnam is gonna get up and sail over here to force us all to be commies? Come on. Putting the fear of God into people is just another way for them to control us. By filling us with hate and suspicion of our fellow men, they win. Because we're too busy fighting each other to notice their profit." Sam's eyes were filling with tears as she spoke, but she kept talking even as they ran down her cheeks.

"I stood there back in April at the Christ Church Parish House off this Square when Dr. King came to speak about the war. More and more people are against it and there's a movement started by Harvard faculty called 'Vietnam Summer' to get even more people to organize peace movements opposing the war in their communities. He came here to support it. And he said – and I'll never forget it – 'there comes a time when silence is betrayal,' that the soul of our nation had been poisoned, that it had isolated us morally and politically, and most importantly, it was diverting civil rights aims. So, I'm sorry, but I don't understand how your intellectual college boyfriend who also happens to be a Black man, would ever support death and exploitation when there's already historically been enough of that right here on our own soil."

Dawn's expression dictated that she'd heard this speech a thousand times. She leaned against her closet door, her face a passive blank until Sam finished her rant. "How did you get this high strung, huh? To hear you talk, anyone would think you're the Black one in this room."

"Don't make a joke of me," Sam said, plopping down on her bed.

"Look, I'm not making a joke. I get it. I agree with you, but you just can't go around judging people because they happen not to. I mean, shit. I'm a Black girl at Radcliffe. What do you think my life is like here? You think it's all moonlight and magnolias? Humph." She threw on a wool coat. "Now, I'm not complaining. I didn't grow up poor. My parents worked hard to give me opportunities that a lot of other girls like me don't get. I know that. I went to the same private school as you did. Now I'm here, but a lot of people still see me as they would if they passed me on the street. Imagine growing up and simply because your skin is a few shades darker, your hair is a little wooly, everything else about you is under constant scrutiny. Your intelligence. Your character. Your honesty. Your worth as a human being. And then try being a woman on top of that. It's funny, but being Black in America is a no-win situation. You see, if we stay in the poor part of town, if we're loud and disruptive, if we own our Blackness and don't assimilate by ironing our hair and dressing like preps, then we fit the common stereotype – your typical lazy, entitled, disgruntled, volatile American Negro. But on the other hand, if we do assimilate, if we get our education, if we dare to get accepted to a place like Radcliffe or Harvard, well then, we're just uppity, and more importantly, we're a threat. We're the competition. But enough of this. We're scaring your friend."

"No, no. Not at all," Sally sputtered. She'd been transfixed by this dialogue. "On the contrary, really. I've never listened to people talk like this."

"See? I told you." Sam broke into another grin.

Dawn shook her head. "Tell me this – how did this poor girl get stuck being friends with you?"

"She was at the right place at the right time."

"Famous last words. Let's get out of here."

Pictures hovered behind her lids like a phantasmagoria, changing ever so slowly, morphing and twisting their vibrant colors into new images. It was hypnotic. Sally felt dizzy even though she was lying perfectly still on her back, the orange shag carpet coming up between her fingers like grass that needed to be cut.

"Are you still tripping?" asked a mellifluous voice from next to her.

"Mmm-hmm," she said, remembering now that the owner of the voice was named Stew and he lived here.

Once they'd arrived at the walk-up, Dawn was in the arms of her boyfriend, and Sam made a bee-line for a flower child with hair to her waist who was sitting on the arm of a couch in the crowded living room. The cramped five rooms started to feel cavernous for Sally, who didn't know anyone except the people who had brought her. So, she moped about in the kitchen, pretending to concentrate on a bowl of pretzels, when Stew sauntered in. The first thing she noticed were his eyes because they were his only feature not hidden by a mane of hair, between his shaggy head and a beard that reached his chest. But the eyes themselves may have stood out, anyway, since they were the brightest tone of azure she'd ever seen. He wore bell bottom jeans, a billowy white shirt covered with a brown suede tasseled vest, and around his head was a red bandana. For all the prejudice that people like her brother and Joey held about hippies, this man seemed perfectly genial to her.

And after a few pleasantries, she agreed to go in his room to try something life-changing.

"This stuff is transformative, right? Do you feel transformed?"

Sally opened her eyes with some effort, like prying open an envelope after you've just licked it shut. She looked over at him. He still had his eyes closed and his grin exposed two rows of teeth that were surprisingly white.

"You said you're an artist?"

"Shhhhhhhhhh…" He placed his index and middle fingers over her mouth, pressed gently and then released.

She turned her gaze to the ceiling and its plaster swirls began to move in an undulating pattern. After minutes of this, they seemed to start dancing, she could hear faint voices singing. As this heavenly choir came to a crescendo, the center of the ceiling opened, and a face started materializing before her eyes. The world was complete euphoria, and she was transfixed at the sight of those familiar gray eyes, the button nose, the cleft chin. There he was, smiling down at her.

"Dad." She spoke but no sound came out. She tried to reach out her hand, but the face only wavered in and out of focus. Her whole body was shaking. Then she realized there were two hands on her shoulders and another face above her. This time, Stew's.

"What are you doing?!" she screeched and squirmed away. She had just woken up to her compromised situation. Here she was alone with a strange man on the floor of this bedroom with only a dress and a pair of tights protecting her virtue.

"Sorry, hey. Hey, sorry. I didn't realize you were still in yours. Your eyes were open."

Sally smoothed her skirt and tried to stand, but was still too dizzy, so she held on to the edge of the bed to steady herself into a sitting position.

"You okay?"

She shook her head and tried to fight the urge to cry or slap this person. Each time she closed her eyes, more lacey patterns traced their way across her vision.

"You ruined it. He was here and you ruined it."

"Who was here?"

"Never mind. When does this wear off?"

"Like maybe four, five hours."

"What?! Ugh."

"Just relax again. Maybe whatever vision you were having will come back." He smiled and patted the floor next to him.

Sally wanted to see her father again or else she wouldn't have been so easily persuaded. But she was certain he was about to say something to her, so she put her attention back on the swirled plaster that formed its pattern around the hanging light fixture. In a moment, the swirls began their dance again, the choir voices echoed, yet the ceiling remained intact, like a veil drawn between her and that other realm. She could not penetrate a second time. The way was closed.

She sighed, blinked rapidly to stop the visions. Here was Stew's face over her again, like all those baby dolls and the Gallagher clan with his manufactured blue eyes and white teeth.

"You asked if I'm an artist. Why'd you think that?"

"I dunno. The way you look, I guess."

He laughed. "I'm pre-med at Harvard. I go to school with Reggie."

"I see. So, you're a wolf in sheep's clothes."

"How so?"

She sat up and their faces were too close, but she didn't care. "You dress like you're this free-spirited flower child, but you're really just a capitalist in disguise. And a medical degree, that's brilliant of you. It looks like altruism, but most likely it's to avoid getting drafted, right?"

Stew snorted. He leaned in to kiss her, sliding his hand up her skirt as he did, but she pushed forcefully against his chest. She could tell he was dizzy, but he didn't back off. He forced his weight on her, pinning her to the ground.

"What do you even know about anything, you sheltered, suburban bitch?" he murmured coarsely in her ear.

"I know you gave drugs to a minor, and that's probably a felony."

"You're a minor?" He paused his aimless groping.

A hurried knock on the door and then Sam was there. She saw what was about to happen and yanked Stew by the back of his shirt with all her might, effectively choking him. Slamming him back down on the floor where he writhed and gasped, she bent down and got right in his face. "You don't touch my Sally. You hear me?! You don't touch her!"

Stew caught his breath and looked at her, a bit dazed, but compliant. He nodded and put his hands up in a surrender pose. "I'm cool, Sam. Look, we're both high as kites. I didn't know."

"What didn't you know?" Sam hissed.

"I mean, we're both high...stuff happens."

"Here's some advice, asshole. Just because a girl is under the influence, doesn't mean she wants to have sex with you. If she's struggling beneath you, that's a clear indicator. And just because you're also high, that doesn't give you a free pass to stick your dick wherever you want, whether you have permission or not. Got it?"

Stew nodded and lolled his head back to look at the ceiling and avoid further humiliation.

Sam helped Sally to her feet. "We need to go. We just heard there's gonna be a raid tonight."

"Shit. It's that mayor, man. He won't leave Kinnaird Street alone. He calls it 'Hippie Row,' and he thinks everyone who lives here is a deadbeat on drugs," Stew lamented, still with his eyes on the ceiling.

"Well, I guess you're doing your part to keep the stereotype alive," Sally said as Sam maneuvered her arms into her coat for her.

"Geez, Sam, what's with your girl here? I gave her some premium LSD, and all she's done is insult me for it."

"This girl isn't used to drugs. She just had her first joint earlier tonight, so maybe it was too much for her." Sam winked at her while buttoning her coat.

"I want to go home."

"We're going home."

"How are we getting there? Are the trains even still running?"

"I have some money. I may be able to score us a cab."

"All the way home?"

"Got any other ideas?"

"Maybe I should just call my brother. What time is it?"

"Almost one."

"What?!"

"Sals, you were on an acid trip. Those take forever. You're probably still on it."

"I am in so much trouble if they've realized I took off."

Sam watched her with a kind albeit unsympathetic countenance.

"You don't understand this, do you? Because you don't care if your parents are worried about you?"

"No, see that's the thing. I don't care because I know they're not worried. In fact, more like the opposite. They're probably just wishing something bad happens to me, and then they won't have to be bothered pretending to care anymore."

"That can't be true."

"It can't be untrue just because you don't want to face it. The world is full of sadness and cruelty and injustice. The sooner you acknowledge that, the better off you'll be. Because I accept that these things are realities, I worry about nothing and I live freely. Now come on, let's get you home."

As the cab pulled up to her house, she could see only one light on in the kitchen, which meant Lorraine was still awake. And the pole light was on out front. Sam patted her hand and tried to be reassuring.

"Don't worry, it'll be okay. What's the worst she can do?"

"Forbid me to be friends with you."

Sam looked taken aback. "You think she'd do something like that?"

"Maybe. At least outside of school, but possibly in school, too. She has Paul there as a spy."

"Yeah, but you still have his little military secret to hold over his head."

"I hadn't thought of that. I should go. I'll see you Monday."

"You won't see me, unfortunately. You'll see Samantha."

"I'm sorry."

"It's okay. I guess we all have our crosses."

"Goodnight."

"Hey. If you don't speak to me on Monday, I'll understand. So, you don't have to feel badly about it."

Sally nodded, trying to keep her sorrow at bay. She shut the door and climbed the front steps. No use trying to sneak in around back. Her key stuck in the lock and she could barely see. She struggled noisily for five full minutes until Lorraine's face appeared in the small middle window of the three on the wooden door. She glared at her daughter before opening it and stood silently to the side as Sally passed by her.

"Mom, I –"

"No." Lorraine held up her hand. "There's nothing you can say to explain the way you've behaved today. It's been ugly and very unlike you. Since you've never acted out like this before, as a parent, I'm left to assume that it's the new influence of this Sam person that's turning you bad. Maybe you're vulnerable to this because you're still dealing with grief. We all are," she paused and repeated herself. "We all are. That's no excuse for lying and sneaking around, and I will not tolerate this level of disrespect in my home. So, from now on, you're not to speak to Sam Pettyfer, in or out of school. This is my punishment, and if I find out otherwise, there will be worse consequences for you. If you can't imagine what, try to envision no longer working at Adrian's and no involvement with the senior play. You would come home every day immediately after school and work on homework. Do I make myself clear?"

"Yes, ma'am."

Lorraine looked on her less severely. "I'm glad you're home safe. Your poor brother just got back from looking for you." With that, she left the room, her flannel nightgown kissing the floor.

Sally trailed her down the hall and shut the door to her bedroom before allowing herself to break down. Even that was silent, though, because she didn't want her mother and Paul to hear her. Flicking on the light in her closet, she could see the outline of a note on her bed. She picked up the folded paper and opened it. It was Joey's messy cursive and it read:

Sally, please don't be upset with me. I only said something because I love you. Joey

Chapter VI

That Monday in school, the whispers down the hallway as Sam strolled in wearing a chic burgundy frock with heels, pearls and a bit of rouge and lipstick were even more startled than the first day when she showed up dressed like a boy. She ignored them in the same way and marched over to Sally's locker.

"So? What's the verdict?"

Out of the corner of her eye, Sally saw her brother standing with Marie, just waiting for her to slip up. She shook her head.

"I'm sorry. I can't. My mother will take everything away if I do. My job, the school play. I just can't risk that."

Sam half-laughed to mask her hurt. "Yeah, those sound really important. God forbid."

"I said I was sorry. Look, I still don't feel that well from the other night. That stuff took forever to wear off, and I've hardly slept."

"Don't sweat it. I said I'd understand if it had to be this way, and I don't lie. We're cool, Sals." With that, she walked away.

Sally turned to watch as she passed Paul and Marie without a look in their direction. She returned her brother's hard look. Thanks to him not sticking up for her the other day, she was now just an outcast again, barely treading water in a sea of loneliness, her grief that swelled instead of fading as the days wore on.

At least she still had work to keep her busy, and she'd been given the title of costume mistress for the senior show. Most of the students were in charge of putting together their own ensembles, but the four leads would have custom made pieces. Too bad that for these she'd have to interact firsthand with her angry sibling and her arch nemesis, Tammy. Poor Marie had been cast as Carrie Pipperidge and would have to suffer through the onstage romance between her boyfriend and former best friend as *Carousel*'s Billy and Julie. Not that it mattered. Tammy was now officially off the market, proudly wearing Lenny O'Malley's varsity jacket.

"What is this, *Bye, Bye Birdie*? What next, is he gonna give her a pin?" Heather scoffed at lunch as the couple walked by hand-in-hand.

"Who knows? If she's lucky maybe he'll lift his leg and pee on her."

Heather choked on her milk and it shot out of her nose. After she recovered and wiped her face, she shook her head in awe. "I don't know what's gotten into you lately, but I like it."

"As badly as I think of Tammy, I still thought she had way more brains than to date that lump of mashed potatoes."

After school, while she took Tammy's measurements in a dressing room behind the stage, she discovered otherwise.

"Is this really necessary?" Tammy glowered as Sally stretched the measuring tape across her perky bosoms blanketed by a fuzzy, pink mohair sweater. "I'm a perfect size six. Can't you work off that?"

"Not really. Believe me, I want this to be over just as quickly as you do. And you know what? It would go a lot faster if you'd shut up."

"What's your problem?"

"I don't know. I think I'm sick of being everyone's punching bag, especially yours."

Tammy squirmed as Sally did her inner seam. "I'm not sure I want you touching me, considering who you've been hanging out with."

Sally stopped and stood up. "What's that supposed to mean?"

Tammy swallowed hard. "Does she kiss you?"

"No. Does every guy friend you have kiss you?"

Tammy rolled her eyes. "No, but I know they all want to, of course. Don't you think she wants to?"

Sally shook her head. "It's not like that between us."

"But you can see how people would think it?"

She now had the measuring tape around Tammy's waist and toyed with the idea of pulling it so tight that she might be severed in half.

"I can see how *some* people would." She took down the measurements in her book. "We're done. Can you send my brother in?"

A few minutes later, her brother entered the space. He hadn't spoken to her since Sam's outburst the week before. Sally began the process, and, all the while, his dark eyes followed her. A couple of times he sucked in breath like he wanted to speak but decided against it.

"Okay, please send in Marie."

He left noisily, clearly exasperated with himself or the situation. Marie came in, wringing her hands. Sally felt maybe she'd make some headway here. She started in measuring across her shoulders and chest. Marie watched her with sad eyes. After a few more seconds, any silence she'd been trying to hold onto crumbled.

"I just want you to know that I'm not mad at you," Marie stammered. "I mean, I was a little at first, but it's honestly better for everyone that it's out about your brother and me. Maybe it was even a bit silly that we were keeping it so secret, but it was only to spare Tammy's feelings."

"Tammy has actual human feelings? I think you're overestimating her."

"I know she can come off as not a nice person, but she's not completely bad. There's good in her. It has a hard time finding its way to the surface, but it's there."

"Perhaps someone should buy it a roadmap. Look, I'm sorry I told Sam. It wasn't my business to tell. I never thought in a million years she'd do that."

"I know. And, of course, Paul knows. I don't really think he's that upset with you, either. I think he's more worried that she'll get you into trouble."

"He needs to let me grow up for myself. He did."

Marie smiled. "You don't realize how lucky you are to have so many people who care for you. I always wished for an older brother to look out for me."

"Looking out for is one thing, ignoring is another."

"He just doesn't know how to express himself. He worries about you and your mother so much, and he's brokenhearted about your father."

"Then maybe he shouldn't be going off to get himself killed!" Sally yelled, unmet anger rising up in her for the first time. "Because how selfish is that? If he cared about us so much?"

She felt the same kind of sobs shaking her chest as the ones that came the day her father died, the ones that were uncontrollable, guttural, and made it almost impossible to breathe. Domenic had been lying unconscious in the hospital, and the doctor told them to go home and rest because he could remain in this state for days. But only a few hours later, the phone rang. Sally bolted herself in her room so she wouldn't have to hear Lorraine screaming when she put down the receiver. She could hear, anyway. Lorraine screamed so much that she tore her vocal chords, ruining forever her once beautiful singing voice. Their neighbor, an abrasive but goodhearted woman named Mary, also heard and came over to see if she could help. She sat on the edge of Sally's bed to console her, her tight white curls giving her the appearance of a lamb. Startled, Sally had shot her arm out and accidentally slapped the poor woman's face.

In this moment, Marie didn't cry. With a maternal grace beyond her years, she took Sally's convulsing shoulders and hugged them to her chest. "I don't want to see him go, either. But I believe everything will work out as it should."

"How can you believe that?"

"I don't know. I just do. And it's a great comfort to me in my troubles."

Sally pulled her head up and wiped her eyes. "Here, let me finish so I can get to work and start making these pieces."

After she finished measuring Marie, she gathered her bags and headed for Adrian's, dreading what kind of reception she'd receive from Rose. She passed Arthur on her way out and stopped short at the sight of him. He seemed to have the same reaction.

"Hi, Sally," he said, warmly but with reserve.

"Hi, Arthur."

"You off to work?"

"Yup."

"Well, have fun," he said, "and be good."

Rose was in the break room making a pot of coffee when Sally got there. The store was quiet, so she sidled up to the counter and pulled out *A Farewell to Arms*.

"Let me guess, you have O'Hoolihan?" Rose set her cup of coffee down and flipped open her copy of *Vogue*.

"You guess correctly."

"Well, I can't believe he's still there. He was ancient when I was in school, and that was practically a decade ago."

"Oh, he's still there, tormenting new generations of students."

"Humph. Did you get your measurements for the play?"

"Yes."

"Have you thought about the costumes?"

"I have some sketches."

"I'm happy to look at them if you want help with ideas and fabric recommendations."

"I'd love that."

Rose smiled down at her magazine.

"Rose, about Saturday…"

But Rose didn't glance up from the page of upcoming spring styles. "No, don't even bring it up. I'll let it go this time. I get it. I was young once."

"You're still pretty young."

"Either way, this one time. However, if it happens again, we'll have a problem. Got it?"

"Yes."

"So," Rose finally lifted her coiffed head and smirked, "what kind of mischief did you end up getting into that night?"

"Well, unless you consider practically getting stranded in Harvard Square while tripping on acid mischief, then it was just a regular old Saturday night."

"Shut up. I don't buy that for a minute."

"I'm many things, but a liar isn't one of them."

"Wow, and here I was thinking I'd finally met someone even more square than me. Well, what was it like?"

"You've never tried it?"

"Please, I've never even tried pot."

"It was strange, kind of awful and amazing at once."

"Just don't make it a habit."

"I would never."

"Were you with a boy?"

"Yes, but not a nice one."

"Keeping control of your faculties when around the opposite sex is as important as keeping one foot on the ground when kissing."

"You don't need to worry about me. I'd rather be home with a book."

"I saw your mom this morning. She worries about you."

"She doesn't need to."

"She's a mother. All mothers worry. Just take it easy on her. Remember what she's been through."

"I know what she's been through," Sally said with a little more curtness than she intended. "I was there. I went through it, too. But that also doesn't mean I need to live in a bottle."

"I'd hardly call your little weekend foray living in a bottle."

"You know what I mean."

The bell on the door jingled as a woman stepped in. Dorris Pettyfer removed her gloves and smoothed the silk, ivory ribbon on her fur pillbox hat. Sally immediately withdrew into herself. How could she face this woman when she'd conspired against her with her teenage rebel of a daughter?

"Hello, Sally."

"Mrs. Pettyfer, hello. How can I help you today?" she asked in a stiff, formal address that made Rose arch a well-shaped brow.

"I'm well. And you?"

"I'm quite well, thank you."

"And your mother? How is she?"

"She's also well, thank you for inquiring."

"Of course. Please send her my regards. Sally, I was wondering if I might speak with you in private?"

"Oh. I –"

"You can use the break room if you'd like," interrupted Rose.

"Okay, right this way." Sally gave Rose a pleading look as she led Dorris into the confined back room that was half kitchen, half den.

"Would you like some coffee? There's a fresh pot here."

"That would be lovely, thank you," she said, scrutinizing the room and subsequently looking out of place in it. She settled herself into a threadbare armchair the color of mustard as Sally handed her a Styrofoam cup of the weak, percolated coffee.

"I'm sorry to show up at your place of employment like this, dear. I wanted to assure you in person that neither my husband nor I blame you in any way for what transpired on Saturday. This kind of erratic and frankly, manic, behavior is very typical of Samantha, and you're not the first unsuspecting friend she's dragged into her mess."

"That's nice of you to say, but I'm sorry for my part in it just the same. I feel terrible for lying to you and for deceiving my mother, of course."

"And you're such a nice girl to say something like that. So nice and respectful. I must say, I hoped and still hope that Samantha might benefit from a friendship like yours – that your integrity might rub off on her. I hate to think the opposite might happen."

"No, you can be assured that's not the case, ma'am."

Dorris smiled. "I know. I believe that. That's the other reason I've come here today, to beseech you. We think you're sure to be a good influence on Samantha, and we want to enlist your help as a preventative measure."

"Preventative of what?"

Here, Dorris sighed. "Well, her father thinks we may eventually have to take more extreme measures with her."

"You mean sending her away somewhere?"

"Yes…it might be our only solution. My husband's family had to resort to that with his own brother when he was younger. He was – troubled. Always acting out. His parents sent him away for a few months, and then he was fine."

"Was he?"

Dorris looked at her with something like accusation, but it only lasted a fraction of a second. "Yes. Granted, he was maybe a faded version of his older self, but he never got into trouble again."

"Pardon my saying so, but I don't think there's anything wrong with Sam. I think if maybe you just let her be herself, she wouldn't need to be rebellious."

"Herself?" She set down her cup on the rickety bamboo coffee table. "Herself is an abomination, don't you see that?"

"No. I think she's great." A hot energy began circulating through her as she comprehended this woman's full meaning. "And besides, she's already the way she is. What would you expect me to do?"

"We thought you might encourage her about the clothes she's now wearing. Maybe introduce her to some boys. Invite her to normal, teenage parties."

Sally laughed. "First of all, I think you grandly mistake my status at school. I'm not really invited to parties. I'm home on Friday nights reading and avoiding seeing boys at all. Second, I've told her I love her clothes. There's not one girl in school who doesn't envy her wardrobe. And it doesn't faze her. She hates them and will always hate them. She'll never be happy until she can look the way she wants, and forcing the matter is only going to make her more determined. I'm not trying to be disrespectful in saying this, Mrs. Pettyfer, but I can't help Sam the way you want me to. In fact, I can't even offer her friendship right now because my mother has forbidden it."

Tears began to surface in Dorris's eyes. "I'm sorry to hear that. Of course, I understand, but I don't want to have to send her to that place. If something doesn't happen soon, though, to rectify her behavior, I'm afraid I won't have a choice. Her father is quite set on it. And I can't even talk to her because she refuses to speak to me. Oh, I shouldn't be telling you this. The last time she said anything was Saturday and her father roared at her that she'd be driven to school and her bag would be checked every morning. She called us both 'small-minded fascists' and those were the last words she said. Maybe you could at least try talking to her, even in secret if you have to. To just let her know not to try and run away or do anything crazy."

"Has she run away before?"

"One other time. She made it all the way to Hartford, Connecticut, then ran out of money and got caught trying to hustle her way to New York. It was right on the heels of a protest she incited at her school – a civil rights protest. Not that it was a scandal. The private school she attended was open-minded, but also very traditional in its politics. The board made it clear they weren't going to stand for that kind of behavior. It's why we decided to move here, really. We thought life in a small town might calm her down a little."

Sally looked down at her hands, unsure of what she should agree to. "I'll see what I can do, but I can't promise anything. I can't risk getting in more trouble at home."

"Well," Dorris stood, "if anything like that should happen, you let me know and I'll call and straighten things out with your mother. Okay?"

"Thank you."

"You're a bright girl, Sally. Have you thought about college?"

"A little. I'd like to go, I'm just not sure for what."

"Keep in touch about it, then. We have a lot of connections."

"You would help me?"

"Of course, as a friend of Sam's. And, well, you remind me a bit of myself. I lost my father when I was about your age, too, and my family wasn't wealthy. There weren't opportunities sitting on the threshold when I opened my door at the start of each day. I had to make my own. For me, that meant marrying well. I would have loved to have gone to college."

"Thank you."

"You're welcome. Take care, now." She nodded and let herself out.

Sally waited to get up until her heart felt less heavy at the thought of Sam in a mental institution, strapped down to a table with electric currents burning up her insides.

The next day in English class, with the stealth of a secret agent, Sally dropped a wad of folded paper on Sam's desk asking her to meet in the girl's lavatory after school. She watched Sam unfold it with the same discreet precision and noted the corners of her mouth twitch up in a wry smile.

When the final bell had rung, Sally took her time arriving at her locker and then remained there, nitpicking over her books. She wanted to decrease the risk of being seen by anyone who might mention this transgression to Paul. After a few minutes, she noticed Arthur in his closet getting out more cleaning supplies. He seemed to be taking longer than he needed to, and she wondered if he was waiting to talk to her.

Sally tried to ignore that empty feeling again, the longing she felt when she looked at him. The business of her daily routine usually kept these thoughts at bay until she turned out her light to go to sleep; but seeing him only a few feet away was like a fresh punch to the gut. She sighed. And now, this errand would pull her away again. She was almost relieved to have it. She turned and headed to the bathroom.

"Hi." He practically ambushed her, his face flushed with childlike excitement.

"Hi, there."

"I wanted you to be the first to know – well, the second – I finished a draft of my book last night."

"Wow, congratulations! What an accomplishment...Who was the first to know?" She feigned effrontery.

"Helen, my landlady. Every morning she asks me where I'm at, so there was no avoiding it."

"That's really wonderful."

"I know you like to read, so I was wondering, would you be interested in having a look at it? Maybe giving some notes?"

"Oh!" She was genuinely taken aback at this request. "I'd love to."

"That means a lot," he said, growing serious. "I'll bring it in tomorrow." He turned back to his closet and his latest read fell from his back pocket. It was a thin volume. He waved it at her as he picked it up. "Have you read this one?"

"*The Picture of Dorian Gray*? No, is it any good?"

"It's a little slow at first, but I think it's just about to turn a corner. It's Oscar Wilde's only full-length novel, and it's about this dandy who engages in a lot of debauchery. And he doesn't age, but he has this portrait of himself that does age, and he keeps it hidden."

"Ooh, sounds intriguing."

"I'll let you know how it is." He went back to his drudgery as she entered the bathroom.

Sam was already there. She stood in front of the large mirror that covered the top half of one wall. Underneath it was a dingy, wooden sill where you could set your makeup while you retouched your face. She looked bored as she pretended to fiddle with the scalloped collar of her indigo cashmere sweater. Sally stood next to her and ran a comb through the ends of her hair, which were always wont to tangle themselves during the day. A few other girls were still occupying the stalls. Each left without taking notice of them, pumped a hand under the bulbous soap dispensers that held a liquid slime the color of cloudy urine, and exited after a quick dry with a brown paper towel. When they were alone, Sam broke the silence, speaking to her through the mirror.

"What's this about?" Her voice echoed on the dark beige tiles.

"I'm not sure how to say this."

"Let me guess." Sam turned away from the mirror and looked at her. "My mother implored you to talk some sense into me?"

"How did you know?"

"You think you're the first friend she's pulled this with?"

"I couldn't know that."

"I'm not blaming you for anything. Maybe I should've warned you, or given you an arsenal of dialogue to throw back at her. She has some nerve."

"I think she did it because she's worried about you. She loves you."

"Are you really this naïve? She's not worried about me. She's worried about how it will look to her perfect friends if my father throws me into a mental hospital. Don't, for one minute, think this is about her motherly affection for me."

"Maybe you're half right, but maybe a little of that is true. She is a mother, and all mothers love their children."

Sam snorted. "God, Sals, you're so easily fooled."

"Say you're right, then. Say she is only doing it for appearances. Still, wouldn't you rather know that your father is serious about this so you can settle down for a while?"

Considering this, Sam leaned against the wall and folded her arms. "No, he can't be serious. He's just as worried about how it will look at the country club as she is."

"But she said his family sent his brother."

"Yeah, and look how that turned out."

"She said he never got into trouble again."

Sam smiled meanly. "Well, it's hard to get in trouble when you're dead." She made a motion of tying a noose around her neck and hanging herself, her eyes staring blankly at the ceiling and tongue lolling out of her mouth.

"Stop it!"

"It's true. If electroshock worked, he wouldn't have killed himself, would he? That's what they call recovery. Death."

"I'm sorry."

Sam smiled. "It's okay. I know you just thought you were helping, telling me something I didn't already know."

"What are you going to do?"

She considered this for a minute, then picked up her book bag and wore a look of stubborn resolve. "I'm going to see how far I can push them until they snap."

"You really think that's smart?"

"Whether it's smart or not, it's my only option."

"Is it?"

"Yes," she said so definitively that Sally felt guilty for even posing the question. "It's my only option, because they leave me with no other. It's either be what they'd have me be – which is entirely the opposite of what I am – or be held prisoner from my life. You see how fundamentally wrong that is?"

Sally nodded but couldn't disguise the tears of worry that now funneled down her face like rain on a windowpane. Sam softened.

"Don't you worry about me, okay?"

"I'm just sick of losing people," Sally blurted, cupping her face in her hands. What an emotional basket case I am this week, she thought, as she felt Sam's arms winding around her.

The door swung open and a laugh fell on them like a thunderclap. Tammy stood there wearing triumph on her arrogant face, shaking her head in disbelief as though she couldn't believe her luck. Sally's instinct was to recoil and jump away, like she'd been caught in the act of something wrong, but Sam kept an arm around her.

"What the hell are you looking at?"

Unflinching, Tammy fixed Sally with a new resurgence of her former poison and said, "Just wait until I tell your brother about this."

Before Sally could protest, she scurried out.

"No!" Sally ran after her, but Sam grabbed her arm.

"She's not going to do anything. And your brother wouldn't believe her, anyway."

"No, she will! And they're all at rehearsal right now. You have to let go!"

She broke free and ran straight for the auditorium where about a third of the students in the senior show convened. They were scattered around the room, some sat in small clusters among the audience seats running through lines and music; a larger group was on stage working with a student choreographer for an ensemble number. Paul was standing up in front by the orchestra pit, chatting quietly with Marie as Tammy made her bold approach in long strides down the aisle. Sally caught up with her and grabbed her arm before anyone noticed.

"Please don't do this!" she pleaded.

"Let go of me!" Tammy shouted, using her stage voice. Now all heads turned their way, and a bevy of whispers peppered the room.

"What's going on?" Paul's voice rose above the din as he and Marie walked over to where she stood.

During the commotion, Sam had followed them in and now inserted herself between Sally and Tammy.

"Funny you should ask." Tammy's grin spread across her round face, giving prominence to her coveted dimples, but also to her slight double chin. "I just stumbled upon quite the scene between these two in the girl's bathroom."

"Scene?" Paul looked confused. Confused and angry.

"If you call two girls making out a scene."

She let her words feel their full effect as the room again broke out into a clamor of incredulous exclamations. In a row of nearby seats, Lenny O'Malley and a few other loitering underclassmen struck up the chant, "Sam and Sally, sittin' in a tree, k-i-s-s-i-n-g!"

"Shut up!" Paul thundered, but he was looking at Sally.

"That's a lie! She's lying."

"What did she see, then?" he asked, but his voice kept its stormy timbre.

"I was upset, and Sam was hugging me. That's all."

Tammy shook her head, still smiling. "Nope, you were kissing. I saw you with my own eyes, and now you're embarrassed. I knew it – I just knew you let her kiss you."

"Oh yeah, Tammy?" Sam said, now getting as close to her face as possible without making contact with it. "You're so interested in who's kissing each other. Tell me this, then, do you let your father kiss you?"

Tammy's face crumbled in a mass of fear and contempt. She fell backwards a little like she'd had the wind knocked out of her and just stared into Sam's face for what felt like a full five minutes while the room waited in silence. Even Lenny O'Malley froze in the spot where he'd stood to come to his sweetheart's defense. Then, with the full force of her body, Tammy slapped Sam across the face. The crack of it reverberated, reflecting with irony the exceptional acoustics of the space. There was a collective gasp as Sam rubbed her scarlet cheek without so much as shedding a tear, and her eyes still held Tammy's.

"Thought so," she said before she walked out, leaving yet another stunned room in her wake.

Sally dawdled at work that day, afraid of what was waiting for her when she got home. Her mother hadn't gone to work because of a bad cold and Paul probably went straight home after rehearsal to inform her that his sister was caught fraternizing with Sam.

Rose watched as she took much too long to close the button box and tuck it behind the counter.

"Well, what's the matter now?"

"How do you mean?"

"You've been a mope all day. Something is clearly wrong."

"It's a long story."

"Give me the abridged version, then."

"I may or may not be in a lot of trouble."

"Again? Wow, this is becoming like another hobby for you. Soon you'll be too busy getting in trouble to sew."

"That's what I'm afraid of."

Rose chuckled to herself. "Oh, you're just going through a little phase. You're acting out, being a normal, teenage girl. Here, let me give you a ride home. It's cold out there."

"I don't know. I'd rather prolong it as much as possible."

"How 'bout I drive extra slow?"

"If you insist."

Her stomach sang a chorus of nerves and hunger as she walked around to the back porch. Tentatively, she opened the door, taking a deep breath and readying herself for whatever scenario awaited her. She imagined walking into a quiet kitchen, Lorraine sitting alone at the table under the dim glow of the Tiffany light fixture, looking terrifying. But instead, her ears were met with the sound of uncontrollable sobs.

When she entered the house, she saw Lorraine bent over the kitchen sink. There was no dinner cooking on the stove. Her brother sat at the kitchen table with his head in his hands. The dire feeling hanging in the air couldn't possibly be about her little bathroom indiscretion.

"What's going on?" she asked as quietly as she could.

Her mother turned to look at her with eyes almost swollen shut from the effort of crying. She squinted like she was trying to ascertain something. "Did you know about this?" She finally blurted before resorting back to full on crying.

"About what?"

"Sally didn't know anything, Mom. Or else she'd have told you," Paul answered, giving her a look. "Mom, come on now. It's not as bad as it seems." He got up and crossed to her.

"Not as bad?" Lorraine stuttered through her heaving. "You're going off to get killed, and I'm supposed to be all right with it?"

"Mom was putting away laundry and found my application to enlist in the army," he said, making a show of giving Sally the context she already knew. Now it was her turn to act shocked.

"What?!"

"Your father wanted you to go to college, he didn't want you to be like him. He wanted you to be like Teddy and become something successful like a doctor or a lawyer."

"I can still do that someday."

"Not if you're dead!" she screamed, starting to collect herself. Now she faced him with a fresh wave of wrath. "And did you ever for a minute think about how this would impact me and your sister? Hmmm? Or were you just thinking of yourself?"

"I was thinking of this country. Of keeping it safe from dangerous ideologies."

"I just lost a husband, and now my son wants to throw himself into harm's way. That kind of reasoning sounds more dangerous to me than anything the communists could come up with." With that, she stormed away from him and into her room.

She didn't come out for the rest of the night.

Chapter VII

The fact that her brother was so serious about enlisting weighed heavy on Sally's heart, but she knew there was no point in trying to change his mind. When it came to carrying out his will, he had an immovable stubbornness identical to their mother's. He was a stone. The one upside, if there was any, was that this new chapter of turmoil in their family certainly took the focus off of her.

That Saturday, her mother's sisters showed up to lend their very opinionated moral support. Nick came along with her Aunt Jo and offered to take Sally out to lunch. They landed at the Adventure Car Hop on Route 1.

"I mean, I can see your mother's point," Nick said as they sat in the car eating hotdogs.

"It's hopeless to try and stop him, though."

"You're right about that. Anyway, what else is new?"

Sally debated about how much she should reveal, but when it came down to it, he was the person she trusted above all others. She retold the past month's exploits and her regrets about them in an almost indifferent narrative. She even told him about Arthur.

"Geez, I added a few more stamps to my collection and I thought that was exciting," he joked.

"Try not to judge me."

"I wouldn't. You know that. But I do worry about you. You're as close to a sister as I'll ever get, and I don't know what I'd do if something happened to you."

"Stop, I'll cry."

"That was the goal. When I woke up this morning, I said, 'You know, I think I'll make Sally cry today.' For real, though, kid. I'll never tell you what to do like Paul does, but take care of yourself."

"I'll be more careful from now on."

"And what about this older guy? Do I need to threaten him or anything?"

"No, he's harmless, and we both know it could never work. He was a gentleman."

"Speaking of Joey, when's the last time you talked to him?"

"You think he's a gentleman, really?"

"By my standards. He sure seems to care about you, and he handles rejection better than anyone I've ever seen. I'll give him credit for that."

"I'm not talking to him after what he did the last time. And don't say it's because he cares about me. I'm sick of people saying that."

"Well, I feel stupid now because I just said it."

"I don't mean you." Sally was starting to tire of this conversation, of the feeling of always having to explain herself. "He betrayed me. There was no need for him to point out that I smelled like pot, but he did it anyway."

"I can understand that, I guess."

"I'm not some reckless hippie, and everyone should know that I'd never be like that. But, Jesus Christ, I should at least be able to go live life and experience things for myself." She momentarily thought of Arthur's manuscript that she'd started reading, all the gritty adventures he'd had on his way there, and she felt a sudden surge, an inexplicable want for the same kind of unbridled freedom. "I should be able to figure out who I am and what I want without everyone chiming in with their two cents and planning out my future. Maybe I don't want marriage and children. Maybe I want to do something else. So what if I do? It's my choice. Should I be cast off as someone who gave up? As a spinster? As a cold-hearted ice queen? What if I just want to go to college, have a career, and travel? That should be okay. If I'm happy, no one else should be bothered about it. And sure, maybe Joey is a nice guy, but he'd marry me and stick me in a house where I'd just be expected to pop out babies, wash clothes, make dinner, and clean."

For the first time in their relationship, Nick was speechless. He stared wide-eyed at his steering wheel and shook his head a little.

"I had no idea you felt that way."

Sally paused before she answered. "I didn't either, until just now. I guess it's something that's been boiling up in me over the past few months and – I don't know. It kind of all just bubbled up. You know how sometimes when you cook potatoes and it seems like the water is still for so long, and then once you look away your pot is overflowing with starchy suds?"

Nick shook his head. "I don't know that. Because I'm a man and I don't have to cook."

Sally punched his arm, and the last nub of his hot dog went flying onto his lap, smearing ketchup on his crotch.

"Really? Because you look like a girl who's just become a woman."

His show of disapproval culminated in a giggle. "You're crass, Sally. But you're clever, I'll give you that."

"Speak of the devil," Nick said as they pulled up to her house to find Joey's car among the family vehicles.

"Ugh, I don't even want to go in there."

"Let's just get it over with. I'll take my mom home, and the others will follow."

"I know, but I also don't want to have to deal with Joey."

"Better get that over with, too. Hear him out. Maybe he'll redeem himself."

"It's going to take a lot more than words for that to happen. And he's not even that great with those to begin with."

"You are harsh, Santa Vittoria. How is any guy supposed to live up to your impossible standards?"

"I don't think literacy should classify as an impossible standard."

"All the women in our family are like this. It's beyond a miracle that any of them got married at all, let alone procreated. Do you know what they all heard from Nonna when they were growing up?"

"No, what?"

"My mom told me this, she said they were taught that, 'The man is always supposed to love the woman a little more than she loves him.' Do you believe that?"

Sally snickered. "From Nonna? Yup."

"Hopeless. Good luck, mankind."

"Yes, you poor, helpless, oppressed little dears."

"My sentiments, exactly. Oh look, here they all come."

Her aunts were making their way down the walkway on the side of the house, chattering on like a flock of flustered birds.

"They're probably plotting the end of men right now."

"I'm telling."

"Of course, you're one of them."

"Anyway, bye, then. I'll see you soon." She leaned over and kissed his cheek. "Ooh, I felt some stubble there. Someone is going through puberty."

"Just get out."

Sally was inundated by her gaggle of relatives as she met them on the walkway. They were concerned for her mother. At least Lorraine had stopped wearing black. It was unnecessary, and Domenic always hated the color, anyway. She should let Lorraine rest and take care of dinner. She should also try to convince her brother that his decision will destroy the family. We'll have Ralph call him, too, to tell him it's not all it's cracked up to be. But she should lead the charge as his sister. She should do all of this as soon as physically possible. And what about that nice boy, Joey? Why wasn't she dating him? What's wrong with him? He's been in love with her for years – that's saying something.

And, as if she knew what her own son had just been talking about, Aunt Jo ended the flurried storm of dialogue by pointing her finger in Sally's face and saying, "After all, the man is always supposed to love the woman a little bit more than she loves him."

"But what if she's not even sure she likes him yet?" Sally asked, attempting to throw them all for a loop.

Aunt Jo just shrugged and said, "Then have fun with him until someone better comes along," like that was something she should've already known.

Inside, her mother sat with Joey having a civilized cup of tea in the front parlor. Lorraine was the epitome of calm and poise. The hysterics and constant stream of tears of the past two days had been neatly tucked away in the presence of guests. And perhaps her sisters' animated presence and advice had cast a serenity over her. Either that or she didn't even want them to feel the depth of her aching. Whatever the reason, she now sat as demurely as any housewife. She even turned on a half-smile as she stood to collect Joey's empty cup.

"Well, now, why don't you young people go out and have some fun. Joey's coat is in the closet, dear."

Joey stood now, as well. "Would you like to go see a movie and maybe grab dinner?"

"Not really," she said, handing him his coat.

He put it on, still watching her with a pathetic expression. She felt a morsel of regret. He looked different today, too. What was it? His hair. Yes, instead of slicked back, he'd parted in on the side and put on much less pomade. He almost looked like he had when they were children. She fought the urge to hug him despite a fresh wave of anger about last weekend.

"You really have some nerve coming here, inviting me out to a show like you did nothing wrong."

"I'm sorry. I just – I got worried about you. And I thought if you got in a little trouble then maybe you'd be safer."

"I don't need you to protect me." She folded her arms across her chest.

"Am I not allowed to care about you?"

"It's a free country. You can care about whomever you want. But you can't expect them to care back."

"Look, I'm trying to be here for you. You're good at putting up a brave front, but I can tell that you're hurting. Just be friends with me again, will you? For old time's sake?"

She dug her shoe into the floral print rug under the coffee table. There was something about his earnest way that she couldn't refuse, that was drawing her in like a moth to a flame. Maybe it was a similarity she saw between them. Vulnerability.

"Fine."

He smiled now. "Really?"

"I'm still pretty sore at you, but I'll try to get over it."

"Let me take you to a movie and dinner, hmm? *Planet of the Apes* followed by Hazelwood's famous chicken croquettes?"

"Okay. But only because the chicken croquettes are my favorite."

After dinner, they parked by the lake. It looked like a frosted mirror surrounded by trees all coated in snow, casting a surreal glow over the evening like a silvery enchantress.

"Humph," Sally muttered, taking it in.

"What're you thinking?" Joey whispered, taking her hand. She allowed it.

"It's pretty, the lake. Isn't it?"

"It is. Not as pretty as you, though."

"Cut it out."

"I mean it."

"Do you always have to be so sincere?"

"Only with you." He smiled. Then he leaned in to kiss her.

She allowed this, too, once again comparing it to Arthur's. It wasn't smoldering, but it wasn't unpleasant. It carried a certain innocence. Yes, that was the difference, wasn't it? Arthur's kiss was the kiss of a man, of a man who more than likely wasn't a virgin. Joey was still pure, like she was. Because he was waiting for her. He held her face as he kissed around her jawline up to her ear and made his way to her neck. Then his hand slid tentatively into her open cardigan and cupped her breast. This bold move startled her, but she didn't stop him. Sometimes curiosity trumps moral fiber and this was one such occasion.

"Sally," he murmured while he nuzzled her ear. "Say you'll be my girlfriend."

"I can't."

He pulled away and looked out the window.

"Joey –"

"No. This isn't fair, and you know it. You can't just kiss me like that and then take it away."

"I'm sorry."

He turned to her. "What's so wrong with me? What's so wrong with me that you can spend time with me, and you can kiss me, but you don't want to date me?"

She stared at her hands where they rested on the black leather seat. "Nothing is the matter with you. I just don't know how I feel about anything anymore. I'm confused. I miss my dad."

"I know.

"The days all meld together sometimes, and I find myself wondering why things like this happen. Why did they happen to me? It makes me question everything. Life. God. Is there even one? If there were, how could He let so many horrible things happen?" The words came out with the same fluidity as they had during her earlier conversation with Nick.

"I think that's normal. Most people, at some point, probably have doubts. I did when my grandparents died. I thought, why them? Why both at once in a car wreck? It didn't seem fair."

"And then there's you. I've known you since we were little kids so it's hard to picture you romantically sometimes."

"That just means I know you better than anyone else ever could."

"That's what I'm afraid of."

"Why? What could be more special than that?"

"I don't know. But I like you, I do."

"I more than like you." He leaned in and kissed her again.

Sally felt herself unable to counter anymore. She kissed him back and lost herself in his ardent touch. While night unfurled behind her closed lids, she could still see the reflection of the moon on the frozen lake.

She woke up the next morning wracked with a guilt she'd never quite experienced before – a dull ache cutting through her insides like when she was little and used to lie on her stomach across the bench of her mother's organ. As she hung over the side, the wooden edges would press in on her stomach and make her feel an odd sort of longing. Last night, she'd gone a little too far, and if her mother ever knew, she probably could be rid of Joey for good if she wanted. Only now she didn't want that. She didn't want to be his steady, though, either.

It was lucky it was Sunday, and she decided to go to confession. Talking to Father Carl always made her feel better, though she was thankful for the screen between them. He had to know her voice, but to hear his unbiased penance, one would think not. Today, she'd have to pretend he was a stranger in order to unburden her spirit. She closed the heavy drapes of the confessional and settled herself on the velvety kneeler. But the voice that spoke when the screen slid open wasn't Father Carl's gentle tenor, but dreaded Father Canning. Father Canning was such an austere presence and flared out his vestments in a way that had earned him the nickname of Dracula.

There was no turning back now. She was determined to maintain the utmost degree of candor. "Bless me, Father, for I have sinned. My last confession was two weeks ago, and these are my sins. I've been struggling lately...with my faith."

"In what way, child?"

"I've been having doubts about God. About whether He exists at all."

"That is not for you to question."

Sally froze, but then gathered her wits in a rush of defiance at his condescension. "What's wrong with questioning, when people are dying for a war that no one understands? When people are forced to fight for basic civil liberties in our own country just because of their skin color? You're telling me I haven't the right to question? Isn't it natural to question the existence of God when the world is falling apart?"

Dracula bristled, and she could make out his shadow roughly adjusting his long robes. "Well," he said with gruff admonition in his voice, "I have a good mind not to give you absolution!"

Sally stood so quickly that the kneeler fell forward onto its side. "KEEP IT, THEN!" she shouted, snapped the window shut, and threw open the curtain. She ran around the corner to the side entrance, salty liquid escaping down her cheeks.

"YOU COME BACK HERE!" Father Canning bellowed after her. She could hear him scrambling up to try and chase her.

As she pushed open the door, she ran smack into Father Carl. Into his arms, she collapsed, a sobbing mess.

"Whatever is the matter with you, girl?" He steadied her and looked deep into her eyes with as much concern as her own father. This brought about a fresh round of sobs. "Now, now. I'm sure whatever it is, it'll be okay. Come with me. Let's take a turn around the neighborhood.

"Can someone be fired from the priesthood?" Sally asked after she'd spent the first few minutes of their walk trying to swallow her hiccups.

"Why? What happened? Don't tell me old Dracula scared you off now?"

"Ha! You know what the kids call him?"

Father Carl pretended to misunderstand her. "The kids? What do you mean? I thought that was his actual name."

"You're not supposed to be saying things like this."

"No? You think just because I'm a man of the cloth that I'm not allowed to comment on the ridiculous?"

"I don't quite understand how the church works. That's kind of what I was saying in confession. I'm starting to have doubts about God." She stopped and looked him squarely in the face. "If there's a God, why would He take people too soon away from loved ones? Why allow wars, suffering, and hatred? If He has the power to stop it, why wouldn't He? And why would He make someone so different from everyone else around her so that she was resented and shunned?"

Father Carl looked on her without judgement, his face full of benign patience. When she was done, he folded her arm in his and kept walking as he spoke.

"The only way I think I can explain this to you is in terms that you'll understand – in other words, I won't be quoting scripture. First of all, these feelings are natural, I'll say that. Because I have them often myself. It's hard not to when you look at what's going wrong with the world. But here's the other thing – as humans, we all have free will, and none of the things you just mentioned happen because of God. They happen because of people. God doesn't cause wars – people do – sometimes in His name, but certainly without His endorsement. God doesn't take life. People die when it's their spirit's time to vacate its earthly vessel. We see this as an end, of course, but I tend to believe not. Things are seldom ever what they seem. And God doesn't create anyone differently with the intention of them being shunned or ostracized. People are created as they are. We are all originals cut by the same eternal fabric. It's we who've refused to understand that. We've blinded ourselves by color, by prejudices, by misconceptions, and we've failed to see that there's only one truth. That everyone is equal in God's eyes, for we're but mere mirrors reflecting one vast and unending stretch of infinite. Though our miens and paths may differ, we're all brothers and sisters just trying to make our way back home. It's good to ask questions, though, Sally. It's good to wonder. It's healthy to deal with your anger. Because giving God the silent treatment will only alienate you more from the unconditional love that's all around, present in everything. But when you're asking questions, make sure you're asking the right ones. Instead of 'Why me?' maybe 'Why not me?' In all that happens to you, look for the lesson because there is one. And there's also a choice. You can choose to enjoy the short time you have here to be happy and do good things, or you can choose to waste it in worry and a warped sense of unfairness. Life is neither fair nor unfair, it's what we – people, not God – choose to make of it."

A warmness crept through her that brought her peace, but it gave way too quickly to a guilty remorse.

"What's wrong? Haven't I made you feel better?" His frown was saturated with such genuine disappointment that she almost laughed.

"Yes, of course. You have, really. Thank you. I was just thinking about something you said. The part about giving God the silent treatment."

"Yes?"

"Well, haven't you noticed? Mother and Paul don't come to church anymore. They stopped right after Dad passed."

"I've noticed." He sighed. "Everyone grieves in their own way, and your mother and Paul are both stubborn lots, but I think they'll come around. At least, I have faith that they will." He smiled and tapped her on the nose. "You be kind to them, all right?"

"Thank you. I was going to stay for mass, but I should go. I'm afraid of running into Dracula."

"Oh, don't worry about Father Canning. He's not so good about putting voices to faces. And besides, the poor old coot is so senile, he already forgets you came in."

"If you say so. I think I'd rather go home, anyway."

"As you wish. Bless you, my child. Go in peace."

The climate of the Fiore home fell under a shadow once more. Lorraine started wearing black again. Bleak dinners with drab faces and no conversation prefaced the nights as though another family member had left them. Lorraine went about her regular business making their meals, washing their clothes, and working, but she ignored her son with purpose. And whenever he would even dare to glance imploringly in her direction, it would spark an argument so loud that Sally thought a few times the house might collapse.

"Are you still under orders to ignore me?" Sam leaned against her locker one morning in late February. "I miss hanging out and I think my parents are starting to cool down since I've been behaving myself. What about your boss lady?"

"Honestly, she's so upset with my brother that I don't think she even notices me anymore."

"Well, that's good. What've you been doing without me, anyway?"

"I've actually been spending some time with Joey."

"Ugh." Sam pulled a face like someone had just thrust a mound of manure under her nose. "Sorry, I didn't know this little separation would be such torment for you."

"No one forces me to go. I don't know…he's kind of growing on me, I guess."

"You can't be serious."

"You don't even know him. How can you possibly have an opinion?"

"I know what you've told me about him, which was never anything complimentary. And, are you forgetting that he's basically the reason you aren't allowed to see me anymore?"

"I know. You have a point on that one. It's not like we're going steady or anything. Besides, what was I supposed to do?"

"I dunno, stay at home and read classic literature? Isn't that what you do?"

"Yes, but a girl has to get out once in a while."

"Let's get out this Saturday, then. My parents have an event. We can go to Harvard to see Dawn, but we'll leave early enough to take the train back. Yes?"

"I'm not positive, but I can try."

"Fair enough. Let me know when you figure it out."

Sally planned to ask Lorraine that night when they drove home together after work, but there was no need. Her mother showed up looking more drawn and weary than ever. Rose rushed to the break room to make her a cup of tea.

"What's wrong?"

"Your Aunt Catherine came by this morning with some bad news. One of our childhood friends passed away. The funeral is Saturday."

"Oh, I'm so sorry."

"Lois had been sick for a while, but we thought she was getting better. We were playmates when we were all little girls. She was a good friend, too. A generous spirit. She had a younger brother who passed away when we were in second grade. I remember, it's why I threw my teddy bear away. Have I ever told you about that?"

Sally shook her head. Rose returned with a steaming cup. Lorraine took it and pulled a handkerchief from her purse before she continued with her story.

"Freddie was his name, and he was always sickly. He'd been born very premature. At one point, he became bedridden and grew weaker. Near the end, we were in his room visiting with him, and I had my favorite stuffed teddy bear with me. Leopold, I called him. I slept with him every night and always took him for adventures around the neighborhood. My father brought him back from one of his trips home to Italy, so I treasured the gift. Well, this day, little Freddie saw Leopold cradled in my arm and asked if he could have him. Thinking of only myself, I said no and that I was sorry. He passed away that night. When I heard the news, I was so angry with myself for not giving him the toy that I threw it in the trash. My father found Leopold and came to see me. I had squirreled away in my room, lying on my bed in a heap of tears. 'What's the meaning of this?' he asked me in his gentle way – oh, I know, you were scared of Nonno with his bald head and his severe looks, but he was really a lamb. If he ever had to spank one of us, he'd go out by the barn and cry after. He set Leopold on my bed, and I told him what happened. 'Well, it's not too late to fix the situation,' he said. 'What do you mean?' I asked, anxious to right what I'd done. 'If you've decided you're okay parting with Leo here, maybe Freddie can still have him.' And sure enough, we visited the family later that evening, and when Freddie was finally laid into the earth, my beloved little bear was in his arms. I'll never forget the way Lois looked at me that day. She loved him so much. Well, now they're together, aren't they?"

Lorraine lapsed into another wave of tears, and Rose wrapped an arm around her. Sally wanted to, but she was so used to sadness that she felt herself becoming detached from it. Tears and emotion exhausted her. It was almost easier to not react, the way her mother and Paul usually were, strong and silent. She stood there helpless, crippled by the months of her previous sorrow.

That Saturday, she waited until Lorraine left in the morning for what would surely be an all-day event and met Sam at the commuter rail. The same as before, they got off at North Station, hopped on the green line and switched to the red at Park for the few stops to Harvard. Dawn met them, and they wandered around. It was still so cold that the wind chilled them to the bones, but it was a lively place with a unique collection of stores to explore. They stepped into Cardullo's, and Sally thought about getting something for her family, but then thought better of it since she probably wasn't supposed to be here. The tempting shelves were lined to the ceiling with all manner of Italian imports – olive oil, olives, jars of marinated mushrooms and peppers, fancy jams, teas, coffees, candies, wine, and cordials. There was a deli counter offering specialty meats and cheeses, little peppers stuffed with mozzarella and prosciutto, pâtés.

"How are things with Reggie?" Sam asked as they meandered into the Coop bookstore.

"There's more of boy than boyfriend about him."

"Sounds like trouble," Sally said, trying not to be left out of the conversation.

Dawn snorted. "It's no trouble, just a minor irritation, but my classes this semester are turning out to be pretty challenging, so I'm happy to forego dating for studying."

"I agree."

"Oh, do you?" Sam mocked. "Meanwhile she's been seeing her pal, Joey."

"Wow." Dawn stopped and set a hand on her hip. "Tell me, how long have you been sitting on that pun?"

Sam blushed and looked embarrassed for the first time. She rolled her eyes. "Just since the beginning of this week."

"What pun? Oh right…the musical, *Pal Joey*. I mean, that might have been funny a decade ago," Sally shot back.

"It's still witty, and you know it."

"Let the girl have her romance, and leave her alone."

"I would hardly call what I'm having a romance."

"You wanna see what it's really all about?" Dawn asked. "They're always playing *Casablanca* at The Brattle Theatre."

"I love that film! Let's go."

They both looked at Sally.

"I do, too, but I don't know. I want to make sure I get home before my mother."

"Here we go again." Sam threw up her arms. "Will you live a little? You're already out with me when you're not supposed to be. Can't you just say Joey picked you up?"

"That's risky. His dad is always over going through my mom's finances with her. Plus, if I get home later, she'll know I'm lying because he'd never just drop me off. He would come into say hello."

"The perfect little Italian boy."

"You've no right to be so critical of him. You don't even know him."

"Let's get to know him, then," Dawn suggested.

"Great idea." Sam caught on and smacked her shoulder.

"What are you two talking about?"

"Call him up. Invite him out with us. That way you're covered for later." Dawn grinned at her own cleverness.

"He'd never come out, especially if he finds out I'm with you. He thinks you're a bad influence."

"I see this as the perfect opportunity to rectify that," Sam countered.

"I'm sure I'll regret doing this, but it could work."

They scouted out a phone booth and she dialed the Mosca's number. Joey answered.

"Hi, it's Sally."

"Oh, hi!" his voice went from apathetic to enthused. "I was going to give you a buzz soon and see if you wanted to do something."

"Funny, I called to see if you'd want to meet up with me in Harvard Square."

"What are you doing there again? Not hanging out with that girl you aren't supposed to be seeing, are you?"

"Well, she's here, yes. But look, she and her friend are all right, and they'd like to meet you. We're planning to go see *Casablanca* at The Brattle Theatre at four-thirty, and I want you to come. Will you?"

The stillness on the other end was heavy as he mulled it over. "I dunno. I don't want to get into trouble with your mother, Sally, that's for sure."

"You can give me a ride home after, and it'll just seem like we were on a date."

"I guess. Okay, I'll come."

"That's great! I'll see you then."

"Hey, hold on. Are you just asking me to come so that I'll drive you home and your mother won't know you've lied to her again?"

"No...Well, to be honest, that's definitely a plus, but it's not the reason."

He sighed. "You're lucky I like you as much as I do. I'll see you." He hung up.

"So, we're getting to meet lover boy, are we?" Sam wore a mischievous look.

"You better be on your best behavior."

They filled the next couple of hours with more window shopping, stopping in Grolier Poetry Book Shop, Leavitt & Peirce where Sam bought some cherry cigarillos, and the subterranean Café Pamplona for hot chocolates.

"Let's go in this boutique, I think Sally will like it," Sam said, holding the door open for them.

"Hi there, can I help you with something?" asked the perky salesgirl.

"No, just looking," said Sam, giving the girl a lengthy once-over.

"Can I help you with something?" the girl asked Sally.

"Nope, also just browsing."

"Okay, well, let me know if there's anything you'd like to try on," the girl offered, ignoring Dawn completely, but then following her like a reverse shadow while they looked around.

She visibly flinched when Dawn slid her hand over a silk scarf that was on display. Dawn didn't seem to notice, nor did the other few customers in the store, but Sam did. She winked at Sally and then began to talk really loudly.

"Hey, Sals, do you like anything you see?"

"Hmmm..." Sally looked around. "You know, I don't think so."

"Yeah, you know what I think?"

"What?"

"I think these clothes are the ugliest pieces of shit I've ever seen."

"Sam!" Dawn gave her a look and nodded her head to indicate that the salesgirl was in earshot.

"I agree. They're hideous," said Sally. She then added, "What kind of tasteless person would even try to sell these to people?"

Dawn's mouth fell open, but then a knowing look crept into her face.

"Excuse me, but you're being very loud and rude, and I'm going to have to ask you to leave the store, please," the salesgirl said, addressing Dawn.

"Why are you talking to her? We're the ones being loud and rude. Or did you just not notice that because we're white?"

"Excuse me?"

"You heard me," Sam said, perfectly calm. "I asked you why you're telling her to leave when she didn't even say anything."

"Well, you're all together, aren't you?" The girl, now irritated, crossed her arms and cocked her head.

"We are, but it seems odd to me that the only person you'd address when asking us to leave is the same Black girl whom you purposely ignored when we came in."

The girl blushed. "I didn't mean to ignore anyone."

"No, you probably didn't. It's probably just second nature to you to act like Black customers don't exist, but then to follow them around the entire time they're in here just to make sure they don't steal any of your overpriced trash. Let's go."

Sally and Dawn followed Sam without a word, but once on the street, Dawn broke her silence.

"You had no right to do that."

Sam stopped, but didn't turn to face her. Dawn walked up to her and spun her around by the arm.

"I had to say something…"

"No, you didn't. You wanted to say something. In fact, you were just hoping to start something with someone today, weren't you? That's why you wanted to go in there."

"No…" Sam looked at the ground.

"Please, girl. I know you."

"How could I have known that would happen?"

"Because it happens everywhere I go. That's how. How many salespeople have you told off on my account? What's the running tally?"

"Like twenty."

"You've got to stop. First, I don't need to be rescued by you. Second, your rescuing me like that for your own self-indulgent reasons is more offensive to me than being followed by ten snooty salesgirls. I get that you're in the fight for equality. I appreciate your solidarity, I do. But creating situations and problems just to spout off about your cause is disrespecting that very cause."

"But shouldn't you be able to go in a store without being followed like that?" Sally asked.

"Yes, of course. But things like that don't change overnight. I'm not a pessimist like this one, and I'm not an idealist like some of these hippies around here. I think in logical, practical terms." She smiled. "Let's just say I pick my battles a little more wisely than this chick."

"I get it."

Dawn wrapped her arm around a properly chided Sam. "Now, let's go."

By the time they arrived for the film, Joey was already there, bundled up in a plaid wool jacket with a furry collar and a ski hat, its flaps pulled down over his ears. Sam, now fully recovered from her scolding, walked right up to him and held her hand out.

"Hey there, I'm Sam. It's nice to finally meet you."

"Nice to meet you, too." He looked wary.

"I'm hoping we can get to know each other so you can see for yourself that I'm not such a bad influence."

"I never said you were, actually."

Sam continued smiling. "No, but you believe it, don't you? You'd rather sweet Sally here not be hanging around someone like me."

Joey laughed out of nervousness and glanced over at Sally, who was shrinking with humiliation at her friend's aggressiveness. "What is this, some kind of ambush?"

"Not at all, I'm just laying it all out there."

He may have been a coddled Italian prince, but this didn't make him stupid. He remained calm through Sam's ill-timed tirade and said, "I have no issue with you, so…Let's go see the film because that's what I came for."

Sam gave him the once over. "Okay man. You're an okay guy. And even if you weren't, I'd still go see the movie with you for a look at Ingrid Bergman."

Dawn snickered. "Don't let the judge hear you say that."

"No kidding. He would stick me right in McLean."

Dawn looked concerned. "Don't play around with that, girlie. You know my neighbor, Rae, is the nurse on night duty there. She has stories, and it's not a place you wanna be."

The four of them sat in a row with Sally on the aisle. There was a spattering of people, and, as the lights dimmed, her eye caught two older ladies sitting across the aisle behind them at a diagonal. They were scowling in her direction down their long, bespectacled noses like two superior hens on a roost. Unaware that their words were loud enough for her to hear, they clucked their unfiltered hate to each other.

"Now what's that nice looking young couple doing with those other two? That's an unlikely group, don't you think?" the first said.

"Certainly so. And the dark girl with that hair."

"I know. Whatever happened to assimilation?"

"What are you looking at?" Sally heard her own voice ring out over credits.

Her friends and a few neighbors turned to the commotion, but the two ladies were so startled by her scolding that their mouths snapped shut like clams. Joey grabbed her hand.

"I heard them, too," he whispered. "I'm glad you spoke up."

Dr. Mosca hurried down the side walkway as Joey escorted her back inside her house.

"Hi, kids," he said, his breath swirling in the glow of the pole light. He looked tired and battle-worn.

"Is everything okay?" Sally asked.

"Your mother is upset today for many reasons. You should probably go in and comfort her. Son, maybe you should say goodnight to Sally here and spare Mrs. Fiore her hospitality." Dr. Mosca patted Sally lightly on the shoulder and resumed a brisk pace back to his shiny, blue Bonneville.

Joey gave her a peck on the cheek. "I'll call you tomorrow, okay?"

"Okay."

"I hope your mom isn't too sad. Better get inside and help her out."

"Yes, well, thanks for coming out with us."

"I had a decent time. Sam seems like a nice kid."

"She is. She definitely is. Well, goodnight, then."

"'Night."

The light over the kitchen table was on its lowest setting, and Lorraine sat there, small and defeated. Sally hadn't noticed lately how frail her mother was looking. Normally she was a healthy weight, if not a little plump, with a round face and forearms that belied her petite stature. She had an unexpected vitality about her, a hidden strength that allowed her to once raise a heavy tool cabinet off a young nephew trapped under it when it toppled over. But now she looked frail and gaunt, her watch sliding far down on wrist, so bony and birdlike it seemed the slightest pressure would snap it. Several stark, white hairs now lived among the sea of inky black that framed her face.

"Mother?" Sally moved to the table and rested her gloved hands on the back of a wooden chair. "Mother, are you okay?"

Lorraine lifted her head and looked at her daughter with disoriented eyes, like she'd somehow forgotten that she was in her own house.

"Where have you been all day?"

"I was out with Joey."

"Did he drop you off just now? Why didn't he come in?"

"We ran into Dr. Mosca on our way up, and he felt like you shouldn't be troubled with company. What's going on?"

"You might as well know." Lorraine fumbled with a pack of cigarettes in her apron pocket. She only smoked one a day when she read the newspaper, but the full ashtray next to her indicated that today had been an exception. With trembling hands, she lit another, inhaled deeply, and blew it out before she spoke again. "Teddy thinks I must sell the house. He's been going over the finances with me for months, and I was determined to show him I could do it." She shook her head. "We're barely getting by. He thinks we'll struggle if we stay."

"He's sure? Isn't there a pension?"

Her mother nodded and took another drag. "Yes, but your father made some unwise choices. He put a lot into this house – buying the land, hiring his cousin's construction company to help build it. He started gambling here and there to fill the gaps – friendly card games mostly, only a lot of the time, he lost, and so any cushion we had in savings is gone. I should have been harder on him when he lost, but it was his only vice, and he worked so hard. When I think of having to leave..." She looked down at the table while tears spilled from her eyes and onto its surface. "I feel like such a failure."

"Maybe I can work more hours at Adrian's. And in the summer, I could work full-time practically. That could help."

"It's no use. And if Paul did reconsider enlisting and wanted to apply to colleges, how would I pay for that? Then you the following year?"

"I don't have to go to college."

"Oh, yes. You're going. You'll be the first woman in this family to get a degree. Do you know who else stopped by my work the other day? Mrs. Pettyfer."

"Really?"

"A nice woman. We had a good talk, and I feel badly for forbidding you to see her girl. She explained to me that she hoped you'd have an influence, pleaded with me to reconsider. So, I suppose it's okay if you're friends with her again. Just don't let her get you into trouble, okay? I certainly have enough to deal with without having to worry over your comings and goings."

"I won't. I promise." The weightlessness of relief washed over her, but like most good feelings lately, its visit was brief when she remembered their new set of troubles. "Well, what are you going to do about the house?"

"I don't know, dear. I don't know. But I have a lot to think about."

The news said that Dr. Martin Luther King, Jr., was dead.

On the fourth of April, an unassuming Thursday, Sally and Paul did the dishes while Lorraine read the paper and watched television in the den. They'd gone to join her as the evening news was finishing and Walter Cronkite announced that Dr. King had been shot dead in Memphis as he was standing out on a balcony. With blood racing, Sally sat there in shock until her mother wrapped an arm around her.

Paul stood abruptly. "Sonofabitch!"

"Paul, calm down." Her mother had begun speaking to him again only recently.

"A peaceful leader, and he's taken out like that? How does this happen?"

Lorraine shook her head because she had no answer.

"What's the difference between him and the innocent kids you'll be killing in Vietnam?" Sally asked, the question came out before she had time to fully consider it, or the ramifications of asking it. She and Paul were also just starting to be on good terms.

"That's different!" he shot back. "They're the enemy."

"Are they? Death is death, isn't it? Killing is killing no matter how you spin it. Either way, it's wrong to take a life whether you believe it's a good life or a bad one. To stand there, holding a gun, pointing it at someone you don't even know and extinguishing them – there can't be any justification for such an act, even if your country says there is."

"You're impossible," he yelled and stormed out. He always left the room when he knew he couldn't win the argument.

"Sally," Lorraine said with a slight tone of reprimand in her voice, "what's this attitude? Is this more Sam coming out?"

"I can think for myself, Mother." She then retreated to her own room, partly because her mother was probably right.

Her thoughts turned to Sam and Dawn. If this news was so horrible for her own family, what could it mean for them? She found out the next day in school. Sam showed up with bloodshot eyes, their rims rubbed pink.

"Come on, we need to go."

"Go where?"

"To Boston Common. People are going there to mourn. Dawn said."

"You mean skip school?"

"Sals, this is really important to me."

She knew Sam was right. And even if she'd disagreed with the sentiment, her friend looked so down-trodden and pathetic that she'd have gone, anyway. They snuck out the back of the school by the gymnasium and headed for the commuter rail. Dawn met them right outside Park Street Station looking like she hadn't slept. Her hair was tucked under a felt beret and there were no traces of makeup on her face. She grabbed Sam in a tight hug, and they cried into each other's shoulders for a while before letting go and merging with the gathering crowd.

The last time Sally had been on the Common was when she and Paul were much younger, and her parents took them into town for a picnic there. She remembered playing in the mottled sunlight, but it didn't seem anything like this space now that was teeming with people of all ages, colors, and walks of life. People held each other, some sang hymns, some condemned the rioting happening in several corners of the country, including locally in Roxbury. Everyone was sad.

She noticed a young Black man holding a sign a few feet from them. It read: "Peace is what he stood for: And peace is what we'll remember him for in our hearts." His face was hopeless, but maybe his spirit wasn't fully broken. And even though there were other white people there, Sally felt like an imposter, like an intruder on this despair that she could never understand. She turned to Dawn, who stood shaking her head with disgust.

"How do you feel right now?"

"How do I feel?" she repeated, shifting from one foot to the other. "I feel sick to my stomach. I feel like – and this is nothing against you or my girl here – but white America has done nothing but systematically disenfranchise us and not only has no one ever taken accountability for that, but you keep doing it, and you're going to keep doing it. First, we're ripped from our villages and put in shackles, sold into slavery by other Africans, yes. But that doesn't excuse the fact that white Europeans took advantage of our exploitation. We're stacked on top of each other like dry goods in the bellies of boats and shipped here where we're worked to the bone on plantations. Our women are raped by white slave masters, forced to bear their children in shame. Our men are whipped until the skin on their backs is a fleshy, unrecognizable mass. We're treated as less than human because of our darkness. And do you know how many times I've heard the contrary argument from one of your *Gone with the Wind* lovin' mothers about how some masters treated their slaves like family? I think the word to pay attention to there is 'slave.'

"Then we're freed, but are we equal? No, even now, a century has come and gone. We've been kept separate because, God forbid, we start breeding with you and muck up that pristine gene pool. We've watched our towns and houses burn at your hands. And every time we get a leg up, you do something to bring us down again, whether it's keeping us ignorant, mired in poverty with no opportunities, or denigrating our men until there's nothing for them to do but live up to your stereotypes of angry, gambling, drunken, thieving heathens. You've used us for your entertainment. You've sexualized our women for our big lips, our high behinds, and our thunderous thighs. Yet you continue to somehow cast the blame our way, and you do it so well that we even sometimes believe you and walk around like we have to be sorry for being Black. And now, just when there's a leader like Dr. King – a smart, respectable, religious, peaceful leader who might succeed in uniting not just the Black community, but all of us as a people – what happens? Some hateful scum shoots him in his damn face. So, how do I feel? I feel angry. I feel so angry that my hatred may just get the best of me today."

"I'm so sorry."

"Like I said, I know it's not you. It's not any one person. It's a cycle that'll take probably another few centuries to right itself."

"I feel guilty being here because I'll never understand this. I'll never face that kind of discrimination. But what can I do? What can I do?"

Dawn smiled at her. "I think all any of us can do is to try to have compassion for everyone we come across in this life. To be kind to everyone you meet no matter who they are. To treat everyone with dignity. And to try and understand one another through a dialogue. You're doing it right now. It's called empathy. You can't feel what I feel, but you're trying to. That's enough. And if you see hatred happening firsthand, I think having the courage to speak out against it will change things. Because if one person speaks out, then others will follow."

Sam looped an arm around her friend. "Couldn't have said it better myself. Sals is okay, isn't she? I think she's one of us."

"I think so, too."

The crowd had now started singing "Precious Lord, Take My Hand," Dr. King's favorite hymn. Dawn reached out to take Sally's hand and the three of them stood together, their voices raised in unison for the departed.

Chapter VIII

It was a slow day at Adrian's, and Sally sat at the counter breezing through Arthur's work for the second time. She lingered on one of her favorite passages.

The pueblos of New Mexico were silent and strong where they stood. The vibrant red earth beneath my feet was just starting to feel normal, but it was already time to go. This was the traveling life I'd chosen and, unlike many wanderers before me, I had a destination. The evening before last at Tiny's Dine and Dance, Henry looked over at me with his face dirty from sweltering days on the ranch and said he was setting out in two days to visit his great aunt in St. Louis. That I could tag along for the ride if I wanted. Of course, I took him up on it. I bade my little Galenia goodbye, kissed her on her mouth and then on her smooth forehead. She cried and shook without making a sound as I walked away and it was all I could do not to stay with her and her warmth, her delicious cooking. But that drive through Oklahoma, all 400 miles of Route 66 – some of it open fields of farmland spanning on forever, some of it odd roadside curiosities – that long stretch of road seemed never-ending, full of potential and possibility, that Mother Road was bringing me to a new home. Something in me kindled, and, as the wind blew through my hair, I heard my mother's voice whisper, "Go Artie, you're free. We're both free now."

She'd nitpicked over it on her first round, reading as carefully as possible and coming up with helpful notes for revisions, but now she was reading for pleasure, indulging in his innermost thoughts. Her childish fantasy of him had become a fantasy far removed and only existing through the thirdhand experience of reading his words. Somehow, she figured, this daydream of him as an unattainable artist was more fulfilling than anything reality might offer. His words were raw and real; they reflected the beauty of his honest soul. They inspired. They reminded her of someone.

"Whatcha readin'?" Rose appeared next to her as if the thought had conjured her from a distant part of the store. "Some kind of Harlequin romance?"

"Why would you assume that?"

"You look very dreamy."

"No, I was actually thinking of you."

"Excuse me?"

"No," Sally giggled. "I mean, this memoir. My friend wrote it, and I think you'd like it. Maybe you'll want to have a look through it when I'm finished? I'll ask him if it's okay to share it."

"Oh. You've a friend who wrote a memoir? How intriguing. A student?"

"He's a little older. He works at the school."

"That's so interesting. I've never met an actual author before." Rose simpered and went back to curating their fabric inventory.

"How come you're in such a perky mood today? Did you have a winning date or something?"

"Hardly. Quite the contrary to be sure. Nothing but duds for miles. I just feel happy today, that's all. It's starting to feel like spring, and it's the time to wear cute dresses and go out. Pleasure Island will be opening."

"You go to Pleasure Island?"

"Of course, I do! Why wouldn't I? I love the Moby Dick and the pirate boat – and all the celebrities who perform. You're telling me you don't like it there?"

"It's okay. It was better when I was a kid. Now it's getting sort of rundown, and how many times can you enjoy it, you know, before you've seen all it has to offer?"

"Now, how do you expect to get through life with that attitude? There's joy to be found in the familiar, Sally. You'll figure that out someday."

"If no one comes in for a while, can we work on my prom dress?"

"Sure."

Her junior prom was coming up, and she'd decided to take her favorite person – Nick, over Joey, even though he was slowly but surely making his way back into her good graces. This slight, as he referred to it, had become such a point of contention between them that he currently wasn't speaking to her. Lorraine took her side indefinitely in this because family always came first, and she thought it sweet that her girl still possessed enough innocence to choose a best friend over a potential boyfriend.

Part of Sally also didn't want Joey there because she hoped to maintain a modicum of privacy. She didn't want people like Tammy and Lenny gaping at them slow dancing, nor risk any kind of a fight where Joey may be injured or humiliated. This is how she tried to explain her decision to him last weekend, but he wouldn't hear it.

"I'm so sick of being jerked around like this. This is hurtful," he said as he dropped her off.

"Please try to understand." She ducked her head back in under the open car door.

"Oh, I understand. You want me when you want me, right? And that's when there's no one better available. I understand more than you think, and I'll tell you what – I'm sick of being second string."

After that, he sped off down the street, motor blaring.

"He'll get over it," Lorraine told her over supper. "He's a boy. They're resilient, and they don't hold grudges as badly as we do."

"Yeah, but he is Italian, so the grudge part is already a given."

"Not to mention he's always been the sensitive type," Paul butted in, wringing his fists by his eyes to indicate a crybaby.

Her brother still wasn't fully out of the woods when it came to Lorraine's anger. She gave him a hard look instead of laughing.

"I think some young men could do with a little more sensitivity if you ask me," she chirped and roughly doled out more salad.

Even with the damper of Joey's displeasure, Sally couldn't help but feel excitement about her dress. The color was a lovely dark coral, somewhere between a salmon and dusty rose. It had a fitted bodice with a ruffled, tulle bust and sweetheart neckline. From the trim waist, a translucent layer of tulle flared over a ruffled, lace skirt that would be even fuller with a crinoline underneath.

"You look so beautiful," Nick said, two weeks later as Sally emerged from the hallway into the kitchen where he, her mother, Aunt Jo, Paul, and Marie waited.

Rose had come by earlier to help with her hair and makeup. She'd left her hair down, but curled the ends, teased the crown, and gently pinned back the sides. For Sally's fair complexion, Rose used a sparse amount of pink rouge on the apples of her cheeks and lined her top lids with a black pencil, flicked up at the edges. She finished with some mascara and a few dabs of a nude lipstick that she topped with some Vaseline. Sally borrowed a pair of fragile earrings from Lorraine, silver rhinestone-studded cones that each held a pearl in their bottom opening. For Sally, who was only a little taller than Lorraine, but whose limbs felt as long and gawky as her father's when he was a boy, she didn't walk around all the time feeling this pretty. But something about this dress enhanced her blossoming womanhood, and she considered herself almost alluring. Vanity made her wish Joey and Arthur were present to witness her entrance, but that hope was almost instantly replaced with another.

"I wish Dad were here to see me."

Nick stepped forward and fastened a lily wreathed in baby's breath around her wrist, giving her hand a comforting squeeze when he finished.

"He's here, doll. He's here."

Lorraine wiped her eyes and endeavored to distract herself. "Let's take a picture of you two, shall we? Go in the living room, right in front of the fireplace."

After a few pictures were snapped, they headed over to the high school. Students piled out of cars in fluffed, pastel droves and poured through the doors just the same, as if the bell had rung to signal the start of a school day.

"Hey, will you check us in and then wait here for me? I need to just use the ladies' room real quick," she said to Nick with a particular thought circulating its way through her mind.

"Sure thing. But don't leave me standing here too long like a weirdo."

"Well, I'll be as fast as I can, but there's nothing I can do about the weirdo part."

"If you didn't look so pretty, I would punch you in the arm."

"You wouldn't even, because I'd punch you back, and we both know I punch harder."

She headed down the corridor, annoyed at the school's insistence on such harsh, unforgivable lighting. As she reached the girls' room, she could see that the supply closet door next to it was slightly ajar, and someone was puttering around inside it. She leaned into the swinging bathroom door just as a burst of classmates were leaving in a cloud of perfume and giggles. There was only one other person in there. Tammy. She stood looking at herself in the mirror, her face crestfallen, her eyes a bit puffy, and the tip of her nose a little red. She dabbed at it with a tissue and looked at Sally in the mirror without turning around. A few moments of silence passed before Sally felt compelled to speak.

"Are you okay?"

Tammy's eyes narrowed. "What do you care?"

"I care. If you need help, I'll go get someone. Do you need help?"

Now Tammy turned. She straightened up and walked to the waste basket to drop in her damp tissue. "No. I'm fine." She now appraised Sally in the same fashion as she always had, only this time something out of character escaped her lips as she took in the coral gown with its under layer of prim ruffles, the classic hair, and the pretty face with its concerned luminescent eyes peeking out from a heavy fringe of bangs. "You look really pretty," she muttered as she brushed by and out the door.

Sally didn't even glance at herself again but tried to follow Tammy to see if there was anything she could do. Clearly, the girl was lying. Instead, she ran directly into Arthur in her haste, better than even she'd tried to plan. He grabbed her gently by the shoulders to prevent a full-on collision, and as he looked down into her face, she remembered why she'd ventured down this way to begin with. She looked past his shoulder to see Tammy storming back to the dance, far out of reach at this point, and she momentarily absolved herself by vowing to return to that deed later.

"Sally, wow." He let go of her and stood back to have a better look. "You look so lovely. So…grown up."

"Thank you, Arthur."

She expected a lost piece inside of her to click into place at these words. Maybe that's why she wanted to see him, for validation from an adult who wasn't a relative, but from a grown man who found her desirable, to confirm that she was, in fact, a woman. And yet, she had known it before, earlier. She mused on this point as he continued to smile at her. There wasn't a lost piece clicking into place because it was already there, placed solidly by her own capable hands.

"You know, I was hoping to see you tonight all dressed up. I don't know why, but I was," he was saying, hands in his pockets.

Now it was Sally's turn to smile. "Because we're friends, that's why."

He nodded. "That must be it. Well, you go and have fun now. Make a complete mess, trash the cafeteria as best you can because I'm getting paid overtime to be here. Better make it worth what the prom committee had to spend on me."

"I'll sure try."

She found Nick standing by a set of lockers looking more annoyed than ever. "What the hell took you so long? Were you making another dress in there?"

"Oh, leave me alone and let's get this over with."

Even though it was only adorned with colorful crepe streamers and balloons, these simple decorations managed to erase the room's humdrum existence, transforming it into a ballroom she'd never before seen. A local cover band was already playing Neil Diamond's "Girl, You'll be a Woman Soon," which she giddily took as a sign of affirmation from the powers that be. Everyone turned to watch as she was escorted in, like this was all a teenage reenactment of the scene in *My Fair Lady* when Eliza Doolittle appears at the top of the stairs in her flowing gown. Many smiled as she passed, as if to acknowledge that she'd made it to this point, and not only that, but she'd done it with class. At least that's what she imagined them thinking. Stepping onto the dancefloor, she was struck with a strange affinity for these classmates, some of whom she'd known since kindergarten.

Girls clustered around her to inquire about her dress. Had she made it? It was so lovely. How long did it take? Sally graciously answered their questions while Nick excused himself to get them some punch. In the far corner of the cafeteria, the junior football players, soon to be taking on senior rank once Paul and his classmates graduated, were already acting like it. Lenny O'Malley, especially, was swaggering about, not-so-discreetly slipping a flask out of his inside pocket while his teammates screened him from the eagle eyes of the chaperones. Tammy was with him now, but she stood a few feet away in her minty green frock, looking out of place at this underclassmen fête when her own senior prom was the next month.

"I swear, those morons couldn't be more of a cliché if they tried," Heather's voice sounded off next to her.

"I couldn't agree more."

"Although, I'm not one to talk. We band geeks flock together, too. I'm here with a trombone player, but that's the most interesting thing about him. Well, that, and he has six toes on his left foot."

"Hey, you look so beautiful!"

Sally had turned and noticed her friend, normally one of the only people she had to bend her head to see, was now much closer to her own height in a pair of beige, patent leather heels. She wore a dusky yellow, chiffon cocktail dress, and her tiny waist, so often hidden by boxy sweaters, was cinched with a charming satin bow. But more than this contributed to her transformation: her eyebrows were less like two caterpillars shading her bright, brown eyes, and, by far, the most dramatic change about her face was her new, straight smile.

Heather brushed off the compliment. "Thanks. This dress is my mom's. She also came at me with the tweezers this morning and made me get my hair done."

"And your braces are gone."

"Oh yeah, that. They came off yesterday after school. I almost miss them, the feeling anyway. This smoothness is the oddest sensation." She ran her tongue over her upper teeth, then noticed Nick, who stood watching her with an amused expression. "Say, who's this fellow?"

"This is my cousin, Nick. Nick, this is my friend Heather."

"Nice to meet you. Wait, you have a friend?"

"Har, har."

"I like him," Heather said.

But Sally's attention was diverted back to the entrance. Sam stood just outside the cafeteria doors at the check-in table, handing her ticket over to the teachers in charge of admission; but something was wrong, and the faculty had their heads together in conference. Then one stood and came into the cafeteria to grab the dean of girls.

"What's going on out there?"

Heather craned her neck to see if she could offer an explanation, but she couldn't see any better.

"Let's go up the ramp and have a better look."

It became obvious what the fuss was about once all of Sam was in view. She was wearing a white shirt, white tuxedo jacket, black bowtie, and pants, and looking as debonair as James Bond himself.

"You can't come in dressed like that, Samantha," the dean of girls said in her patient way.

"What's wrong with the way I'm dressed? It's not offensive. I'm all covered up, unlike some of these other girls with their knockers hanging out all over the place."

"Samantha, please don't make a scene. I'm not sure how you got this attire past your parents, but I'm sure they'll be very displeased to hear about it."

"They didn't see me because they didn't even know the prom was today. Or that I was planning to come."

The dean of girls frowned slightly at this neglect on the part of the Pettyfers, but her sympathy wasn't enough to let Sam get away with what classified as deviant behavior. "I'm sorry, but you'll have to leave."

Sam kept her composure, but Sally could see her jaw twitching with a flip remark. Whatever it was, it didn't come out. As inherently rebellious as she was, she'd still been raised to respect her elders, and she never faltered on that, the one exception being those who'd taught her manners in the first place. This is also where she noticed Sally, Heather, and Nick watching, along with the rest of the small crowd that began to swell near the door.

"All right, have your perfect prom, then. See if I care." She turned and stalked off.

She did care, though, Sally knew it. "Come on, I have to go after her."

"What? You have another friend?"

"Don't be funny. She's upset, I can tell. I'm going. Are you coming with me?"

"Well, I'm not gonna stay in here when I don't know anyone."

"You know me," Heather said, trying to add a sultry tone to her voice, but it came out like she was clearing her throat.

"Yes, Heather. It was so lovely to meet you." He took her hand and kissed it with excessive chivalry. "I hope to see you again, but duty binds me to my unruly cousin, so I must take my leave."

"Bye," Heather sighed, still looking down at her hand.

"You've a fan," Sally said as they hurried after Sam's retreating form.

"My first."

"That can't be true."

"I hate to admit something like this to you since I'm sure you'll use it against me, but I'm not that suave with the ladies."

"I'm shocked. Speechless."

"Finally. Mission accomplished."

"Sam!" Sally yelled, bursting through the heavy doors and into the evening air. It was oddly warmer than the air inside the building, and the breeze carried the scent of flowers.

Sam stopped where she was on the sidewalk and didn't turn around. Her head was bent, and her shoulders shook a little. It was strange to see her display emotion or weakness, as she would call it. A few minutes later, when she finally faced them, there was no trace of such defeat to be seen. Her mouth broke into a wide grin as she reached inside her jacket pocket.

"Wanna go smoke behind the school like juvenile delinquents?" she asked, producing three hand-rolled joints.

Sally knew she did but wasn't sure what Nick would have to say about all this as the world's biggest prude. He cocked his head at Sam and threw a quizzical look.

"Let me get this straight. You and I haven't even officially been introduced yet, and here you are offering me drugs like some street corner dealer?"

Sam continued smiling and shrugged. "Looks that way."

"Oh, come on, don't be such a granny." Sally grabbed his hand, and they trailed Sam around to the back of the school.

What they didn't know was that they were being followed. They were huddled around taking their first puffs when it happened. First, two of them jumped Nick. The joint fell from his fingers onto the grass as he struggled. Another grabbed Sally roughly by her arms and held them behind her. Then two more set upon Sam. They were members of the football team, and Lenny strode into the center of the ring, swigging more on his flask. Even though something bad happening was imminent, Sam still wore a look of resilience.

"Let her go!" Sally screamed, but Lenny put his finger to his lips.

Her captor's hands bore harder into her arms, and she guessed by the supreme halitosis wafting into her nostrils that it was none other than Richie Jennings, good ol' fish breath. Next to her, Nick thrashed violently until one of their assailants punched him in the gut. Out of the corner of her eye, Sally saw a bright speck of mint green moving towards them, but then backing away and making haste. Rendered powerless, she prayed that Tammy was going back to retrieve a teacher.

"Well, look what we have here, boys. The little troublemaker who likes to humiliate my girl and hustle my brother on top of it. Yeah, we put two and two together on that one," he said and pointed to his head, indicating where a brain ought to be. "The nerve of you, swindling a veteran. He went to war to make the greatest sacrifice for your stinkin' freedom, and all you do with it is dress like you got a dick. Well," – he took another swig – "maybe you do. And that's what me and the boys here were getting curious about lately. What are you, anyway, a boy or a girl?"

"Why don't you ask your old lady?" Sam smirked at her own joke, but it wasn't long before her face met the full force of Lenny's fist.

There was a sharp crack, blood trickled down from her brow onto her unspoiled white lapel, and her eye began to swell. Sally couldn't fully tell, but it may have knocked her out completely because she didn't struggle in the aftermath.

"HELP! HELP! HELP!" Sally screeched, finding her voice. Once she did, she couldn't stop, and it was like that morning as a baby when she'd discovered her ability to scream. Lorraine said she nearly went mad with the sound of her shrieking infant.

"Shut that bitch up!" Lenny demanded, and Richie switched positions, holding her tight around the middle with one arm and clamping his sweaty right hand over her mouth. It smelled like salted peanuts.

"Turn her around!" he barked at his friends who held Sam. They obeyed, spinning her around and pinning her arms up against the brick wall. "We're gonna see once and for all what you are." He unzipped her dress pants and started tugging them down.

"WHAT is going on here?" The dean of girls stepped into the circle and threw back Lenny's offending hands.

He was so startled that he forgot his words and sputtered, "Ugh, ugh," over and over like he was having a case of the dry heaves. The look on the dean's face was venomous and Sally thought she might even slap him, but instead she lightly brushed a shaking hand across the double strand of pearls around her neck.

"You've got a lot of explaining to do, Mr. O'Malley. Frankly, I'm sick of your checkered existence at this school and am loathe to say that some of the administration here have turned a blind eye when you've used your size to intimidate other students simply because that also happens to make you a good football player. But not in my mind, sir, no. Violence on the field is not to be so commended, especially when one almost entirely lacks character or intellect off the field. And this, my friend," – she pointed to Sam – "is assault. Plain and simple. So when I say you've a lot of explaining to do, I don't mean to me or to others who may give you nothing but a cautionary slap on the wrist. I mean to the police."

The police were there within minutes to interview all parties involved. The dean called Sally's house, and Paul was there nearly as fast to come down and pick them up. Of course, he wanted a go at Lenny, but he and his cohorts were already in police custody. Word spread inside the dance of what had transpired, and students seeped out of the two sets of double doors that led to the lawn.

"I'm fine, really. I don't need to go to the hospital," Sam said to the dean. "Believe it or not, this isn't the first time I've been punched in the face."

"Come on, guys, I'll take you all home," Paul offered once everything was settled.

"I can drive myself," said Nick. "And I need to stop by your house and pick up my mom."

"Okay, we'll be there after we drop off Sam."

"No –," Sam pleaded. "Please, can I come to your house?"

"Don't you think your parents will want to know what happened to you?"

"They'll be out late. They're at a benefit. I really don't want to go home to an empty house."

"Okay, sure. Of course," Paul said, his features softening at the sight of her mangled eye.

"Where'd you learn to do this?"

Sam sat perched on the lip of the bathroom sink while Lorraine cleaned and dressed the wound on her brow with as much tenderness as she would've shown one of her own children. Sam looked around curiously at the quaint pink and gray tiles, taking in the sheer compactness of the room.

"Oh, you know. During World War Two, Sally's father was stationed out in California at a Prisoner of War camp. I traveled out there to be with him, and I'd make use of my time by volunteering at the hospital there."

"What's the worst thing you saw?"

"Nothing too bad. I was never in with the surgeons or anything. There, that should do it." She looked at the broken blood vessels under Sam's eye that were already starting to darken and her lips tightened in fury. "Boy, if I had five minutes alone with the one who did this to you, what wouldn't I do?"

"He's pretty big, Mrs. F. Maybe even too big for you to take on."

"The bigger they are, the harder they fall," Lorraine recited. "That's what my father used to say whenever anyone would pick on me at school."

"There's truth in that."

"Do you want to borrow one of my nightgowns?" Sally asked, holding up two in front of her.

Sam grimaced at the heaps of feminine ruffles. "Sure, whichever is fine. Thanks for letting me sleep over, Mrs. F."

"You're welcome. I'll phone your parents later to let them know you're here."

"Can we watch a show in the den?"

"Sure, don't stay up too late. And Sam, you can sleep in Sally's bed. Sally, you can share with me, unless you'd prefer the couch."

"Okay."

"If you need any snacks, I'll be in the kitchen."

"Your mom is amazing. I hope you appreciate her," Sam said, once they were sitting in the den in their pajamas.

"I try. I still think your mom doesn't seem so bad, either."

"She's not all bad, but she never stands up to my father because he's her meal ticket. That makes her weak and sad, and I'll never be able to respect her." Sam turned to seriously regard her. "You looked really pretty tonight."

"Thanks." Her cheeks were burning while Sam continued.

"Promise me that no matter what happens, like if we don't know each other someday or something, that you'll never let that happen to you. Don't ever depend solely on a man."

Sally nodded, unsure of how to respond.

"Because you're too good for that. Too creative and too talented. You promise?"

"Sure."

"Pinky swear." They linked pinky fingers.

"I swear."

"So, what are we watching?"

Lorraine got up early the next morning and made a breakfast of pancakes, eggs, and bacon. Sam was dressed in her white shirt and a borrowed pair of jeans, already eating like a farmhand and having a lively conversation with Lorraine, when Sally wandered in still in her nightgown and robe. The sound of a lawnmower churned outside in the yard as Paul did his weekly chores. Sally had just sat down to a plate when there came an angry rapping at the front door. Then the doorbell rang. Then another fierce knock.

Quickly, her mother removed her white apron. "Sam, this must be your parents."

Sure enough, Judge Pettyfer stood, tall and stormy in a gray coat and hat, with Dorris lingering behind him. Lorraine opened the door.

"Good morning, Judge Pettyfer. Mrs. Pettyfer."

"Where is she?" the magistrate bellowed, barging in past her mother, through the living room, and straight into the kitchen.

Sam continued eating, unperturbed by her father charging in and towering over them like he was waiting for someone to grovel. Even at the sight of her black eye, he showed no sympathy. Dorris came in behind him with cooing attempts to mollify his rage until she saw her daughter's face and whimpered into her baby blue glove. It was obvious that while they liked to maintain appearances, he had little regard for what the Fiores might think of them. This gnawed at Sally, and she wondered if it was because her mother had catered their holiday party – if it was because in his superior, Boston Brahmin eyes, she and her first-generation immigrant mother were just the help. From the look flashing in her mother's eyes, she knew they were realizing the same truth, and, if it bothered her, it bothered Lorraine tenfold.

"Oh, hi there, Pop. Didn't see you come in." Sam scooped up another forkful of eggs.

"You shut your smart mouth." He wagged a hostile finger at her. "You tell me how this complete debacle happened. Some boys in your grade are in custody because of you. A promising football player will most likely be expelled, even if we don't press charges."

"And why wouldn't you press charges?" Sam yelled, slamming down her fork. "I was attacked." She pointed to her eye. "In case you hadn't noticed. Attacked by grown men much bigger than me, and you couldn't care less. You only care that people at your precious country club might find out about it and snicker at you behind your back for having a queer daughter who likes to wear pants. Oh, no – not that! I have news for you. People already snicker behind your back, and it has nothing to do with me."

The joules on Judge Pettyfer's face shook as he spoke his next words, words that would cut not just Sam, but everyone else present in the Fiore's kitchen.

"Look at you. This attack was your own fault."

"Excuse me, Judge," Lorraine's voice rang out. Judge Pettyfer blinked at her like she was an animal that had magically begun speaking. "I think you're being a bit unfair considering what your child has just been through."

His livery mouth twisted itself around again like a perplexed kaleidoscope of flesh. "I don't give a damn what you think. You mind your goddamn business!"

Her mother's lips formed a thin line, and Sally knew Judge Pettyfer had no idea that he'd just unleashed a beast. She walked up closer to him, barely coming to his shoulder and spoke with a voice firmer and more resounding than his.

"In case you've forgotten, this happens to be MY house. And anything that happens under this roof IS my business. And if you don't like that, then you can just get the hell out!"

He stared down at Lorraine in disbelief. The lawnmower outside stopped, and Paul hurried in through the back door because the din of their shouting was louder than the machine.

"What's going on in here? Is everything okay, Mom?"

"Everything's just fine." She smiled, her eyes still on Judge Pettyfer. "Judge and Mrs. Pettyfer were just leaving, that's all."

"Get up," he hissed at Sam.

If looks could kill, he would have been dead and buried, then exhumed, his corpse beaten and ravaged by wild animals, and buried again. But at the end of it, Sam stood and followed her parents out the door without a word.

"We shouldn't have let her go." Sally turned to her mother, a knot forming in her insides. "Who knows what they'll do to her."

"We had to. We couldn't forcefully keep her here. You know that," Lorraine said with conviction, though it was obvious that even she didn't believe her own words.

They watched through the living room curtains as the Pettyfers pulled away. Sam looked up at them from the backseat but didn't wave. The corners of Lorraine's mouth turned down as she shook her head. She was the kind of mournful that Sally knew all too well.

"Poor darling."

Chapter IX

Sam didn't show up to school on Monday. Or Tuesday. When she was absent again on Wednesday, Sally decided to do something about it. During lunch, she stood in line and when she reached the lady who doled out soupy peas or chalky mashed potatoes, she made a face like she was about to vomit, set her tray down, and swayed a little.

"I feel sick."

"Honey, why don't you go see the nurse. You don't look so well."

Out in the empty hallway, she quickly stopped by her locker to grab her things. Her last period after lunch on Wednesday was a double study hall, and Mr. Nebbins only remembered to take attendance half the time so she was sure she wouldn't be missed.

"And where do you think you're going?"

Heather was a hall monitor during this period. She sat at a flimsy desk at the end of the junior corridor and inspected passes. Most kids thought she took this assignment much too seriously. Sally hoped she wouldn't throw her weight around on today of all days.

"Oh, hey."

"Pass, please." Heather's open palm shot out in front of her without looking up from the issue of *Seventeen* she was reading.

"Look, will you help me out? Sam hasn't been in school all week, and I'm taking off to go see how she is. I'll have a couple of hours to do it before I have work, and I only have double study periods with Nebs."

"You realize what will happen to me if you get caught, and it comes out that I let you by without proper permission?"

"I dunno, you lose your Miss Hall Monitor 1968 sash?" Sally was quickly losing patience. But Heather chortled at this.

"You just sounded a little like her, you know. I guess you can go. But I never saw you, and this conversation never happened," she said, engrossing herself again in an article called "Who'd Go Out with a Girl Like Me?"

"Thanks, you're a friend."

Sally walked down Main Street as discreetly as possible, holding her stomach a little so that if anyone did question her, she'd just say she was going to see her mother at work because she felt ill. No one seemed to notice her at all. It was an unseasonably warm day for early May, and by the time she arrived at Sam's address, she was lightly sweating through the back of her cotton dress. Molly answered the door and looked distraught upon seeing her.

"Oh, Sally dear. You wait right here while I go get Mrs. P."

After some muffled, raised voices in the background, Dorris came to the door, dressed very casually and wearing no makeup. Without it, she looked older, the lines around her mouth seemed dry and cavernous, and her cheeks sunken and puckered.

"Sally, please come in."

They sat in one of the front parlors, a cheerful room with poppy and cream striped wallpaper framing a pleasant hearth.

"I have to apologize for the way I look. I should have at least put my face on this morning."

"That's okay."

"No, it's not. If my mother taught me one thing, it was to never let anyone see me without my face on. 'People have to look at you,' she'd say. 'So you should make it as easy as possible for them.'"

"Where's Sam? Can I see her?" Sally blew past these trivial pleasantries.

Dorris swallowed and studied her folded hands, which, without their gloves, also resembled something less lovely, like two overcooked pieces of chicken.

"Oh, my dear, Sam isn't here."

Sally stood. "Where is she?"

"Her father. He sent her away like he said he would."

"To that place in Belmont? McLean?"

Dorris nodded.

"How could you let him do that?"

"What was I supposed to do?!" She spat this out in a way that made it seem like Sally wasn't the first who'd challenged her.

"You're her mother. You were supposed to protect her!"

She ran outside, slung her bag over her shoulder and walked as fast as she could up the side of the lake. Skirting the town green, past the little stone church and through the historic cemetery, there was a row of flowering trees known as "floral way." Sally set her bag down and wiped the tears from her face. The wind had blown them into her temples, and her hairline there was damp. A sense of helplessness overcame her. What was happening to Sam right now? How long would she be there? Would Sally ever see her again?

Her throat began constricting, and she tried to take deeper breaths, but the air only kept funneling itself in through what seemed an opening the size of a pinhead. She sank to her knees and buried her face in the fibers of her book bag. Then she blacked out. When she opened her eyes again, she saw shoes, black shoes with a familiar scuff. Someone was rubbing her back and humming a song. *"It was fascination, I know. And it might have ended right there at the start."*

"Hey, kiddo," a voice she'd almost forgotten whispered in her ear. The smell of Old Spice lingered in the air. "Better get up now. You know, you're right near my old route. Why not walk a bit of it? You might find it easier to breathe if you move about. Come on, little one. Wake up for Daddy."

It took every bit of strength she could muster to lift her head, expecting to see her father in front of her. But there was no one, just the breeze through the dogwoods and some stray turtle doves waddling about in search of bugs. She took another deep breath, put her hands on the gravely dirt beneath, and hoisted herself up. The pathway was empty. The breeze blew her hair back, kissing her face. She watched while sunlight glittered across the rippling water of the lake. After a brief spell, she took up her bag and started in the direction of Prospect Street, winding her way over her father's ghost footsteps until she came to the point where she knew his route ended.

She stood on the corner of Prospect and Sheffield, staring at the house where the Stodges family lived. Because she'd made a promise to a young boy, she plucked up the courage to go knock on the door. An older woman answered. She had her hair pulled back in a tight gray bun and wore a high-necked blouse fastened with a cameo. Paired with a long skirt, it gave her the appearance of a schoolmarm.

"Yes?"

"Hello, I'm very sorry to bother you, but my name is Sally Fiore. My father, Domenic, was the mailman in this area and used to come by and visit Danny."

"Oh, yes. Danny's been hoping you'd visit soon. Come in, he's right in the living room."

"You came!" Danny crowed from his chair when he saw her.

"Here I am."

"Well, have a seat. Your dad used to sit right there." He pointed to an olive-colored couch opposite him.

"I'll bring you two some fresh lemonades." Mrs. Stodges left the room, trailing her skirt behind her like a governess out of literature.

"So, how've you been?"

"Not so bad. Glad the school year is almost over."

"Do you go to regular school?"

"No, my mother teaches me."

"I see." The outfit now made more sense. "What's your favorite subject?"

"Math. What's yours?"

Mrs. Stodges came in again and set down a tray with two lemonades and some shortbread cookies. She handed Danny a glass and two cookies before she wheeled him closer to the coffee table and exited the room with another graceful swish of fabric.

"Oh, I like English. So, basically, the complete opposite." She laughed, trying her best not to show she was upset about other things. But the boy was too intuitive.

"Is something wrong? You can tell me." He bit into a cookie and looked at her with sincere concern.

"Something is. It's hard to explain."

"Try me. I may be able to help. Just because I'm in a chair that doesn't mean there's anything wrong with this." He knocked on his head.

"Well, I have a friend, and she's different, I guess you could say. She's not like a regular person."

"Okay, I can already relate." He smiled.

"Her parents don't understand the way she is, though. Even though she's been unique in her way since she was a very little girl. They think there's something wrong with her, and they want her to change. So they sent her away to this place that's sort of like a hospital where doctors will do things to try and fix her."

Danny's blue eyes were wide. "That sounds just terrible. You have to try and help her."

The urgency in his tone made her think. He was right. She couldn't just stand by and allow Sam's spirit to be broken, possibly destroyed. If she was ever in a situation like this, she was sure Sam wouldn't rest until she'd done everything in her power to change it. But where to start? Judge Pettyfer was a powerful man with much influence, and she couldn't very well march into the place and sign her friend out.

"I agree. I'm just not sure if there's anything that will work."

"You still have to try. Just don't try to do it all by yourself. Tell someone else who might be able to give you some help."

Dawn. She had to get ahold of Dawn.

She smiled. "Say, how'd you get so wise?"

"Let's just say I've gotten a lot of good life advice from a great guy."

A framed picture of a young man sat on an end table a few feet behind him. They looked so much alike it was as though time had moved forward to capture his older self. He was dressed in an Air Force uniform.

"Who's the boy in the picture behind you?"

Danny's toothy grin closed in on itself, and his eyes dropped to his lap. "That's my older brother, Nathan. He was shot down last year in the war."

"I'm so sorry."

"My folks begged him not to go. Even tried to give him money to go to Canada, though that's not very patriotic. Dad says patriotism is all well and good until it's your own blood about to run off into danger. I sure wish my brother had listened to them."

"I have an older brother, too. He's only a year ahead of me, though. There was quite a gap between you two, huh?"

"Yeah, well. Mom calls me her little surprise." A smile surfaced again when he said this.

"My brother plans to enlist when he graduates, too. We're all pretty upset about it, but he's very proud and stubborn."

"I wish my brother were still here. It makes me feel bad sometimes when I think that my parents had such a perfect son, and now all they have is me."

"No, don't say that. You're perfect just as you are."

He smiled, but it was morose. "I'm sorry your brother will be going off. Maybe the war will end soon, and he'll come back. A lot of them do, you know."

"I know. Well, I should go. Thanks for all the wonderful advice. I need to hustle to make it to work now, but I'll be back and stay longer next time, okay?"

"Okay. Goodbye, Sally."

She gave his shoulder a little squeeze as she stood.

He grabbed her hand.

"That's how your dad always said goodbye, too."

"Boy are you lucky it's slow today. You're a half an hour late!" Rose folded her arms across her chest in an attempt to be cross.

"Please don't be upset. I have very good cause, even though it's still not an excuse."

"What is it?" Rose's tone softened at once.

"Sam's father sent her away like he's been threatening. I just have to do something about it, and I think I need your help."

"Of course, I'll do whatever you need."

"The main thing is that I have to get in touch with her best friend, Dawn. She's a student at Radcliffe, and I know where her dorm is but nothing else about her. I'm sure Sam said her last name when she introduced us, but I can't remember it for the life of me."

"So, you need me to drive you in?"

"It would be quicker than having to take the train."

"Absolutely. I can take you on Sunday if that works."

"It does. I'm just not sure what I'll tell my mother. I know she wouldn't blame me for trying to help, but she also wants me out of trouble. Judge Pettyfer seems really vindictive and, on top of that, he has a lot of influence."

"Well, we could say we're going there to visit the Design Research building to look at the Marimekko fabrics. I've actually been wanting to go, so it wouldn't be a total lie."

"You'd do this for me?"

"Of course, I would. You're like a little sister to me now. Besides, what else have I got to do on Sunday, sit in church and pray for a decent man? I've been doing that for the last year, and guess what? I'd have been better off shopping."

The days until Sunday felt unending, and her mind was wracked with thoughts of what Sam could be enduring at any given moment. She didn't have a clue as to how these places operated, so she was left to imagine the worst: Sam lying on a hard table, her arms and legs strapped down, and electric currents coursing through her lithe body. But she also knew that Sam was a fighter and tried to comfort herself with the fact that if anyone could make do under dire conditions, it would be her.

As she waited for Rose to arrive that morning, Paul and her mother were in a discussion that seemed like it would explode into a fight at any moment.

"I wish you could try and see my side of it. I want to serve because Dad served. I want to be the kind of man he was."

The breakfast dishes clanked in the sink as Lorraine washed them, much more roughly than she would under normal circumstances.

"I will never understand why you're doing this. Your father wouldn't be doing this. He'd be staying and taking care of his family."

Sally stood and moved into the front parlor to see if Rose was there. To her relief, she'd just pulled up in her Beetle. The conversation was wearing on her, and she wanted to get out of there before anyone asked for her opinion, and she was forced into taking a side. Which side would she take if given a choice? She didn't even know. It was impossible. Her brother's motives, while noble, were still somewhat selfish in her eyes. There was a good chance he could die, leaving her and her mother all alone. On the other hand, why shouldn't he be able to follow his own path just because their father had unexpectedly died? Why should he be kept from the future he wanted? Why should he forego a dream for familial duty? It would only make him resentful. He would turn inward even more, keeping company with himself like a mollusk. No, she wouldn't know what to say if asked, and thanks to Rose's impeccable timing, this was a dilemma that could be avoided.

"I hope this plan works." Rose's voice, with its chipper warmth, carried tones of skepticism.

"It has to."

Retracing her way to Dawn's dorm posed more of a challenge than she thought. Once inside, she knocked on the door with an urgency that turned her knuckles red. A slim girl with mousy hair answered and furrowed her brows at the two unfamiliar faces.

"Yes?"

"Hi, I'm looking for your roommate."

"Oh." The girl motioned her closer and lowered her voice. "Dawn went home a couple of hours ago. Her parents called with some news about something, and she took off in a hurry."

"Can you tell us where she lives?"

"Who are you, exactly?"

"I'm Sally. Her best friend, Sam, is a friend of mine, and she's in trouble."

The girl looked Sally up and down and seemed satisfied that she was who she said. "Sure, I'll write it down for you. It's not too far."

The modest, gray home looked like a house should, noted Sally. Two stories with a pointed roof, a decent yard, and black flower boxes on all the windows, which were a classy touch.

A pretty lady who looked like an older version of Dawn opened the front door. The sounds of raucous play drifted out from inside. She looked kindly at them.

"Hello, are you girls lost?"

"No, ma'am. And we're sorry to barge in on you like this, but my name is Sally. I'm a friend of Sam Pettyfer's, and I really need to speak to your daughter."

The woman smiled, warmly this time. "I think you'll want to come in."

The house smelled like freshly baked bread and a roasting chicken. To the left was a living room where two younger boys were laughing and roughhousing with an older boy. Dawn sat in an armchair, a book poised open on her lap, but her face turned towards the merriment and set with a languid grin. On closer inspection, it wasn't an older boy they were play-wrestling with at all.

"Sam!"

Sam froze, looked up from the mayhem, and broke into a wide, Cheshire grin. "Sals!"

In a second, she'd made it to the lip of the room and had Sally in a tight embrace.

"How are you here?" Sally pulled away and did a quick inspection of her friend, taking inventory of every bit to make sure she was all there. Aside from appearing a little gaunt with one eye still a bit black, she seemed like her normal, jovial self.

"How much time you got? It's kind of a long story."

"It's one I need to hear."

Sam had noticed Rose in all this, standing in the background like the most vivacious wallflower to ever grace a room. "Who's this?"

"I'm Rose. Sally and I work together at Adrian's." Rose stepped forward and put out her hand.

"You drove her all the way here?" Sam asked, taking it.

"I did."

"That was real good of you. Any friend of Sally's is a friend of mine. This is my best friend, Dawn Elder, and her family. Her mother, Flora. Her father, Abe," Dawn gestured to a man Sally hadn't even noticed before, who sat looking professorial in a bow tie and sweater vest, his soft, closely-cropped hair just graying. "And her two younger brothers, Lamar and Isaac."

"Girls, please. Come in and sit down," said Mr. Elder.

When they were all seated and at attention, Sam began to retell the week-long ordeal she'd been through.

"My dad drove me there last Sunday, right after we left your house. There was a packed bag in the car for me. He had me admitted. It wasn't entirely bad, not like you'd think. A lot of people are helped by places like that if they actually need the help. Some of the girls were even pretty cool. At first, though, I was so shocked that I was there that I kind of went along with everything. I knew if I went into hysterics and demanded to be let out that it would be worse, so I played nice. My father had paid extra for me to have a single room, given my 'condition.' He told them I might be predatory to another female. So, I didn't want to give them anything to react to. I played docile, kept my cool, and tongued my meds. They gave me sleeping pills. These I saved to trade with the girls who'd been there longest. I wanted as much info on the place as I could get.

"The second day, they gave me shocks. This slowed me down a little." She grimaced, remembering. "Just a little. I found out about the tunnels that run beneath the whole place, largely used for transporting patients between buildings in bad weather. They gave me shocks again. My body felt numb from it, like when you burn the inside of your mouth, and because it's so burnt, you can't taste anything for a while. I felt like that, only all over. I kept tonguing my meds and plotting my escape, although it wouldn't have happened if it wasn't for the Elders' neighbor, Rae, the evening ward nurse.

She remembered me, and she knew I shouldn't be there. Last night, I'm fairly sure she 'forgot' to double lock my door, and I was able to slip out undetected through the tunnels just in case anyone was looking outside. And I walked here. Stayed off the road, of course, just in case they figured it out before morning. I hope Rae doesn't get in trouble. I left a bobby pin on the floor to make it look like I might have picked my way out."

"She can't stay here, though," Dawn said. "So, it's lucky you two showed up."

"What do you mean, she can't stay?"

"We're too close for comfort. This is the first place her parents will look."

"I see. I bet they'll suspect my family, too," Sally mused aloud.

"Likely. They may assume she tried to run off to New York again, but they'll look locally first. Do you have any ideas of where she might stay temporarily? Just until they think she's unable to be recovered? I'm working on leaving a fake trail."

"I'm not sure why they'd even care at this point," Sam said. "Maybe this time, they'll give up easier, now that it's obvious I'm beyond their idea of repair. It's probably just an exercise in power for my old man. He's determined to have me be normal. He's obsessed by it. But this might be enough for him to forget me."

"Either way, you need to figure something out and fast."

"You could stay with me," Rose offered. "I live with my parents, but I'm sure they'd be okay with it."

"That's so kind of you," said Sam. "I mean, you don't even know me."

"Well, like you said. Any friend of Sally's…"

"I really appreciate it. I'm just not sure staying in Wakefield at all would be smart, but it might be my only option at this point."

As they were talking, an idea started churning in Sally's brain. It was a long shot, but it was their only chance of successfully protecting her friend.

"I think I know what to do."

Twenty minutes later, she was knocking on another door with the same kind of blind hope in her throat. Joey answered. He looked surprised and happy to see her, but quickly masked this with the anger he was resolved to hold onto.

"What do you want?"

"I need a favor. A big one."

"Are you serious?"

"This is an emergency. You know I'd never come to you like this in the middle of a fight if it weren't."

He caved a little, leaning his lanky frame against the door. "What is it?"

"Your parents are away for a bit, right?"

"They're in Florida dealing with my grandpa – my mom's dad. He hasn't been well. Why?"

"My friend Sam is in trouble."

"Your friend Sam. It's always about her, isn't it?" He shook his head. "Now she's in trouble. Shocking."

"She needs a place to stay where she won't be noticed." Sally pressed on with her request.

"And you think I'm gonna let her stay here?"

"I'm begging you to let her stay here. I promise she won't get in your way. Please, for the sake of years of friendship."

He sighed. "Just stop. I can't stand to see you looking so pathetic…She can stay here."

"Thank you, thank you." She wrapped her arms around him and kissed his cheek.

"Okay, you don't need to kowtow to me."

Rose and Sam had been watching this entire exchange with rapt attention. Sally motioned to Sam to get out of the car. She bolted up the steps with her small duffel bag.

"Joey, wow. I can't thank you enough, man."

"It's fine. So, do you have a plan? Because my parents will be back within a week, so it's not like you can stay here that long."

"There's a plan. Dawn is going to leave a fake trail that makes it look like I headed to New York again, but really, I'll be going to D.C."

"Do you have friends there?"

"I have some people I can stay with."

"Come on in, then." He stood aside to let her through.

She hugged Sally. "I don't know how to thank you for this."

"You don't have to. Just promise me I'll see you before you leave."

"I promise. I wouldn't dare leave without saying goodbye to my Sals."

"You're really lucky, you know," Rose said during the ride home after several minutes of comfortable silence.

"How do you mean?"

"I just think it must be nice to have a man like that who'd do anything for you."

"You mean Joey?"

"Sure. I mean, I know maybe he's not your ideal, but there's something to be said about someone who'd bend over backwards like that, even when he's still upset with you. To have someone who'd die before hurting you. There's something to be said."

"You've never had anyone like that?" Sally asked this, knowing the answer.

"Oh, the closest I got to that was Roy." She looked over at Sally. "You know, I haven't told many people this, but I was married before."

"Really? You're so young."

"Well, it was soon after high school. I was still floored by Roy's death, and I was easy prey, I guess you could say. He was the younger brother of one of my uncles by marriage and several years my senior, but to a young woman, a twenty-seven-year-old, well-established salesman is an exciting prospect. The summer after I graduated, we were at a family barbeque, and we'd run out of ground beef for burgers, so I ran to the store with him to get more. On our way back, he pulled over on a side street and put his hand on my bare leg. 'I'm real sorry to hear about what happened to your friend Roy,' he said. 'I just want you to know, I'm here for you if you need me.' At first, I thought he was being sincere. So, I thanked him. Growing up, I'd always nursed a bit of a crush on him. My grandparents had a pool put in a few years before, and he was always such a specimen at these gatherings. He had wavy, dark hair like a movie star and the broadest shoulders you've ever seen, but the rest of him was narrow and lean. And here I was, sitting in a car with him, his full attention on me and his massive, hairy paw completely covering my knee. When he leaned over and kissed me, I jumped. My heart raced, but I couldn't get Roy out of my head, and that made me resistant. His hand bore down on my knee. 'Stay still,' he said, 'and show me how you kissed Roy.'

"I should have known then that marrying this man would be a colossal mistake, but I was easily swept into the mutual excitement of our families at such a match. It all happened very quickly. We married around Christmastime, and I convinced myself that I was happy. My parents were relieved that I wasn't moping about anymore. They were proud that I was already going to be a homemaker and married to a successful, handsome man who was strong and charismatic in every way. So off I went, from the safety of my loving parents to my own home – a cozy little mansard in Reading, but still close enough to visit regularly. Only I wasn't allowed to unless he said I could. I was a prisoner, beholden to a daily schedule set by him because he said I was 'young and without proper training to take care of a man's needs.' If I strayed from routine in any way, there was punishment. Sometimes it was physical. Mostly it was humiliation. His expectations and demands would always have to be met, and that included my duty in the bedroom. There was no such word as 'no,' you see. I found that out the hard way."

Sally looked down at her own body, and she'd instinctively curled up in her seat, winding her arms and legs as close to herself as she could.

"How did you get away from him?"

"After one particularly bad spell, I found myself sinking into a depression. I had no friends, no one to call about what was happening to me. I was thinking of just ending myself and meeting Roy over on the other side. But I realized that was foolish. I was nineteen, and I had a family who loved me. Even though he'd fooled them all, I knew they'd believe me if I showed them the bruises. And that's what I did. I drove to my parents' house; I even called my aunt over, who was married to his brother. I got down to my bra and panties in front of them – talk about humiliating. But he never hit me where anyone could see. They cried. They all cried. When he arrived home to an empty house with no dinner waiting for him, he came looking for me. And my father and his good friend, the chief of police, met him at the door."

"My gosh, Rose."

"It's all right. I live at home with my parents still. I'm afraid to leave them. I go on dates to convince them I'm okay, and for the most part, I am. But I'm just not sure that I'll ever trust a man again."

She pulled up in front of the Fiore house, turned off her engine, and sighed. Reaching across Sally, she opened her glove compartment and pulled out a pack of cigarettes.

"I didn't know you smoked."

"I don't normally. I think it's a filthy habit, but there are occasions." She looked down at the one in her mouth that she was about to light, but then took it out and set it back in the pack. "You know what? He's not worth lighting up over."

"That's for sure." Sally grabbed the pack and shoved it back in the compartment. "I feel so sheltered after hearing that story. After seeing what Sam's going through."

"You're going through something, too, don't forget that. I think it's quite brave of you to be such a good friend to that girl. As for my experiences, you don't want them as your own. That's why I shared them with you."

"Thank you."

"Can I say something else?" A new worry etched itself across her lovely features. "I'm concerned about your mother. For a while, I thought she was getting through things. Granted, I knew she was putting on a brave face for everyone because that's how she is, but lately she looks thinner and worn. She's wearing black again. I see her outside downtown on her breaks smoking like a fiend."

"It's because my brother is enlisting after he graduates. She's not handling it well."

"Men can be so bullheaded about war."

"He wants to go because my dad served, and he thinks it's a way to honor his memory."

"By going off and getting himself killed? That's the most foolish thing I've ever heard."

"Maybe you should talk to him, then, because he won't listen to a thing we say."

"Look, your mother needs you now. You'd better pay special attention to her. That's all I'm saying."

"I will. The house looks dark. I'd better go in and see how she is. Rose, thanks for driving me today. It meant a lot."

"It was no trouble at all, honey."

Sally went up the side of the house again to give herself time, thinking about how Rose was right. She was lucky that all the men in her life – her father, Paul, Joey, Nick, even Arthur – were all such gentlemen. This thought diverted her from what she wasn't ready to face. Her mother. At this hour, Lorraine would be in the middle of making Sunday dinner, either a roast or a pasta dish with her famous meatballs, some family might even be over. But the lack of activity in the house was alarming. The kitchen was dark when she walked in. There were no sounds of television or radio or record player. There was no movement at all.

In the living room, she found her mother sitting in the dark. The air was cloudy with cigarette smoke. Anger swelled inside her as she flipped on the light. Lorraine didn't look up but kept looking off into the distance at nothing.

"Why are you doing this?" Sally demanded.

Her mother didn't respond but turned to her with the same faraway gaze like she didn't know where she was.

"Answer me! Why are you doing this? You're just giving up!"

Lorraine cleared her throat and set her current cigarette in the little gold ashtray carved with delicate butterflies. "I'm starting to think you'd be better off without me."

"What?! What does that even mean?"

"I can't face all this. I don't want to. You'd be better off without me like this."

"Like I'm better off without Dad?"

Lorraine closed her eyes as if she didn't want to hear anymore, but Sally couldn't let go of this argument. It was, in fact, long overdue.

"Maybe you're right," she said now. Lorraine's eyes snapped open at this. "Why don't you just go kill yourself, then? You can kill yourself, and Paul can go off to war and get himself killed, too. And I'll just change my name to Little Orphan Annie and get myself a dog."

"Santa…" Lorraine warned. "I don't need this from you right now."

"You think Paul's being selfish? What do you call this? Sitting in the dark like a vampire. You don't even care how this affects me! How anything you've done affects me! You only care about your own goddamn grief!"

"You haven't exactly been that helpful around here lately," Lorraine yelled, now standing and recovering some of her lost energy. "You teenagers are so caught up in your own drama with school and friends and clothes. Who cares if they make fun of you for wearing secondhand things? That was more important than the fact that your father dropped dead!"

"Really? Did he? I wouldn't know since you immediately got rid of everything!" Sally screamed back. "Maybe that's not what I needed! Maybe I needed to still have his things around! But you did what was good for you – to forget! I can't forget!!! I can't forget because I never told him I was sorry!"

She fell to the floor and her mother's arms were instantly around her.

"Oh, Sally," she said in her old voice like her spirit had been wandering and had just returned to her body. "I'm so sorry. You're right. You're absolutely right. I didn't pay enough attention to what you and Paul were going through. Maybe if I had, Paul wouldn't have made this decision he's made."

"No, it's not your fault."

"I was just trying to be as normal as possible so we could all get through this. That might have been a mistake, too. Look…" She took Sally's face in her hands. "Don't you ever worry about me leaving you, okay? You and I, we're going to be just fine."

"We're all going to be fine," Paul said from behind them. He'd just come home with Marie, who nudged him forward.

Lorraine stood and held her arms out for him. It was the first time they'd embraced since Domenic's funeral. "My Paul," she cried into his shoulder. "My brave Paul."

Sally still knelt on the floor, watching them hold each other. Marie's head was bowed as if in reverence, and the way she held the silver heart-shaped locket Paul had given her, Sally knew that she, too, was sending silent prayers out into the Universe.

Joey had been in touch a few times over the next week. He said Sam was doing okay, and he didn't mind having her around. In the meantime, Dorris came into the store twice. Once to inform Sally of Sam's escape and the second to see if her daughter had reached out. Sally took some satisfaction in being no help, but made certain that was well hidden by sullen, if not accusatory, looks. Seeing Dorris so broken and haggard did stir something inside of her to temporary sympathy. She looked like a woman who had lost two children, and there had to be nothing sadder than that.

In their free time, Sam and Joey would also do regular drives by her old house to check whether her parents were home. Before she departed, she needed a few of her personal effects and some money she had stashed away in her room. Unfortunately, they'd been home every day that week, and Sam needed to be off before the Moscas returned, so they were cutting it close. By Friday, they'd lucked out. At eight o'clock in the evening, Sally was immersed in sewing when there was a tap on her window.

It was Sam. In the twilight that lingered in purples and oranges, Sally could just make out what she was wearing – a dandified look of seersucker pants, a short-sleeved shirt of pastel blue with yellow suspenders, a yellow bowtie with blue and pink dots, and immaculate boat shoes. She put her finger to her lips.

"I don't have that much time," she whispered. "Joey's waiting for me a couple of houses up. I did it," she said with an almost crazed anticipation in her voice.

"What?" Sally fought to find the words as she processed what was happening. This was another goodbye and probably one that carried some permanence.

"We watched my parents leave the house dressed fancy, which means they were going to some dinner or benefit, and they'd be out for hours. So, I snuck in and got what I needed, but then I did something else, so they'd know I was there. I took almost everything out of Lottie's room – her perfect clothes, her toys, her books, her bed linens, and I put them in a pile on the front lawn. I lit a match to it, and we watched it burn from the car." She wiped some tears away.

"I don't know what to say."

Sam waved her hand as if to dismiss this cathartic act. "She's in peace now, that's all I care about. I couldn't burn this, though." She thrust something up into Sally's hands. It was the stuffed bear that had been on her little sister's bed. "His name is Chauncy, and I want you to keep him for me. Okay? Someday, I'll have to come back for him," she said through gulps of air.

"No, I couldn't. You should have him."

"I'm afraid something will happen to him. I'll be flitting around, staying with different people on and off. I know he'll be safe with you. Please, will you take care of him for me?"

"Okay." Sally held the bear to her chest.

"I like the thought of the two of you together."

"Where will you go?"

"There's a movement happening, even though Dr. King was killed. A revolution. It's inevitable. You can only push people so far. You can only demoralize and dehumanize people to such an extent before they realize they have nothing left for you to take and the only thing to do is act. It's like the buildup of pressure behind a champagne cork once you start to open it. Nothing can stop it. Change is coming, and I need to be part of it."

"Just be careful, please. Take care of yourself. Promise me."

"I promise. Sals, I know we haven't known each other that long, but you're one of my favorite people of all time."

"You're one of mine, too."

"Sally, who are you talking to in here?" Lorraine asked, opening the door. Sam was on tiptoe, resting her head on the windowsill, and there was no mistaking her. But Lorraine didn't say anything. Instead, she nodded and shut the door.

"She won't tell, will she?" Sam's question was more of a statement.

"No, I'm pretty sure she's on your side."

"Hey, Sals? You told me once that you had a fight with your dad and never got to apologize before he died. What was the fight about?"

This question threw Sally for a loop. What was the fight about? Not a fight really, an argument more like. But it seemed bigger than it was because they never fought, and he rarely scolded. It came back to her, then, washed over her memory like a silent motion picture.

"My mother wasn't feeling well. She had a headache, and I was in my room reading after dinner. My father came in and told me I should be helping her instead of goofing off. I was annoyed that he had just barged in my room. I could have been changing or something, so I mouthed off and said, 'Don't come in here again without knocking first.' And then I still didn't go help my mother, so he did the dishes that night. His last night on earth and he had to do the dishes because of me."

Sam took Sally's hand and looked into her eyes. "I forgive you."

"Thanks. I think he would have liked you a lot."

"I'm sure I would have liked him, too. Well, I have to run. Joey is taking me to the train station. Hey, be nice to him, okay?"

"I have to now. He harbored a fugitive for me." Making a joke still didn't keep her tears at bay.

"Don't be sad. We'll see each other again."

Sally nodded, her face screwed up in a futile effort not to cry. She bent down and kissed Sam's cheek.

"I left you another present, too. It's in the backyard. Wait until I'm gone to go out, okay?"

"Okay."

Sam sank back down and headed off to where the car waited, but she turned back one last time. "Here's looking at you, kid." She winked and then was gone.

Sally held the stuffed bear and closed her eyes. She didn't move until she heard the engine of the GTO speeding off down the street. In the hallway, Lorraine waited to comfort her.

"It's okay. It's okay. Just think about how much better off she'll be on her own."

"She gave me this. It was her little sister's. She wants me to keep it safe for her."

Lorraine looked at the stuffed animal. "Did she?"

Remembering her mother's sad story about Leopold and Freddie, she held it out to her. "Would you like to have it in your room? She said she left me another present that's outside, so maybe this can be yours. I think she'd like that. She thinks so highly of you."

Her mother's mouth twitched into a smile, and she took the offering. "Thank you. Outside? What could she have left for you outside?"

They wandered onto the porch, but there was nothing there or on the steps. In their backyard stood a rock ledge about forty feet high. It sloped down into a hill laden with majestic pine trees, the floor of it covered in fragrant needles that stopped where their lawn began. There was a gathering of ferns over to the left and, on summer evenings, this area lit up with fireflies that she and her cousins would make a game of counting. Sally always loved looking out and seeing the woods right there at the edge of her insular world. It felt like being on the cusp of a wilderness, the kind where fairytales were made.

"Look! In the trees!"

She looked now to where her mother pointed, and she could see the outlines of garments in the swiftly approaching dusk. Dresses and blouses swayed in the evening breeze like ornaments.

"Oh!" Sally burst out laughing.

"What are they?"

She walked up to the nearest tree and ran her hand over the deep emerald party dress Sam had been wearing the first night they'd met. Around her, the cashmere sweaters, the wool coats, the demure blouses, all blew about like they were imbued with Sam's vigorous spirit.

"It's her wardrobe...She's left me all of her clothes."

Lorraine came up and met her. "Well, my goodness. That was generous." She smiled, but Sally could see distraction and worry in her expression as she shifted on her feet and pretended to examine the ground.

"What is it?"

"What do you mean?"

"I can tell when you have things on your mind. You acted off all during dinner."

She examined her mother in the glow of early night. Her face was still young and supple, but so much harder than it was nine months ago. Lorraine took a deep breath and made her announcement like she'd been rehearsing it.

"Sally, I've decided to sell the house."

Chapter X

Paul's graduation had come and gone, and now he'd enlisted and would be shipping out soon for basic training in Texas. Sally went through the motions in school, making grades that were passable but unimpressive. Every week, she waited for a regular letter from Sam, who reported she was safe and engaging in activism as much as she could. She was staying with old friends from Cambridge who were out that way and even had a job at a record store. Sally wrote back informing her of the new address she should write to after the fifteenth of July, when a new family would be inhabiting their house.

She paid a few visits to Danny and tried to force herself into a sense of normalcy with an occasional cherry Coke at Colonial Spa. But the town felt different to her now, like when you wake up from a dream but can't remember the details. These places were all still there – the Spa, the Bowladrome, the lake – but she took no joy in them. They were no longer hers.

A few weeks after school was over, they'd be moving. Her Aunt Jo had invited them to live with her family. With one son in the army, one in college, and Paul heading off, there was more than enough room for Lorraine and Sally. And this way, from the sale of the house, there would be money to send Sally to college when the time came. She knew her mother was trying to do what was right, so she didn't protest, even though her heart ached to leave the home her father had made for them. On the other hand, she'd be spending her senior year of high school with Nick, which tempered the ache more than a little.

During the last day of school, Sally hoped to run into Arthur. She'd said her goodbyes to Heather and a few other girls who'd become friends during the senior play, promising to keep in touch and hang out over the summer. Now she milled about the bathroom, pretending to fix her makeup, before heading off to work. Arthur was in his closet when she came out.

"Hi, there."

"Hey," he said. "So, last day. Are you excited for summer?"

"I dunno. I'm kind of on the fence about it."

"About summer? I thought everyone liked summer."

"Well, we're moving, see."

"Oh?" He looked up now from filling his bucket with cleaning product. "So, you mean, you won't be going here next year?"

"No, I'll be at Winchester High."

"That's a shame. Who's gonna read my next story for me?"

"Ha, I see how it is. You only like me for my proofreading skills."

"Really though," he said, more serious. "How do you feel about moving? Isn't that the house you grew up in?"

"Yes. I'm sad, I am. I feel like we're leaving my father's memory behind. It wasn't easy for my mother to make this decision, though, and I know she's doing it for my future, so I can't really say anything. I'm just…dealing with it as best I can."

He nodded. "I understand. Well, let me know if there's anything I can do, okay?"

"Thanks."

At work, she tried not to focus on the fact that she'd also have to part with Rose at summer's end, though Lorraine promised she'd find a way for her to still attend sewing class on Wednesdays. As she thumbed through new samples, the bell jingled on the door, and Mrs. Gallagher and Tammy walked in. Sally braced herself for one final confrontation after Tammy whispered something to her mother and made her way up to the counter. Instead, Tammy smiled shyly.

"Hi, Sally."

"Hello." In the awkwardness of a few seconds, she added. "Look, thanks for doing what you did for us at the prom. Sending for help, I mean."

"Of course. Lenny took it too far. I'm not seeing him anymore. Not sure why I ever was. Anyway, I heard you're moving, and I just wanted to say that I'm sorry for everything I did to you. I really am."

"Oh." Sally was almost too shocked to speak.

"I know that can't mean much to you since I've been so horrible, but I wanted to say it."

"Thanks."

Tammy hesitated. "And your friend Sam was right about something." She looked down at her feet and said in a lower tone, "My mother has asked my father to move out."

"I see. I'm sorry."

"That night at the prom, you offered help because you could see that I wasn't okay – I'll never forget that. No one else ever brought it up, even after I reacted the way I did with Sam. People don't like to know things like that, they get uncomfortable. They'd rather be silent than know the dark things that sometimes happen in homes that are supposed to be safe. But they still gossip. My younger brother got wind of it, and it took him a while, but he eventually confronted my father. If you see Sam, will you send her my apology for the slap?"

"I will, but I'm sure it's not even necessary. Sam's not the type to hold grudges."

"Well, it would mean a lot to me."

"Okay then, I'll pass it along. What will you do now?"

"I'm going to Salem State to become a teacher, and I'll be able to stay at home. I'll be fine. My family – what's left of it – we'll be fine."

"I'm glad to hear that, Tammy."

"So, good luck with your senior year."

"Thanks. Good luck in college. Take care of yourself."

Tammy's former veneer of arrogance was untraceable when she smiled. Sally wondered if Sam's hurtful implication was help in disguise, if she knew what she was doing, or if it was just by chance that she was correct. In either case, there could be no argument against the good of its outcome, whether intentional or not.

"Who was that?" Rose asked, coming out of the break room.

"That was Tammy Gallagher, whom I just actually met for the first time."

The morning Paul left was overcast and unseasonably cool. The entire family was over to comfort Lorraine, but Sally needed space. She walked downtown and made her way to the Stodges to commiserate with Danny.

"How did he say goodbye to you?" Danny asked, sipping another lemonade. "Remember it now so you always will…I mean, I'm sure he'll be fine, but just in case."

They sat out on the front porch, Sally rocking in a cushioned swing. She thought back to only a few hours earlier when her brother stood with her on the side walkway. She regretted avoiding him all morning even though she could see his attempts to have a moment alone with her; but whenever he'd walk into a room, she'd find a reason to leave. She didn't want to face what was happening, this goodbye that might be a final goodbye. So, she pretended like it was just another normal day. Soon, her family swarmed in, and it irritated her that she had to fight through aunts and cousins to claim a minute alone with Paul. She thought she should apologize for this while she still could.

"I'm sorry I've been ignoring you all day."

"I wondered about that, but I figured you were just upset."

She nodded, focusing her gaze away from him. He had some words for her, and she listened, staring hard into the row of Rose of Sharon trees that lined the side yard along with a giant rhododendron bush. The white and lavender blossoms muddled together like one of Monet's impressionistic paintings behind the water, veiling her eyes.

"Sally, I know that I haven't been the brother you wanted. I'm too serious, and I'm a grouch, and I've never been fun like Nick. And maybe I haven't always been there for you in the way you needed me, especially after Dad passed, but don't doubt for a minute that I love you, that I always tried to protect you, and that I'm protecting you now, only in a way bigger than either of us. Always remember that, okay?"

She nodded. He grabbed her in a hug so all that was visible was the crown of her head. He kissed it.

"I'm scared, Sally," he whispered.

"What?" She looked up at him, and he suddenly seemed like the kid that he was.

"You're the only person I can say this to. I'm really scared. I'm scared of what it's going to feel like to kill someone. I'm scared of being killed or hurt." He sighed and let out a deep breath. "Just between us, okay?" He held out his pinky, and she took it in hers.

"You're human, Paul. I know you try to be harder than you are because you think it makes you a leader and maybe it does, but it's okay to be afraid. It doesn't make you any less of a man, or less courageous. Everything will be all right."

He smiled. "You're starting to sound like Ma." He grabbed her in another all-encompassing hug.

"I want my girls to take care of each other, okay? And if anything happens to me," – here his voice broke – "you be there for Ma." He turned and stalked off to the car where Uncle Ralph and Marie waited to drive him to the airport.

"You should go home and see how your mom is," Danny advised after she related this.

"Once again, an eleven-year-old has more sense than I do." She stood and brushed cookie crumbs from her sundress.

"Will you still come to visit once in a while even when you've moved?"

"Of course, I will. You're not getting rid of me that easily." She bent and kissed his forehead.

On her way home, she passed the library right as Arthur was coming down the steps. She hadn't seen him since school had let out. He was holding a book, thicker than his usual fare.

"Hi there, I was hoping to see you before you moved," he said. "Do you have time to come with me?"

"I guess so. I should get back home soon, but I can spare a few minutes. What do you have there?"

"Oh, I decided to branch out a little." He held it up so she could read the title.

"Oooh, *The Age of Innocence*! I'm a huge fan of Edith Wharton."

"I could've guessed that. What is it that you like about her?"

"For one, she was the first woman to win the Pulitzer Prize, basically self-educated by her father's library. Secondly, she grew up in extreme wealth, but she saw the underlying hypocrisy in New York high society and then spent her entire career exposing it. She didn't care what any of her rich contemporaries thought of her, and she didn't have to. You know the phrase, 'keeping up with the Joneses'? She was born Edith Jones, of that very family."

"Fascinating. I knew the part about the Pulitzer. That's why I was interested in picking this up. And what about her writing?"

"Well, she's a satirist, and I like that. I guess you could say she's like the American version of Jane Austen, only minus the happy endings."

"Doesn't everyone prefer a happy ending?"

"Oh, I don't know. Happy endings are all well and good if you're a child, but I think unhappy endings are far more plausible and relatable. Or at least, ones that are ambiguous."

"You're a funny one, Sally."

"No, just a realist."

"A realist, not an idealist? Aren't you going against your generation with that one?"

"I don't think the two need to be mutually exclusive."

"Oh no? Do they complement each other like the Bible and Darwin?"

"You think you're going to reference *Inherit the Wind* without me noticing, do you?"

"Can't slip anything past you, can I?"

She followed him back through the square making small talk until they reached Armory Street where he led her up the steps to his apartment. She stood in the open doorway, reluctant to go all the way inside because of what had transpired the last time she was there. He didn't seem to notice.

"Wait here," he said, rushing into his room for something.

He returned with a flat clothing box.

"I was going to mail this to you, but I'd much rather give it to you in person. Here." He handed it to her.

Sally stepped in a bit more and set the box on his kitchen counter. Inside, was the familiar plaid of her father's favorite shirt. She touched it, the buttons, and the slightly frayed front pocket.

"You'd said that you felt like you were leaving your dad's memory behind, and so I thought you should have something of his."

She stared down at it for a moment before carefully putting the lid back on. "This is beautiful, Arthur."

"Of course. If there's anything else you want that I have of his, it's yours."

"No, I kind of like the fact that his clothes are having a second life and being worn by another good man."

"Sally, I wish –" he started, then stopped. "I wish only happy endings for you from now on, however unrealistic or idealistic that may be."

"Thank you. I wish the same for you."

A thought came to her then, and she was ashamed that she hadn't thought of it sooner.

"Well, I know you're in a hurry, so…" Arthur was saying.

"Actually, I need to make one stop before I head home, and I'd like you to come with me this time."

The bell jingled as they entered Adrian's. Rose sat at the counter in an aqua-colored dress with an enticing scoop neckline and capped sleeves, flipping through dress patterns for her sewing class. She beamed as she saw Sally, but then noticed Arthur and self-consciously draped her light cardigan over her shoulders.

"Sally, whatever are you doing here on a Saturday?"

"Paul left today, and I had to go for a long walk to get away from all the people over at the house. And I ran into Arthur here, my friend who wrote a book."

"Oh?" said Rose, standing now. "This is the book you recommended I read?"

"Yes, that's right. Rose here is also a literary buff, so I thought she'd enjoy it."

"Well, I'd love another set of eyes on it. I'm thinking of maybe submitting it somewhere."

"I'd be honored to read it."

"So, you like to read? What's your favorite book?"

"Oh, I'm a sucker for the classics."

"Like this one?" He brandished the Wharton title.

"Exactly like. That's in my top five of all time!"

As Sally inched her way to the door without them noticing, she thought this must be what Sam had felt that first time she'd left her alone with Arthur. Seeing Rose's cheeks flush as she dived into her affinity for the canon and Arthur's intent expression as he leaned into the counter, fully engaged, Sally left thankful that she could repay the favor to someone who truly deserved him.

Her relatives were gone, and the house was empty. Some boxes were strewn about because Lorraine had started to pack up the china and formal dishes that they may not use for some time. She could hear music in the living room. "Stardust" was playing on the record player, and her mother stood in the middle of the room swaying back and forth like she was dancing with an invisible man. Sally watched her for a few moments then quietly inched over and stepped in to dance with her.

"You scared me!"

"Sorry, you looked like you were enjoying yourself."

"This is the song your father and I danced to at our wedding. He was such a good dancer."

"I know, I remember. He used to let me stand on his feet when I was little, and he'd waltz us around the floor."

"That weekend before he passed, if you recall, we went to his niece's wedding. Do you know we danced every single dance together that night? I wanted to sit one out and rest, but he wouldn't let me. It's like he knew it would be the last time."

"Oh, Mom, I'm sorry."

"I shouldn't cry. Even though he died young, we were together longer than most couples get to be. If you count childhood, that's more than thirty years." She took out her handkerchief and dabbed at her eyes. "What's in that box?"

"Here, open it." Sally laid it on the couch.

"Where did you get this?" Her mother lifted out the shirt.

"It's a long story. But someone knew it was his and thought I should have it."

Lorraine put the shirt up to her face and smelled it. "It still has his scent. Just faintly around the collar." She held it out to Sally.

"You're right."

"Come here, dance with your mother." Lorraine pulled her close, and they held her father's shirt between them while the song continued its nostalgic refrain.

This building was similar to her old school – the bricks, the front entrance where students gathered – only it wasn't her school. It was a brand-new school full of people she didn't know, who didn't know her. She took a deep breath. At least she had Nick with her, and he seemed to know everyone. He kept introducing her as "Sally, his little cousin," until she reminded him that she was a full month older.

"I'm just trying to protect you. I don't want any of these chumps getting ideas about you," he said.

"Who cares? Let them get ideas."

"Santa Vittoria –"

"Do not call me that here."

"Your mother made me swear to guard your virtue at all times, and I take my oaths very seriously."

"What are you, a human chastity belt now?"

He wagged his fist at her. "Don't you start with me."

She laughed. It had been easy to settle into Aunt Jo's house. Lorraine seemed more at peace around her sister, there was money in the bank, and Sally had Nick as a constant companion. After the pain of leaving the old house behind, the rest of the summer had been almost enjoyable, and, at the very least, relaxing. She'd learned how to make a full dress and had gotten her driver's license.

The week before, she'd taken the car to visit her father's grave and was in the middle of reciting his favorite poem, "The Darkling Thrush," when a loud engine startled her. Joey was walking towards her carrying a bunch of Black Eyed Susans to put on his grandparents' plot that was in the same row a few stones away. They'd only seen each other a handful of times over the summer, and she assumed he was still cross with her about everything. Whenever he'd visit or they'd hang out, it felt sterile. This made her sad.

"Didn't think I'd run into you here."

"I know. I got my license, and I wanted to come while I can before school starts."

He nodded and placed down his flowers.

"Are you still upset with me for not taking you to my prom?"

"No."

"Then, what?"

"Then, nothing. Geez, Sally, I can't figure out what the hell you want." He threw his hands up.

"What do you mean?"

"I mean, I'm trying to give you some space."

"Oh."

"I do everything you ask me and it's still somehow not enough. You ask me to take in your friend and I do it even though, yes, at that point I felt slighted that you didn't take me to your prom. But I still helped you. You told me you were confused, that you were sad about your dad and needed to grieve. So, I backed off a lot. And now you're wondering why. That's why – because you asked me."

"Okay. I get it."

He squatted down and mumbled a prayer, made the sign of the cross, and stood again.

"So, we're good, right?"

"Yes. Look, Joey, I really appreciate all you've done for me. I do. And I miss our time together when you were acting more like yourself. I'd like to have that time back if you're up for it."

He cocked his head and smirked at her. "Sally, are you asking me on a date?"

"Maybe. If I were, what would you say?"

"Hmmm..." He tapped his chin. "I'll consider it."

The bell rang now, interrupting her reverie to signal the first day of her last year of high school, and what a monumental one it would be. As she smoothed out the lace collar of one of Sam's finest day dresses, she inspected the faces around her while she and Nick made their way down the senior corridor. They were staring, wondering, speculating, and admiring. The trail of whispers didn't bother her. Nothing did anymore.

"You ready for this, Sally?" Nick asked, steering her to her homeroom.

She shot him a look, invoking every woman in her family as she answered him.

"What do you think?"

THE END

Book Club Discussion Questions

Hi reader,

If you enjoyed this novel, please consider leaving a review on Amazon and Goodreads. It helps, and I appreciate it more than I can ever say. Also, check out my other novels at lskilroy.com!

Happy reading,

1. This book contains strong sociopolitical commentary about issues within our own society – sexuality, race, class. How do you feel about that? And how are these issues still (or not) relevant and represented in today's world? What are the differences in how we view and deal with similar problems in the present?

2. Kilroy has said that she chose to set this story in real locations with historically accurate details versus a fictional town because she thought it would create a more authentic story. For example, the rally in Wakefield center that Paul and Sally attend together actually took place. Words on posters that Sally sees at that rally and the gathering for the death of Martin Luther King, Jr. later in the book were based on actual photos Kilroy saw when researching. How did it enhance or

take away from the story? Did you feel more connected to this place and its characters because of the true details?

3. What themes are emphasized throughout the book? What do you think Kilroy is trying to convey to readers?

4. What's the overall message of the book?

5. Is Sally a likeable protagonist? Why or why not? What do you think of her evolution?

6. Who is your favorite character and why? Who is your least favorite character and why?

7. Who was your favorite supporting character and what did they add to the story?

8. Gregarious Sam is presented as almost a foil to shy Sally. What did you think of Sam and how does the story start changing when she comes into it?

9. Sally's relationships with others are central to the story. What did you think of the dynamics between Sally and Sam, Rose, Joey, Paul, Arthur, Nick, Father Carl, and Lorraine?

10. There are several antagonists in the book: Tammy, Lenny, Judge Pettyfer, Stew, the war itself. What function does each of them serve in the story and what do we learn from them?

11. The role of clothing is present in the title and woven throughout the novel. What did you think the significance of this was and how did it reflect in each character's identity?

12. There are some very disturbing depictions of sexual violence or aggression throughout the book – in Sally's trip to Cambridge, in the prom scene, in Rose's story, and in what's revealed about Tammy. Did these parts make you uncomfortable? Did they lead you to a new understanding or awareness? Did they make you consider sexual violence or our reactions to it in a different way?

13. Do you have a favorite line, passage, or scene? If so, what is it?

14. The story is told in third-person limited omniscient, meaning Kilroy sticks closely to Sally's character, but the narration remains in third-person. What did you think of this narrative voice?
15. One of the main threads in this book is how Sally deals with the grief of suddenly losing a parent. Her main outlet for healing is taking up sewing, followed by her budding friendship with Sam. Her mother and brother deal with it in different ways. What do you think this says about the grieving process in general?
16. Dawn Elder is a supporting character who gets an epic monologue later in the book. What is the significance of her speech?
17. Dawn is the only person who really holds Sam accountable for some of her actions. What do you think of their friendship?
18. How did what was happening in their small town reflect the greater turmoil of the decade?
19. If there were to be a movie adaptation of this book, whom would you cast?
20. Imagine Sally and Sam run into each other as adults after some years have passed. Where are they in life and what's happened to them?

Other Works by L.S. Kilroy

The Vitruvian Heir Trilogy

Heart Like Eyes

lskilroy.com

About L.S. Kilroy

"The first thing I do in the morning is brush my teeth and sharpen my tongue." – Dorothy Parker

L.S. Kilroy is an irreverent sort of person who likes to write about things. Growing up an asthmatic only child in a neighborhood of geriatrics, she made friends with books at a young age because she had to – luckily, she also really liked them. Early exposure to the classics fueled her own writing. At fifteen, a man in a bookstore asked her what she wanted to be when she grew up and she replied, "Writer," without hesitation.

Writer is a title that has driven her both personally and professionally. She holds a Bachelor's degree in English from Merrimack College and a Master's degree in Writing, Literature & Publishing from Emerson College. By day, she's a communications professional; by night, she's an award-winning indie author.

Kilroy lives in a rural community in Massachusetts with her husband, stepson, and three naughty cats. Aside from writing, she loves being creative in the kitchen, belting out show tunes, traveling, throwing epic dinner parties, reading, and scouting out vintage finds at consignment shops.

Made in the USA
Middletown, DE
09 July 2021

43652813R00136